ALL GOOD THINGS

LINDA SHANTZ

All Good Things

Cover Artwork by Linda Shantz

www.lindashantz.com

eBook edition ISBN: 978-1-7773003-4-0

Paperback ISBN: 978-1-7773003-5-7

IngramSpark Paperback ISBN 978-1-990436-01-7

Hardcover ISBN: 978-1-7773003-8-8

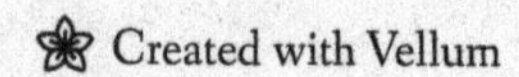

Out of suffering have emerged the strongest souls. The most massive characters are seared with scars.

EDWIN HUBBELL CHAPIN

CHAPTER ONE

Voices, nervous laughter, peripheral movement; on the fringes of her consciousness, none of it important. All that was worthy of her focus was skin sliding over muscle, muscle extending and contracting. Liv analyzed every stride down to each footfall, and tried to gauge the ever-unknown unpredictability factor in the sleek filly before her.

Chique was light years away from the unraced two-year-old she'd been a year ago. There was a swagger to her step now, the glint in her eyes behind the blinkers self-important, if you could say that about a horse. With eight races under her belt, at five different tracks — five of them wins — the professionalism she displayed here in Woodbine's walking ring, willow branches whispering overhead, wasn't unexpected. Liv just didn't trust it.

A touch disrupted her concentration, her head snapping to the side like the wind whipping from the northwest had picked it up in a gust. She didn't bother to fix the dark hair flying around her face. She should have put it up. She was usually practical about such things, like the "turf shoes" on her feet — flats, when heels would have punched through the rain-soaked carpet of grass. Not that she ever wore heels.

She extracted a hand from the depths of her trench coat pocket, and Nate returned the firmness of her grasp, the amusement playing on his features a contrast to the seriousness of her own. She could tell what he was thinking. *No, Miller, it would not be appropriate for the rider to kiss the trainer in the walking ring.*

"So?" He crossed his arms, stick tucked under his elbow.

"Stay off the inside," she responded, though she wasn't saying anything he didn't already know. They'd discussed strategy ad nauseam, walked the full mile-and-a-half of the rain-sodden E.P. Taylor turf course that morning, and he'd ridden over it in an earlier race. The course was soft, but safe.

"Breathe," he said. He squeezed the elbow of the arm that was now folded over her chest in a less-assured reflection of his posture.

"Sure, Miller. It's only the Canadian Triple Crown on the line. But if you're cool, that's what matters."

This was the first possible first in her fledgling training career. A woman trainer had won the Queen's Plate before her. A woman trainer had won the Prince of Wales, the second jewel of the crown. A woman trainer had won this, the Breeders' Stakes, third and final jewel. But no woman had won all three in the same year with the same horse.

The paddock judge gave the riders up call. Liv glanced at Nate.

"Let's do this," he said with a nod, trying to be serious before he let go the grin that was the only thing with any hope of distracting her from the stormy sky, the very un-August-like cool, and everything that was on the line.

"*Bonne chance.* Don't screw up. Come home safe." She threw him up onto the moving filly, and felt the too-familiar helplessness seep in.

He was so sure about Chique. Like he was so sure about them. Liv envied that, but now wasn't the time to think about it.

"Don't worry, princess, you don't have to run in this," Nate said.

Chique balked at the on-gap, as if she didn't believe him, her ears swiveling to the grey slab of sealed track in front of them, a wet gloss to its surface.

Nicole nudged Paz into a jog to lead them up for the post parade, the stable pony happily punching through the surface like a kid playing in the mud.

"You worried about the turf?" she asked.

"Nah. Just worried she might hate me after warming up."

The filly minced over the bog, and actually seemed happy to downshift to a walk while the announcer introduced the starters. Thank goodness they were running on the grass. Chique might have overcome her differences with the slop enough to win the Plate, but she was in a mood today.

Nate glanced at Nicole as soon as the roll call wrapped up, eager to get the filly doing something constructive. "Turn us loose. We'll see you behind the gate."

The slop slapped up onto her belly and soaked her tail, backing her off from her usual pre-race enthusiasm. At least it wasn't raining. Despite the conditions, this was almost Nate's favourite part. Just him and his little big filly out here, leaving the others behind – like she'd leave them behind in the race. It didn't matter that she'd never run on the grass before. She'd trained over it like a bear.

Six other racehorse and pony pairs approached the metal barrier looming in front of the grandstand. Nate wasn't in a hurry to join them, but it wasn't as if he could postpone it. When he steered the filly onto the turf, she dropped her head and let out a shuddering breath.

See? Would I lie to you?

Nicole slipped her long strip of leather through Chique's bit, Chique brushing up against Paz. The hairy eyeball she gave the asphalt to their right was a remnant of Nate's wild child — the one who had tried to lie down in the gate in her first start. And refused to run a jump in her second start. Or blown the turn so badly at Gulfstream in January she'd very nearly sacrificed a win in her fourth start.

The apron was bigger, so it didn't appear half as packed as Fort Erie had been the night she'd won the Prince of Wales, but there was a different anticipation in those who congregated at Woodbine. They were here to see which side of history Chique would land herself on. The Breeders' Stakes was a well-established graveyard of favourites — and the Canadian Triple Crown demanded greater versatility of a horse than its American counterpart. But behind the gate, there was no room for doubt.

She loaded without even a hint of hesitation. *So grown-up.* Nate felt her square herself beneath him as they both narrowed their vision to the stretch of blue-green ahead. With the crash of doors and clanging bell, the starter turned the seven runners loose.

Chique's launch projected them to the lead, letting Nate place her exactly where he wanted, just off the inside. The E.P. Taylor turf wasn't a traditional oval, the clubhouse turn's angle obtuse, more like something seen in the UK. Chique's ears flipped forward, eating up the short straight that followed as she sized up the next turn. It would be easy to blow this one — acute and on the home side — but Chique seemed to relish the chance to show off how handy she was. She dropped closer to the rail, hugging it. The turf did have more give there, and though Chique handled it okay, Nate steered her back out as they straightened into the long backside. He didn't think the others were anywhere close to him, and resisted the temptation to glance back.

Chique cruised along like she was on a morning gallop, setting a pace she'd have no trouble carrying to the wire. It was hard not to get cocky up here; hard not to think how close they were to achieving a feat that was still rare, despite a smattering of Canadian Triple Crown winners in the nineties. But she was moving so easily, happy with the springy footing, happy with the cool air, happy on the lead.

Happy, happy, happy.

The final turn was the complete opposite of the other end of the course — gradual, sweeping downhill to the long home stretch. If Chique had been a kid, she'd be squealing *weeeeee* as she reached out with her quick forelegs, thrusting with her powerful engine, accelerating down the incline. So she drifted a bit in the lane. Liv wanted them off the rail, right?

A flash of bay to the inside caught the corner of his eye. *What the...?*

Wampum slipped up next to them — still out from the rail, on that choice path Chique had abandoned.

Where the hell did he come from? That was way too easy.

Wampum looked good, big and strong and fit. And Chique? Chique was suddenly acting like she'd checked out. Still happy, but galloping alongside the colt like she was appreciating the company. Steve Gordon let Wampum out a notch, and Chique didn't fight back. Memories of the Florida Derby flooded Nate — when Chique had let the same colt go on to be third as she finished up the track. *Not today, Cheeky Little Bitch.*

He chirped and threw the lines at her, and her ears flipped forward like she was saying *yeah, I see him*, but she wasn't interested in gunning for the lead again. Like she enjoyed playing this stalking game with the Northwest colt. *Kind of late in the race for games, Cheeky*.

He steered her closer to Wampum, hoping she'd re-engage. But she moseyed along with his tail billowing beside her like she was admiring its flowing length. A heartbeat later, the rest of the field closed in on her, leaving her blocked in tight quarters with limited options.

Oh, she didn't like that. She was back on the bit, her will to run resurfacing thanks to the surge of energy around her. She pinned her ears at the horse next to her and tried to drift over, and Nate hoped that horse would back off so they could break out of this pocket and chase down Wampum on the outside. Except that was Dave Johnson, his main rival for the Woodbine riding title, smiling back at him. It wasn't a friendly smile.

Chique eyed the hole on the inside.

She was dangerously close to Wampum's heels. Nate blew out a breath like it would lighten the weight of his decision. *Liv is going to kill me...*

The filly shot up the inside before he'd even sent her — apparently reading his mind — and caught Wampum in a couple of jumps. Her progress wasn't as smooth on the softer, more tiring ground though, and now that she was back up beside Wampum, she was content to match strides with him again, albeit with ears laced back. Or maybe the Northwest colt was digging in, holding his own. *Didn't think he had it in him.*

Nate took a chance — a big one given Chique's history with such things — and reached back with his whip to smack

Chique on the haunches, hoping to jar her out of her complacency. Chique pinned her ears again and pressed against Wampum instead of shooting forward. Wampum crowded back, the two of them fused like conjoined twins.

He gave up on the whip, relying on hands and voice. Finally Chique broke away from Wampum, pushing her head in front, then her neck. *Yeah, that's my baby.* He exhaled in relief, half a length up, then a length. The colt was game, but Chique would prevail.

Except now Chique was coasting, with a sixteenth of a mile yet to run. Her ears flicked forward, her stride less urgent. Nate flashed his stick, waving it without making contact, but she just swooped closer to the rail. *So much for being grown up.* He switched hands and waved her back off the inside — carefully, because all he needed was for her to encroach on the path of the horse behind them, the freight train breathing getting ever closer. Wampum, fighting back.

All he could do was growl at her and scrub the hair off her neck. Wampum wore down their lead faster than the wire was coming. The colt drew even, and Chique nailed her ears to her head like she was saying *how dare he?* Nate would have laughed if he hadn't been feeling so helpless. *Well, Cheeky...you let him. And it's up to you now.*

She wasn't letting him by, but Wampum matched her, stride for stride, breath for breath. Nate pleaded with his hands, the pop of Steve Gordon's whip in his ears. They drove straight through the wire, Chique still eyeballing Wampum as they galloped out.

"Sorry, Miller!" Gordon was grinning broadly.

Nate looked over sharply. "Don't be so sure!"

Gordon laughed.

He'd better be wrong.

Liv rushed trackside, furious. What the hell had happened out there? What was Nate thinking? If he'd lost this race...

Her best friend Faye Taylor, and Faye's brother Dean — Wampum's trainer — clustered next to her, the three of them huddled on the apron near the scales. Liv searched for Chique as the other finishers returned and were stripped of their equipment. Both Chique and Wampum were still out of sight, held somewhere on the far side of the track with the outrider, who would escort the victor back.

"Your colt ran a hell of a race," Liv said, forcing a smile.

"It's gotta be close," Dean responded, pacing two steps, back and forth like a tall, wiry, broken toy soldier until Faye grabbed his arm to stop him.

Acid churned in Liv's stomach, and she wrapped her coat around herself to keep from shaking. She tore her eyes away from the PHOTO declaration blazing from the tote board, not wanting to know if the filly's number didn't come up first. When a furtive glance showed INQUIRY lit up in red, she turned away and stared up at the grey clouds. Which would be worse? Losing because Wampum had out-nosed them, or losing through disqualification?

The grandstand was humming, a swarm of restless bodies. Liv's chest hurt, and she pushed out a breath when she realized she'd been holding it. Dave Johnson walked by with his tack to weigh in, a smirk on his face.

"I don't know, Liv," he said, and Liv pressed her lips together to keep from snapping.

A surge rose from the crowd, and she heard Faye's squeal.

Liv didn't really need to see the board to know the result, but she turned and stared at Wampum's number on top. Dean crushed Faye in his arms, rocking her back and forth.

"Congratulations, guys," Liv said, not even attempting to muster enthusiasm. It wasn't like they wouldn't understand. The shoe had been on the other foot on Plate Day when Chique had just got up to beat Dean's Touch and Go.

Dean released Faye, and pulled Liv into a hug and kissed the top of her head. "Sorry, kid."

Liv pushed him away. "Don't be. You deserve every bit of that."

Dean and Faye rushed across the turf course, Liv stepping down more carefully in their wake, dropping her eyes to the boards making a path to the main track. She lifted her gaze to the clubhouse turn, Chique a dark smudge cantering back slowly as the other also-rans began returning to the barns. The filly looked fine. When Nate slowed her to a jog, Chique's toes flicked, her ears up, looking frustratingly fresh.

Someone bumped Liv from behind as Jo, the barn's assistant trainer, snapped a lead shank onto Chique's bit. Emilie, Liv's younger sister, squeezed her arm.

"Let it go, Liv."

She glanced at Em. Did she really look that mad? Liv nodded curtly, and took a step toward Nate as he dragged the tack off Chique's back.

His eyes met hers, wary. "Don't speak," he said, and she left him to walk away to the scales, turning on her heels toward the parking lot.

People just showed up.

It wasn't unexpected — racetrackers could smell free beer from the other side of the backstretch. They didn't care that this wasn't going to be a stake party after all. They'd made the assumption the Triple Stripe barn would've been prepared. They'd assumed right.

Two of the grooms, Michel and Sue, were unloading cases of beer from the back of Sue's VW Golf, surrounded by moochers ready to lighten their load. The cases were emptying before they had a chance to set them down. Roger Cloutier — trainer of all of the Triple Stripe horses but the one who had just lost the Triple Crown — watched with a frown. Nate came up behind him and gave him a nudge.

"I'll fix this. I'm sure I'm going to hear it's my fault anyway." Nate didn't look back to check Roger's expression, pushing himself through the cluster. It was time for the scavengers to move on.

"Okay, stop," he called to Michel and Sue. "Put them back. We're taking them over to Northwest. Party's over there, people!"

It didn't keep him from grabbing a bottle for himself before he sent them off. He twisted off the cap and took a swig. He was probably going to need it.

Chique came ambling around the corner as he walked onto the shed. She stopped and gazed over the dispersing horde like she was offended by their departure, then snorted, ducked her head to snatch a mouthful from the haynet hanging on the rail, and dunked it unceremoniously in the water bucket hooked to the post next to it. Munching, she dragged the hotwalker over to Nate.

"How is she?" Nate asked, backing to the inside of the sandy path. Chique poked her nose along his arm, still dribbling freshly brewed hay tea, until he produced a peppermint from the pocket of his suit jacket.

"Finished drinking in the test barn after ten minutes. Was afraid she'd miss the party."

The snort that reached Nate's ears was unmistakably Liv's.

"So sorry to disappoint her," she said. "You can take her out for some grass, Marc."

Nate removed the bottle he'd tucked in the crook of his elbow as he'd attended to the filly's demands, and half-heartedly brushed at the smear from her body search before holding the beer to Liv. Liv crossed her arms. Would he call that a grimace? Yep, it was going to be like that.

"Let's go in the office. I don't want to do this out here."

"What are we doing?" He actually said it out loud. He gulped another swallow from the bottle, and caught the screen door after she breezed inside, softening its landing as it closed behind them.

"You're mad at me, aren't you?"

She gave him a tired look as he dropped onto the small couch next to her. Well. He had to give her an opening, didn't he?

"What was the only thing we talked about?"

He shrugged. "I had no choice, she was getting snarky. I had to take her inside."

"There's no way you should have let her get boxed in."

"She wasn't really boxed in. The rail was wide open." The grin he flashed her did nothing to dislodge her cool expression. "Can you stop being a trainer for a minute and remember what it's like to be out there?"

She sighed, then grabbed the beer and took a swig, features screwing up as she handed it back to him. "I don't know how you can drink that."

"Don't you have some champagne stowed in there?" He nodded at the small fridge behind Roger's desk.

"I wasn't going to jinx us."

"Maybe if you'd had a little faith things would have turned out differently."

She scowled at him, then pressed her lips into a line.

"Maybe we underestimated Wampum. Maybe we were overconfident."

"And by we, you mean me." He drained what was left in the bottle. *Should have grabbed two.* "*We* should get out of here."

She glanced at him sideways. "Chique's not even done up yet."

"Jo's doing her up, right? We'll come back later to check on her."

"We have to go to Dean's barn."

"Sure. Token appearance. Unless you really want to hang out there."

"No."

"Didn't think so."

Liv got up and walked to the door, peering through the screen, then turned back to him, her grey eyes warming a little closer to blue as she met his. "Let's go."

He left the empty bottle on the desk and grabbed her keys, tossing them to her with a smirk. "Probably best if you drive. I might not do it right."

It was hard to find a spot to park at Dean's barn, with cars jammed everywhere. They probably should have walked. Liv locked the Nissan with a beep, and Nate grabbed her hand, meeting her eyes when they turned to his, but she didn't pull away. Not until they were closer to the crowd outside the shed, at least.

No one had to remind him he'd had the mount on Wampum once. He'd been up when the colt had broken his maiden. Been up, only to come crashing down, in the Blue-Grass. That had been Wampum's last race before this, the colt injuring his shoulder in the accident. It was a day forever imprinted on his memory; a *this changes everything* day. Faye breaking up with him. Liv giving him a glimmer of hope, only to figuratively slap him in the face. It had stung, but he'd deserved it.

"Sorry, buddy," Dean said, shaking his hand with a self-deprecating shrug. Dean had always been good to Nate, and the BlueGrass spill had knocked Wampum out of Plate contention, so he couldn't begrudge the trainer the victory.

He moved on to Faye, resting a hand on her elbow as he pecked her on the cheek and backed up to stand next to Will. It still felt strange that Faye had hooked up with his best friend. The four of them sure didn't double date, unless you counted an awkward evening at Will's dad's wedding. It had been more of a mercy mission. If Nate were honest about the last seven weeks, could he really even call this thing between him and Liv dating?

She was talking to Dean now, but glanced over, and Nate had no trouble reading that look. *Have we been good enough sports now to leave without looking like we're skulking off with our tails between our legs?* Nate's nod was slight, the corner of his mouth rising just enough to second the motion.

"Sorry to be party poopers, but we're going to go sulk now." Liv wasn't a fan of pretense. Her eyes shifted sheepishly from Faye to Dean. "Congrats again."

Dean squeezed her shoulders — a little too comfortably for Nate's liking — and Liv gave Faye a quick hug before they slipped away, back to the car.

"Where to?" she said once she settled behind the wheel.

"I just need to eat something. And I'd bet you do too." He paused as she directed the Nissan toward the east gate. "Turn right."

"And then?"

"How does Wendy's drive through sound?"

"I like your style, Miller."

Salads to go with plastic cutlery under the weeping willows

along the track's back access road — not quite the celebration they'd been hoping for. Liv peered up at the grey sky, her eyes reflecting its colour. Serious and sombre was her default. In so many ways, she still felt elusive, a mystery to be solved.

"Do you think this is it for summer? Hard to believe how hot it was in June," she said, cross-legged on the navy night sheet they'd spread to sit on. It was clean, but still smelled distinctly of horse. Neither of them was ever very far away from that scent.

Nate leaned back against the tire. "Is it too early to start thinking about Florida?"

She laughed. "A little, maybe. Soon enough, though."

It might be Florida before they had a shot at some semblance of a normal relationship. Florida would give them the time and freedom they didn't have here, when sometimes it felt they were under a microscope. Liv had taken Chique to Fort Erie to prep for the Prince of Wales after the Plate, leaving him at Woodbine with his riding commitments. Her judgment had paid off — Chique had taken the second jewel handily, bouncing out of it looking for more. After that, the tension of a possible Canadian Triple Crown win had kept her preoccupied. He had to remind himself regularly it was best to take it slow, no sudden moves, all too aware how quickly she might spook — and knowing full well how prone he was to making mistakes when it came to relationships.

"So what do we do with her now?" Liv sipped her water.

"Take the blinkers off for sure," he said.

"Do you think the turf had anything to do with it? Back to the dirt?"

"It wasn't the turf. Trust me on that."

"Trust you? You totally blew off my instructions out there."

"Are we doing this again?" He shot her a sharp glance. "Cheeky blew *me* off out there."

"I'm sorry," she said, the warble of a laugh in her voice. "I guess it was only a matter of time before she started playing games with us." She produced a white booklet from the pocket of her coat, unfolding it and pressing it open to a page he couldn't see.

"What was that, almost an hour before the condition book came out? I'm impressed." He smirked before stuffing a forkful of lettuce in his mouth.

Liv rolled her eyes. "Where do you think we should go next?"

He didn't hesitate. "The Mile."

"Breeders' Cup *Win and You're In.*" There was no missing the incredulity in her tone. The winner of the Challenge race was guaranteed a spot in the Championship, with entry fees paid and a $10,000 travel award that would more than cover transport. "She didn't deign a restricted race at home worthy of an honest effort, and you want to think about the Breeders' Cup?"

He laughed. "It's at Keeneland this year. She loved Keeneland."

"You seem to be filtering out some details. Like when she got knocked to her knees. Or when I had to pull you off Ricky Acosta in the jock's room."

"That was pretty hot." His grin was crooked and bold.

She shook her head, shoving him with her elbow, and went back to the condition book. "In between the Mile and going a mile and a half again in the Northern Dancer Stakes is a nice little mile and an eighth race restricted to fillies. With a $250,000 purse."

"Cutting back to the Mile after today's mile and a half, she'll win for fun."

"That doesn't sound overconfident at all, Miller. But I'll think about it."

"Does that mean I'm forgiven?"

Her criticism rattled him more than he was ready to admit. Her eyes steadied on him, then she wrapped her fingers around the collar of his jacket, and pulled his face to hers. A smile played with her lips before she kissed him.

"I'll think about that too."

CHAPTER TWO

SEPTEMBER BROUGHT with it a heat wave and a flood of memories. The hot spell was almost welcome, after a cold and wet August. Some of the memories were too. Others, not so much.

Liv closed her leg and the yearling colt dropped his head, moving into the bit like he'd been doing this his whole life instead of just two weeks. Chique's full brother, heir to the throne. He never put a foot wrong. He was perfect.

Like Nate, who had just walked up to the ring. He leaned on the top rail, and she returned his trademark grin with a more reserved smile. Thankfully Feste was so easy-going his rider's temporary distraction didn't phase him; he didn't react to the slight tension that overtook her body, or the subtle amping up of her heart rate.

Nate's gaze shifted to the other yearling and rider. "Hey Cory."

Cory wasn't so lucky. With the break in her concentration, the little bay she was on faltered and ducked, leaving the petite rider a dusty heap in the sand.

Liv pulled her colt up as Nate ducked into the ring. Cory's little bay snorted dramatically at his downed rider, one eye bugging out at the loop of rein hanging off the side of his neck as Cory climbed to her feet. Nate's voice came low and lyrical, the bay's eyes flicking toward him, his legs locking long enough for Nate to grab the lines.

"You okay?" he asked, scratching the bay's neck as Cory sheepishly dusted herself off and shuffled over.

She nodded, a bright pink flush rising in her cheeks beneath the brim of her helmet.

"Get Nate to tell you about the time he came off Chique as a baby," Liv called.

Cory straightened, eyes darting to Liv like she couldn't believe her idol had ever suffered such an embarrassment. "Really?"

Nate smirked. "Never going to live that down, am I?" He turned to Cory. "Let me throw you back up."

Cory sprang lightly into the tack, looking only a little less mortified as she thanked him, her voice a squeak. Liv set her dark bay colt in motion again, picking up an easy jog. When she was satisfied with the day's lesson, she parked him in the middle, and waited for Cory to join her.

Nate approached and rubbed the patch of white in the middle of the colt's forehead — a larger star than Chique's mixed swirl, like their dam Sotisse had been more generous with the paint this time. "He seems a lot quieter than his big sister. 'Big' being a figure of speech, of course. He's already as tall as her." He had the same inky coat as Chique though, a colour anyone outside of horse racing might label black.

"I'm not going to complain about either of those things," Liv said, dropping to the ground and running up her stirrup irons before she loosened the girth a hole.

"What do you call him again?"

"Feste."

Nate looked the colt in the eye. "You've got some big shoes to fill, Fester."

Trust Nate to think *Addams Family* instead of Shakespeare's fool in Twelfth Night. Liv couldn't help the wash of affection that came with her smile — freely, for the yearling. Helplessly, confusingly, for the man.

Cory trailed silently behind them as they walked to the barn — totally out of character for the gregarious eighteen-year-old.

"The new kid working out okay?" Nate asked.

Liv nodded, happy to discuss Cory and offset the conflict in her head. "She's a decent rider. And she works hard."

"Let me guess..."

"Of course. She wants to ride races. I'm thinking of asking her if she wants to come to Florida this winter."

They exchanged a look, and Liv tried not to overthink that. What would a winter in Florida mean? Would he expect to stay at the condo? He'd been giving her space, but she feared for her much-needed solitude in such a concentrated environment. It felt way, way too soon to be living together. But how practical would it be to live apart? As usual, she was getting ahead of herself. Time to steer the conversation away from that. "You should bring your boots and helmet next time and get on him."

"Does that mean I get to ride this one?"

"We'll see."

He held her eyes just a moment too long. Damn that grin of his.

It was cool in the barn, Feste snorting contentedly as Liv led him to his stall. Nate rested against the doorframe while she pulled off the saddle and bridle, and slid the door shut behind her.

"Hey Cory, when're you going to start coming into the

track and helping us out? Now that Em's spending so much time with Faye at the café, we could use an extra rider." Nate caught Cory's eye as she emerged from the little bay gelding's box.

Cory froze, her lips parting slightly. "Are you serious?" she sputtered. She looked at Liv.

"It's up to you." Liv shrugged. "Even just get on the pony a few times."

"Oh hell, Liv." Nate choked back a laugh. "Paz? Jay would be easier to gallop."

"Jay? Just Jay?" Cory was gasping again.

Liv resisted the urge to elbow Nate. Like they'd put Cory up on the nicest three-year-old colt in the barn. A colt who was on the cusp of a promising career after a late start, and probably heading to California in a few months with her father's US-based trainer. "That two-year-old filly is super quiet."

Nate grinned. "You're right. Good choice."

He stepped in with the saddle pad and cloth after Liv knocked off the next four-legged student, brushing close to her as he moved out of the way. He slipped around to the other side while she settled the exercise saddle in place, then buckled the girth for her on the off side.

"So how are you feeling about the Mile?" he asked, his tone casual.

He was beside her again, handing her the bridle, their fingers touching as she took it, and she cursed the little tremor that ran up her arm and tingled along her spine. "I'll tell you on entry day." She'd nominated Chique to both the Mile and the fillies-and-mares-only Canadian Stakes — in case she chickened out on the whole Breeders' Cup *Win and You're In* thing.

"Thursday."

She didn't need him to remind her, to state it so affirmatively. Yes, Thursday. Three days out from the race. They'd agreed they'd decide after Nate blew Chique out that morning. Together, though the final word would be hers.

"Still game for blinkers off?" she asked.

"I'm always up for an adventure with the Cheeky Little Bitch."

She snapped a lead rope to the halter she'd left under the bridle, turning the yearling towards the door. He wasn't exactly blocking her way, but he was there; so, so, present.

"Don't you have to be somewhere?" she said quietly, unable to control the amusement playing on her lips. "You're distracting the help."

"Fine. I'll leave. I don't want to be where I'm not wanted," he said, feigning hurt that smile of his belied.

He leaned in, but she pushed him away before he could kiss her. She had to maintain some kind of decorum at work. Backing away, he held her eyes, his grin still taunting her, then sauntered out the end of the barn, leaving her standing there considering his silhouette.

"You are so lucky."

She hadn't realized Cory was behind her, the words a sigh. Liv glanced back. Why couldn't she just agree? Because this was good. This was fun; the back and forth, the teasing, the banter.

But it couldn't go on indefinitely. She knew his history; knew what he wanted. He wanted more, and she wasn't sure how she felt about that. Nate was patient. He'd never push her physically. But that wasn't the part she worried about.

Chique torqued her neck, one eye rolled back far enough Nate could see a crescent of white as she tilted her head away from Paz. The object of her contempt was directly in front of them in the post parade — Youthful, over from France for the Woodbine Mile, his straight-backed jockey cloaked in cobalt blue.

Don't they know that's not how we do things here? Chique seemed to huff.

Nate laughed and reached forward, running a hand down her crest, her mane defiantly flopping halfway to the wrong side of her neck. She shook off his touch, bouncing into Paz for good measure. Youthful strutted, bunched powerfully against his lad's hold. They didn't use pony horses across the pond. One of the outriders hovered nearby, ready to swoop in if the big horse got to be too much.

"You'd think this would be a 'when in Rome' kind of time, wouldn't you?" Nicole, atop Paz said, gently pushing Chique away now that the filly had pushed her nose against Paz's withers to get a good look at the offender with her other eye.

Nate shrugged. "Maybe he doesn't like other horses." Though it was pretty common for runners who came over for the big turf races at Woodbine to go solo to the post. Youthful was favoured to win, so they probably knew what they were doing.

Chique's odds were more a reflection of sentiment from the hometown crowd than logic — she was third choice in the betting, but no one in the *Form* had picked her in the top three. She gawked freely with her blinker-free view, but not once had Nate seen her check out the tote board.

The post parade wrapped up, and Youthful shot away from his lad, settling into a steady but energetic gallop. Nate glanced at the lad — red-faced but eyes still on his charge — as Nicole initiated a jog with Paz.

"You can turn us loose. Maybe keep close though, okay?" He flashed her a grin.

Nicole looked doubtful, as always, but let the long strip of leather slip through the bit. Chique surged forward, shaking it away, her ears shooting up and zeroing in on Youthful as the big horse swept around the clubhouse turn. The filly zipped past the other North Americans, who cantered conservatively next to their ponies. They looked like they were getting ready for a hunter flat class, not a horse race.

This might be fun.

The crowd pressing against the rail was a blur, the current of warm September air lifting Chique's unruly mane as she reached over the track, each stride quicker than the last. At least her fixation on Youthful kept her from the antics Nate had expected — or maybe she was grown-up enough for *blinkers off* to be a non-issue.

"You're determined to get me in trouble again, aren't you filly?" Nate muttered through gritted teeth, picturing the look on Liv's face behind the binoculars that were most certainly taking in his struggle to temper Chique's momentum. "Remember I had to talk her into this, Cheeky."

He pulled her up on the backside, Chique snorting with satisfaction as she finally caught up to Youthful. Nicole was close behind, and reattached herself to the filly, Paz blowing from the effort of keeping up.

"Don't laugh at me," Nate said, his heart still thumping against his chest, a warm ache in his arms.

"I don't know why you do that to yourself. One of these times it's gonna come back and bite you in the butt."

"This was almost the time." He grinned.

Nine starters filed through the gap from the main track to the turf course. Breeders Cup hopefuls, including some of Europe's top milers, and the two best middle-distance horses from south of the border. *Why did I talk Liv into this again?*

"Good luck, Nate," Nicole said when she transferred Chique to the assistant starter.

He chased his apprehension away as the doors slammed

shut behind them, and focused between Chique's ears: a mile from here to the wire.

Chique bounced out when the starter released them, ears flickering as she assessed the footing and the horses around her, the same way Nate did. She wasn't gunning for the lead though. *Why the hell not?* What was she up to today? Youthful glided easily to the front, and Nate felt Chique line him up again, but she was content to let him go on. No sense trying to figure out what version of crazy was occupying her pretty little head. *Ride the horse you're on, Miller* — even if you don't recognize her. Chique skimmed over the turf, biding her time, one eyeball still locked on the dark bay horse on the lead. Maybe Nate shouldn't question. Maybe she had this under control. Now that was a scary thought.

They cruised into the big sweeping turn, the only one they had to contend with today. Chique naturally quickened with the incline, the field bunched behind them, the sense of their collective presence enough to press her closer to Youthful. She hovered just off his flank, ears flickering forward as they straightened into the wide stretch. Chique was in the game now, taking a hold, asking to run instead of waiting to be told, but Nate didn't move. It was a long way to the wire yet.

A horse surged up to their right, and Chique pummeled the turf, moving faster...but Youthful accelerated too, holding her off. She pinned her ears and Nate started to ride, rolling out arms and hands, Chique gaining inches, shadowed by the challenger to her right.

He glanced across — they were part of a four-wide charge for the wire. Youthful hung tough on the rail, Chique wearing him down with fervor, two closers creeping up insidiously on the outside. Nate cocked his stick, flashing it on the filly's right, coming short of actually hitting her. Chique scooted beneath him, veering towards Youthful.

Youthful's head swung towards Chique with a flash of teeth, and Nate's jaw dropped as he stood instinctively to check his filly — but Chique merely swapped leads to rebalance and drove on with a fresh burst of speed. The big horse's rider dragged him away, and Chique shot past, bursting ahead with her ears still pinned flush to her skull.

Nate thrust his arms with each extension of her neck, but it was just for show — Chique was doing it with or without him, jumping clear of her rivals, streaking under the wire alone.

There was a maniacal lift to his laugh as he stood in the irons, the filly charging on beneath him, the trailing thunder of hooves lost in the wind whipping past his ears. Chique careened around the clubhouse turn, ears flicking forward. A bounce finally returned to her gait, Nate able to separate the footfalls of her stride as she eased.

"Did you see that?" Nate said before the outrider could get a word in, picking them up as the also-rans exited the turf. "That bloody French horse tried to savage her! He don't know who he's messin' with, eh Cheeky?" Nate grinned, slapping her heartily on the neck. Chique snorted in agreement as they started towards the grandstand.

Liv was the one coming forward to meet them, taking the white lead shank from the outrider, reaching up to grasp Nate's hand. He wanted to hop off right then and there, throw himself around her. *Keeneland, here we come.*

Nate scrubbed Chique's neck as Liv made the requisite tour for the wall of snap-happy photographers, then they travelled across the main track to the infield winner's circle.

Then somehow, Liv was always where he wasn't. She passed Chique to Jo before his feet hit the ground, pulled away by her parents as he dragged the tack off and went to weigh in. She was distracted as Jo led the winning filly back to the barn; impatience thinly veiled during the presentations, mounting during the post-race interviews. Nate could see it so plainly, but if the reporters recognized it, they didn't care. She broke away before he did — extracting herself from the clinging media, giving Nate an apologetic half-smile.

The back-slaps and high-fives in the jock's room came one after another. Everyone liked to see one of the local riders win. It didn't happen often. Breeders' Cup *Win and You're In*. They were in.

It sucked he had the rest of the card to ride. These big races were broadcast on NBC and the telecast messed up the order of the afternoon, making the Mile the fifth. He grabbed his phone before he changed for the next race.

Wait for me, he typed.

The shedrow was deserted, the afternoon's warmth giving way to a cooler evening. Chique's head hung over her webbing, staring out as if she was wondering why Liv was still there, staring back.

One phrase, filly: Breeders' Cup Win and You're In. It taunted, and Liv envied the filly's inability to comprehend the ticket this afternoon's victory had handed them.

"Do you have any idea how much stress you've caused me?"

Not that Chique causing her stress was anything new, but this was on a totally different level. *Yeah, I'm sure there are eight other trainers tonight who wish they had your problem.* It's like Nate was next to her, she heard his voice so clearly in her head.

She'd told him to go home, leave her here alone with this crisis. He was understanding about so much, but he wouldn't comprehend her reservations. Who would? Who would even consider not going, especially when it was Keeneland and not

Santa Anita? Entry fees covered. Transportation covered. All they had to do was get themselves there, and keep Chique peaking for another six weeks. Keep her healthy. Keep her sound. Get her to the race in one piece, and pray she performed. Pray she belonged.

We ask, and we ask again. When was it too much?

The buzz of her phone startled her, Chique's ears swivelling forward.

Are you still there?

It didn't feel like an intrusion when he checked in on her, but she still wasn't used to it. She wondered how long he'd put up with her, with her fickle ways, her uncertainty. *You don't even know what you'd be getting into,* Miller, she'd told him back in May. When she'd put him off — again. He'd given her space — again. But he'd never given up. His conviction terrified her.

She couldn't ignore him, so she answered. *Yeah.*

See you soon.

So he hadn't gone home. She shouldn't be surprised. He wasn't that easily put off; not prepared to let her struggle alone. He never had been, though at times in the past she'd given him no choice. But this was right. They would talk. They were a team. Even before things had evolved into a relationship, they'd been a team. The three of them.

It wasn't long till she heard the beat-up Mustang's rumble. Chique echoed it with her own before Liv even saw Nate appear. Then he was at the end of the barn, backlit, his expression hidden, though it wasn't hard to imagine. She rose as he drew closer. Chique nickered again, vying for his attention, but he went first to Liv. Unspeaking, hand resting on her hip, lips meeting hers, lingering just long enough to grab wisps of her breath, trip up her pulse. When he went to greet Chique, he left a void.

He glanced over his shoulder. "It's okay. I'll give you a couple of days to process it."

She looked from Nate to the filly, the two of them emanating confidence. Chique's was cocky...Nate's was just sure. Steady. A foundation on which she could build things she'd never thought she wanted.

He returned to her, slipped his hand into hers, and pulled her back in. This time he just held her, arms enveloping her. She buried her face into his neck and breathed, his scent calming.

"Go home. Get some sleep. Okay?"

The voice of reason, in her chaotic brain. He made her doubts seem foolish, and at this moment, the two of them, together, made perfect sense.

CHAPTER THREE

Everything was finally aligning for Just Jay. It felt good to be part of that journey, seeing as Nate had always felt to blame for setting that cascade of one thing after another in motion. If Chique hadn't gotten away from him the day she and Jay had breezed as two-year-olds in Florida, maybe Jay wouldn't have developed tendonitis, the first of a string of minor injuries and ailments that had prevented the promising colt from getting to the races until last month. Now Jay had put together two impressive wins in a row. In the Durham Cup this past weekend he'd faced some tough older horses, and there was talk of him heading to Keeneland with Chique for a race the week before the Breeders' Cup.

But Nate hadn't expected all the good things in his career could turn the rest of his life upside-down.

He set the phone down, staring out the picture window behind the piano in his apartment. He almost hadn't picked up. He hadn't recognized the number, and assumed it was a scammer. It hadn't been, though it felt as if someone was playing a joke on him. He should be dancing around the room with the opportunity the call had presented. Instead, it felt as if the high he'd been flying on had propelled him into a mass of grey clouds.

He glanced at the photo he'd never been able to put away — he and his brothers, and the first girl who'd ever gotten to him. Cindy was so very different from Liv. He hadn't seen her since the night he'd left Calgary, the same day she'd gone and married his older brother. He'd been pretty messed up that night, but found himself wishing he could talk to her now. She was rational. Heartbreakingly so.

You home? he texted Liv.

Liv was one of those people you only called if someone was sick or dying, and showing up at her front door unannounced wouldn't be any more welcome. Sure this seemed like an emergency, the way it had set his world off balance, but she still might not see it that way. No immediate reply, but that was normal. She didn't live with her phone glued to her hip like some people.

The Lachance residence wasn't far. The walk there did nothing to settle his brain. Liv's Nissan was parked beneath the trees at the side of the building, so he'd guessed right. She must be finished with the yearlings.

It was only the second time he'd been to the house, the memory of the first hitting him with a ripple of melancholy as he trudged up the front steps. Liv's father, Claude Lachance had invited him here to break the news of the death of Geai Doucet, two years ago. Nate wondered if he and Liv would have handled the farm manager's loss better had their relationship been more what it was today. Back then, when he'd reached out, she'd pushed him away. Now, just when she'd started to accept she could count on him to be there, whatever the reason, he was going to put a fresh wedge between them.

Liv's mother, Anne, answered the door, stepping back and welcoming him in. "Hello, Nate."

Anne would genuinely inspire compliments that she could be an older sister to her two daughters. She reminded Nate so much of Liv — in looks and mannerisms and reserved demeanor. The same wry humour, once you got past the shield.

"Olivia's in the pool. I'm assuming that's who you came to see." Anne smiled as she ushered him across the sunken living room. There was no doubt Anne was on his side.

"Does she ever stop and relax?" Nate asked.

"Perhaps you can help with that? Sometimes I think the two of you are so wrapped up in that horse and your careers, you don't even know who you are apart from it."

That was exactly what they were supposed to be figuring out this winter. He thanked her and stepped through the sliding doors onto the patio.

The long, narrow lap pool was practical instead of fancy, his eyes going straight to it. Splashes of colour from purple and white petunias filled planters on the terra cotta stones, but they only remotely registered in his vision. Liv was in the water, a clean crawl stroke pulling her through to the far end. Her turn was seamless, and she came back toward him, her face only partially leaving the water to breathe.

He felt guilty watching her, though he told himself he was merely admiring her athleticism, not thinking about that supple body and what he could do with it. When she came to the near end, she stopped, starting when she saw him, though her expression quickly changed to a smile — even if it was a vaguely suspicious one.

She climbed out and he handed her the towel draped over a nearby chair, his eyes falling to the wet one-piece suit clinging to her torso before snapping up. She pulled off her cap and goggles and pressed the towel to her face.

"Thanks," she said, wrapping it around her shoulders, long hair falling stringy and damp about them. She still looked wary of his presence, like he was pushing the boundary too much and infringing on her cherished alone time. "Everything okay? I thought you were going down to Will's."

"Something came up. I did try to text you." He followed her lead and sat on the edge of one of the patio chairs, thinking she was going to get chilled if she stayed out here too long. He should have taken her out to dinner or something, instead of showing up like this. "Your mother let me in."

Liv rolled her eyes. "Next thing you know she'll be out here with refreshments. Asking you to stay for supper."

"Just because you shun guests doesn't mean it's normal behaviour." He grinned, and Liv laughed.

"So what's up?"

"I just had a call from Don." Nate paused. Don Philips trained a few horses for Liv's dad in New York. Liv and her filly L'Éclaircie had been based with him for most of Claire's career, though Liv had never wintered with him. She'd always chosen to go to Florida with Roger and the Canadian string instead. "He invited me to come to California this winter."

There was the slightest hesitation, a shadow passing over her features. Her voice was soft and careful when she responded. "That's great, Nate. You've always wanted to go to California, haven't you?"

He'd hoped for something different, some kind of protest; some indication she was as thrown as he was by the news. Because even though it was true, he'd always wanted to ride there — it was the pinnacle wasn't it? — he was torn by the prospect, because now, he wanted to be with her more.

"I haven't given him an answer yet. I had to talk to you first."

She nodded, but didn't offer anything; didn't rescue him from his predicament.

"Any chance you'd consider bringing Chique to Santa Anita?" It was a shot in the dark, though he didn't have to tell Liv what would be available to the filly there. There were a number of big stake races; rich purses, the best horses. Chique would have no trouble fitting in.

Don had confirmed he was taking Just Jay, hoping to build the colt's appeal as a stallion prospect. The trainer had dangled that information in front of Nate like a bright chestnut carrot, assuring him he'd keep the mount.

But Liv shook her head, slowly. "I'm taking Chique to Florida, Nate. She's had a long, hard season, and she'll deserve the break, especially if we go to the Breeders' Cup. And it's not like I could take Feste, is it?"

Of course — Feste. He'd let the yearling slip from his mind, neglected to assign importance to him, because he wasn't working with the colt, didn't see him daily like Liv did. He'd been living in the here and now, while Liv always, always, skipped ahead, sometimes to her — and their — detriment, mapping out worst-case scenarios. Feste was her insurance, the next in line, the one who would give her purpose once Chique retired. Liv planned to run the filly as a four-year-old, but Nate suspected that would be it.

"You should go, Nate. Don's got nice horses. You'll do well with him."

Every time she said the trainer's name, it twisted his heart. "I was looking forward to this winter."

"You should still be looking forward to this winter. Even more so. It's California."

"I was looking forward to this winter with you."

Her eyes dropped, hands wringing the edges of the towel.

"This is your career, Nate. You can't make your plans around me."

"Damn it, Liv! Why the hell not?" He stood up and turned away, finally showing his frustration, because making plans — around her, with her — was exactly what he wanted to do. And this winter was supposed to be where she caught up with him, with those feelings. But like Cindy, Liv was ruled by logic — even more so. At least with Liv he knew his competition, and her allegiance to Chique and Feste wasn't a betrayal like Cindy's marriage to his brother had been.

He blew out a breath, and turned back to her, sighing. "I'm sorry. You're probably freezing. I should go."

Liv followed him through the sunken living room to the front door. Anne Lachance had discreetly disappeared. They should have come in where it was warm a lot sooner.

She faced him in the foyer, seeming as much at a loss as he was, reaching for his arm, her touch tentative. "When we're both back here in the spring, if nothing's changed...we'll start over, okay?"

It was like a slap to the face. "If nothing's changed?"

"A lot can happen over the winter."

He wanted to argue, but last winter, and how things had fallen apart in his relationship with Faye Taylor despite his intent to prevent it, came sharply to mind. This was different, he was sure, but it was too early to convince Liv of that. "So you want to put it off. Again. Now?"

"Don't you think it would be harder, staying together for the next two months, just to be apart for five?"

"It's going to be hell either way."

"What do you want me to say?"

"I want you to say you'll come too." He dislodged her hand from his arm, lacing his fingers with hers, but knew he was being unfair, no matter how much he meant it. The pain in her face was genuine, but it only amplified his own.

"You're the one who says everything happens for a reason." She countered his plea with a stoic gaze. "Good things come to those who wait?"

And all good things come to an end. "You would throw that back in my face."

He couldn't win. If he forfeited this opportunity, he passed up on a dream. But if he followed the dream, he did it without Liv. There were no guarantees he'd get such an offer again. He'd had a hell of a year — Eclipse Award for North America's top apprentice, Sovereign Award for the same in Canada; Queen's Plate, Woodbine Mile, maybe a trip to the Breeders' Cup — but this time next year there was a chance no one would even remember his name. The racing game was capricious that way.

If he had to make it through the winter without her to prove his point, so be it. He'd waited this long...what was another seven months?

She ran alone today, shoes crunching on gravel, heading towards the sideroad instead of the usual route around the farm — a change of scenery when her head was in desperate need of clearing. Nate's absence would have been more obvious through the trails. Damn him for wiggling into things she'd always been happiest doing alone.

She'd only seen him briefly this morning, when he'd come by first thing at the track to check on Chique. Cue awkwardness, thanks to the status update she'd inflicted on them. His usual end-of-the-morning visit hadn't happened, so apparently he'd taken her words yesterday to heart. It had been what she'd asked for, but she hadn't anticipated how disheartened she'd be that he'd accept it so abruptly.

The unpaved road was quiet, and she ran just off the shoulder where the repeated passage of tires had left a smooth path. She'd go farther today — maybe that would sort her out, bring order back to her brain. But it wasn't going to change reality.

Everything had been too perfect. Scary-perfect. Too smooth. A bump, a hill, or in this case, a roadblock, was inevitable. She pushed herself harder, not wanting to think.

On the way back, she turned up the lane to Northwest instead of going home. Faye's car was parked beside the old red brick Victorian farmhouse, Dean's pickup gone. Liv slowed, walking to let her breathing normalize, hands on her hips. She stretched before skipping up the steps to the back door.

"Hey! Come in!" Faye held the door while Liv walked through. "Forgive me for not giving you a hug. Can I get you a... towel? You're drenched."

Faye was allergic to exercise. It felt good to laugh, augment the endorphins.

"Hungry?" Faye said as Liv mopped her brow. "Will gave me pastries. Coffee?"

"No thanks on the coffee — I think I'm dehydrated enough. I won't say no to pastry, though."

Faye poured her some water and ushered her out onto the deck, setting a plate on the round glass table between the metal chairs. Liv drank half the glass before sitting, propping her legs out in front of her, letting the sun prolong the warmth of exertion.

"From dating a jockey, to a pastry chef. How did that happen?" she asked, grinning as she perused the plate. Maybe protein would have been a better option right now, but carbs would restore her depleted glycogen, right?

Faye closed her eyes as she bit into a flaky brioche. "I think it suits me."

A sigh escaped Liv's lips as the first buttery-sweet mouthful of an almond croissant melted on her taste buds. "This is divine. You'd better keep him."

"I do believe that's worth considering. He is multi-talented." Faye's mouth twisted slyly. "I hope he and Nate find another excuse like the Plate Party to play. Their little unplugged gig at the café was wonderful, but they need a bigger venue so the whole band can be there."

Liv shoved another piece in her mouth to put off a response. The night of the Plate Party had been dreamlike. Champagne on the shed with Nate after the race. The dance that had turned into a kiss. And another. Later Nate had joined the band for a few songs, the crowd loving the Plate-winning rider contributing vocals, Faye and Emilie heading up the dancing. The music had gone on longer than any of them had hoped before backstretch security had shut them down. And Faye was right, the evening at the café — which was now Faye and Will's café — had been magical. All of it had been a wave she'd been riding, but yesterday she'd been knocked off the crest, sucked into the undercurrent.

"You really should come when they practice at Will's," Faye continued.

Liv reached for her water, still not ready to bring Faye up to speed on Nate's bombshell. "That would be too much the doting groupie-girlfriend for me quite yet."

"Please." Faye waved away the protest.

"I think it's important we have our own things. He has his music. I have — "

"What, exactly?" Faye quirked a perfect eyebrow.

"I swim. And I'm starting yearlings." It sounded lame, even

to her. "We work together. I don't want us to get sick of each other."

"You'd better not be sick of each other yet. You're still in the dreamy early stages. You seriously need to relax. You know what's good for relaxing?"

Liv smirked, then sighed, shoving another piece of croissant into her mouth, trying to convince herself she was savouring it, but it might as well have been sawdust now. She stared at the paddock across the driveway where a mare and foal grazed.

"What's up, sweetie?"

That's why she'd come here, wasn't it? To do what she was always disinclined to do. Talk about it. It would be all over the backstretch soon. Faye would never let her hear the end of it if it came second-hand. "We've kind of — I don't know. Broken it off."

"What?" Faye was immediately upright, the plate almost falling off her lap. "Why? What happened?"

Liv glanced at her, and set her own plate aside. It seemed a shame to waste the rest of her croissant on her churning stomach. "He's going to ride in California this winter."

Faye looked confused. "Okay. So, that sucks, sure, but why does it mean you have to break up? Especially now? That's like...weeks away." Faye paused. "I thought things were good."

"They were. Just — too good."

"That's not a thing, remember," Faye scoffed. "You being you, of course, didn't say anything to sway him."

"How could I? I had two choices. Either shut up, or go myself."

"That doesn't sound like a bad option."

"I can't, Faye. Chique's brother is a yearling now. I can't take a yearling to Santa Anita, no matter who he is."

"You know in this business horses come and go, Liv. Guys like Nate Miller don't. You let those horses get in the way of everything." Faye finished her brioche, and reached for her coffee cup. "It makes me want to slap you sometimes. You have no idea."

Liv felt guilty expressing her fluctuating emotions to Faye. Nate was the first guy Faye had really let herself care about, and if it hadn't been for Liv — as unintentional as her part had been — she wondered if the two of them would still be together. But Faye had found Will, battling her own resistance to give him a chance, while Liv kept struggling to do the same with Nate.

Faye's hard gaze hadn't left her. "It's not too late to at least change your mind about now."

"That would just make it all more difficult. Ending things before — " Faye's eyebrows went up, a self-satisfied smirk on her lips. Faye would never understand it wasn't about sex. Liv shook her head, twisting her fingers together. "This is the way it's always going to be. One of us is always going to be where the other isn't. It's part of the job description. So if we can't deal with it now, for one winter, I want to know before we get in any deeper."

That, at least, Faye didn't dispute.

"How are things with Will?" she asked, reaching for her water just to have something in her hands.

"Change the subject, why don't you."

"Not exactly." Liv grinned.

"Besides the fact that this pastry is amazing, and I'm going to have to start exercising too if I keep eating it like this...good. Really good. But if it doesn't work out with Will," Faye continued, "I'm moving to Calgary, because they seem to breed them right out there."

CHAPTER FOUR

Nate stood back, observing silently with what he could only call resignation. Chique was tied to the stall's back wall, her sleek hindquarters bearing witness to absolute fitness, the definition of her hamstrings a sharp contrast to the soft sweep of tail that nearly touched the deep straw. Liv knelt at her left foreleg, quick hands wrapping the lower limb in a white polo bandage — oblivious to his presence.

Chique's head cocked ever so slightly, the low rumble escaping her throat exposing him. Liv glanced over, a half-hearted lift to the corners of her mouth when she saw him.

"Hey, Miller." Her tone was soft, almost apologetic, as she finished with the bandage and ducked under the filly's neck. She set herself by Chique's right leg, wrapping it to match the left.

"How is she?" he asked, coming to the doorway. Best to keep his mind on business. A month out from the Breeders' Cup. He could still be excited about that.

Liv straightened, coming closer, and he held out the martingale and girth as if they could shield him from the draw of her.

She shrugged. "Everything looks fine, but you'll have a better answer after you gallop her."

It was so familiar, their motions rote as they got Chique ready, like they had most mornings this year. He liked to get the filly out first. It had always been the best part of his day. Now it was just a reminder that this emotional separation would be physical, to the degree of thousands of miles, come November.

"I'll take her a turn," he said, breaking the silence once they were done.

It wasn't common knowledge yet, the news that weighed on him — he'd seen no reason to share with anyone other than Liv at this point — but he still felt as if all eyes were on him, judging him. *Deserter*. But Liv had told him to go. Sent him away. Selflessly? Taking one for the team. Or was it defence? It didn't matter. It didn't change anything.

She waited in front of the tack room with her helmet on, taking the shank while he automatically checked the tack, even though he'd been there as it went on. Habit. When she wrapped her hand around his left ankle to throw him up, her touch, even through the leather of his boot, made him want to let go of the lines and grab her by the shoulders, demand they come up with a better answer than the one they'd settled on. But there were more appropriate times. A move like that would no doubt give Chique an excuse to go dashing down the shed without them — not something to even joke about with Miss Breeders' Cup *Win and You're In*. He mustered the inspiration to brace against Liv's hold on his leg and bounced, easing lightly into the saddle. The significance of *getting tied on* seeming deeper each day. Seven months was already feeling like the longest ride of his life.

"Right behind you," Liv called after turning him loose, and he was vaguely aware of her disappearing into the pony's stall.

Chique was uncharacteristically quiet, like she was picking

up on his mood. Liv didn't even take her head as they walked to the main track, Nicole on the other side of her with an unraced chestnut three-year-old filly named Happy Together – a name which seemed a bit too ironic at the moment. The silence was painful.

Liv didn't back up with them, and didn't need to speak for Nate to know they'd meet after at the five-eighths pole. Chique settled into a jog next to Happy, and Nicole glanced over.

"You okay?" she asked. "You're not singing. With the way you're riding these days, I expect you to be singing."

He snorted, lightening up a bit and breaking into the first bars of Wild Light's "California On My Mind." It wasn't an endorsement for the place.

Nicole looked at him strangely, so he'd guessed right thinking she wouldn't know the tune. In an attempt to break out of his wallowing, he shifted to "More Than Fine." Switchfoot usually worked to get his head out of a funk, but it was a hard sell today. At least it kept Nicole from asking more questions.

They turned in at the wire like they always did before setting off to gallop. He noticed it immediately. Chique didn't feel right. It was more than her not grabbing the bit like she wanted to take him for a joyride, her usual MO; there was a subtle hesitation, a less than solid sense of her beneath him. She swapped leads a beat too early as they hit the backstretch, and her ears didn't flip forward like they always did at that point. He shook his head when Nicole glanced back as he pulled his filly up, letting Happy go on without them. Chique shook her head too, annoyed with being left behind.

Liv was already coming toward them, maneuvering Paz to their left. Nate wished he could rub the furrow out of her brow, but it probably matched his own.

"What's wrong?"

"She's off. Left fore."

"Damn it," Liv muttered. "Let's get her back to the barn."

He wouldn't have thought the silence could be heavier heading home than it had been walking out, yet here they were, Liv holding Chique protectively by the bridle like she hoped she could somehow regain control when things were fragmenting like cracks in an old teacup. Chique danced lightly, no doubt wondering why she hadn't been allowed to finish her gallop, even if Nate wasn't convinced she'd been into it today.

The vet wouldn't be around until after training hours, but he still felt bad leaving after he'd removed the tack. Not that there was anything he could do.

Work was only so much of a distraction. It didn't help that everyone asked about Chique. *How's the big filly?* He tried to go along with the fantasy that they were, in fact, Breeders' Cup bound, when he was sure in the pit of his gut now they weren't.

He hadn't noticed Cory earlier, but when he returned, she was there, putting a walker away. Chique waited in her stall, pulling at her haynet, rumbling for peppermints as soon as she saw him. He indulged her, glancing down at her bandageless legs. Open, for x-rays.

Ducking past a mass of bridles hanging on the hook in the doorway, he found a little huddle in the tack room — Roger's assistant trainer Jo sipping a coffee, Liv with her helmet still on, Nicole pulling off hers and hanging it on a nail.

"All out?" he asked.

"All except for Lacey," Jo said. "Liv's going to get on Paz and take Cory out on her."

"I'll take her," Nate offered. "You'll be more useful around here than I would be." He flashed his eyes to Liv with a restrained smile.

"I don't know, Miller. I'm sure you remember how to do

tack, and you're pretty good with a bandage. But I do think she'd appreciate your company more than mine."

Nicole sputtered. "True. Though it might affect her ability to focus."

"Other than that she should be fine," Liv said. "The kid evented. She'll look better than most of the exercise riders out there."

Liv's grin was cute, tugging at Nate's heart, all he saw as Jo brushed past him and called down the shed.

"Cory! Get your boots and helmet on."

Cory was tiny. Saying that in a place where his five foot six was considered tall was quite a statement. It didn't mean anything, of course. It wasn't her size that would determine if she turned out to be a rider or not. Lacey was on the small side too — a late-maturing two-year-old filly who was just in for the experience. She'd go to Payson with the others this winter. The others that didn't include him.

"Ready to go, kid?" he asked.

Cory's head looked too big for her body now that her helmet was on, her tiny feet shifting back and forth, elbows clutched by white-knuckled hands. Liv stopped Lacey next to her.

"First thing? Check the tack," Nate instructed. "I'm not saying Jo didn't put it on right, but never assume the person who did knows what they're doing. It'll save your ass one day."

Liv's smile was encouraging, watching Cory do as she was told. Then Nate legged the kid up, and hauled Paz out of his stall while Liv led the filly off, quietly coaching as she went. *Yes, check your girth again. Got your lines knotted? We call reins lines. She's not tough, but shorten the irons up a couple of holes. Nate will have you, so you can work on standing up. Try it now. Take a cross — like a bridge. You know how to do that, right? That's it. Good.*

Nate swung into the pony tack unassisted. Liv hated it when he did that on Chique, even though Chique didn't care. He'd bet by this afternoon the filly would be at the farm, out with Claire, grazing in the warm fall sun under Triple Stripe's colourful maples. Why had he even bothered to let himself plan? This crazy job didn't lend itself to such things.

Outside Liv walked Cory right up to him, not letting the kid try to get there on her own. He rolled his eyes as he freed the long leather strip from where it hung on the pony's saddle and looped it through the D-bit Lacey wore. It wasn't till then Liv unsnapped the shank. *Not overly cautious at all.*

"Have fun," she called, retreating into the barn.

Nate squeezed Paz forward, holding Lacey with his arm loosely at his side. He ran his eyes over Cory — helmet secured, safety vest in place over her long-sleeved t-shirt, hands clenched on the reins in the same death grip she'd had on her elbows before she'd got on.

"You comfortable?" he asked skeptically.

"Except for being terrified!" she squeaked. "Are we really going to the track?"

"Yeah. The training track. It'll be fine."

Her face suggested that was a ridiculous thought.

The track was practically deserted this time of morning — just the usual assortment of babies like Lacey, and inexperienced riders like Cory. Nate stopped just before the on-gap. Lacey stood like a pony, while Paz dropped his head, mouthing the bit and starting to prance. *Chill, old man.*

"We'll back up to the five-eighths pole, then go once around as long as you're okay. Do you know what all that means?"

She gave a short nod. "Em told me some stuff. You're not allowed to trot going counter-clockwise, so we have to trot the other direction, and stay on the outside rail to keep out of the way of the gallopers and workers."

"Pretty much. Just don't say trot. We say jog." Not that anyone would mistake her for anything other than a newb. At least they hadn't subjected her to an orange vest. "All set?"

Another short nod, and Paz led the way as soon as Nate eased his hold on the reins. He let the pony gelding jog as soon as they were past the clocker's stand, Cory posting automatically to Lacey's lazy gait.

"Plant your cross at the withers and try standing up."

"That's easy," Cory chirped. "It's like cheating, resting my hands on her neck like this. I could do two-point for hours."

"Perfect," Nate said. "I'll make sure Liv knows, so she can send you out on those three-mile jogs we do in Florida." *We*. There would be no *we* this winter.

On the backside he pulled them up and faced the infield. "And then we spend a few moments watching the world go by. We like to teach the horses to relax — but you'll see a lot of people just turning around and taking off, or coming on the track and galloping right away."

He started them at a hobby-horse canter. "Stand up again, and leave your hands down there. You won't be able to do that with every horse — you've got to hold a fit one, and that's a bit different — but don't worry about that for now. Right now just worry about your balance, and stay out of the horse's way. Stay quiet. Not too far forward, or some rat that likes to drop its shoulder will have you eating dirt. With the babies, your balance is important because they're just finding their own, so they need a little more support. But you probably know that from the yearlings."

The kid was a natural, really. Liv said she was chatty, but she'd barely uttered two words. She was concentrating hard. It made him laugh.

"What?" She glanced over, then set her eyes back on Lacey's poll.

"You're taking this very seriously."

"Why wouldn't I be?"

"Well...you've ridden cross-country, right? Like galloping through fields and jumping stuff? This — at least this here, this filly — is a piece of cake next to that. Breathe."

Her cheeks puffed as she blew out a gulp of air.

"Better," he said. "Why do you want to do this, anyway?"

"You're a jockey. You have to ask?"

"Well, okay. But I hope I'm not the first one to tell you — getting an education and a real job is an easier way to go."

"I'm not smart like Em. I'd never get into university. And even if I did, my mom could never afford it. If I have to pick between this or working at Tim Horton's...I'll take this, thanks."

"You know you're pretty lucky Liv agreed to it, right? Most people have to start at the bottom. Walk hots. Learn how to groom. Beg someone to let them get run off with on the pony."

Her serious expression finally cracked, and she caught his eye with a bright smile that lit up her face. "I guess I have you to thank for that, don't I?"

"Maybe you do. You owe me big-time, then. I'll have to remember that." Her body was looser now, her knuckles on the lines not so white. "Once we get past the on-gap, I'm going to turn you loose. Worst case, Paz will run off with me, and you'll have to rescue me. You might get to pay me back sooner than you think."

Her grin only got bigger. The little gallop seemed to work her tongue loose, because she chattered all the way back to the barn. He tried to act like he was listening — and it had given him more of a distraction than hanging out on the shed waiting for the vet to show up would have. He tried to remember the first time his boss back in Calgary had put him up on a horse, that feeling. Even on the old war horse Al had let him gallop, he'd been hooked. Likewise, Cory was hooked.

Liv held Lacey while Cory bathed the little filly. The kid sloshed suds and water about, wearing a third of it, helmet off but her kerchief keeping her short blonde hair back. Now he saw what they were all talking about. He didn't think she'd stopped yakking. Liv stood patiently, tickling Lacey between her nostrils with the end of the shank.

"Thank you," she mouthed.

He shrugged, and had Paz hosed off and out grazing before Cory finished.

Normally Liv was all about geeking out over cool diagnostics, but today she resented the expensive imaging that pinpointed the source of Chique's problem. Dr. Koval, surgeon at the nearby equine hospital, took the time to go over the report with her, even though she already knew the verdict. He'd called as soon as he had the results, but due to the nature of nuclear scintigraphy, it was necessary for Chique to remain in isolation at the clinic until the radioactive isotope had decayed to safe levels.

They were pretty pictures, like colourful pointillism, with the darkest area marking the highest concentration of the isotope, at the site of concern. It wasn't a large area, but it indicated subchondral remodelling — what lay people were calling bone bruising — on the distal articular surface of Chique's left third metacarpal, the cannon bone. Liv was sure only Nate would have noticed Chique was even off, it was such a mild injury. But thank goodness he had, because when something like this went undiagnosed, it could lead to catastrophic breakdown.

She dressed Chique in clean white flannels and cottons, and the clinic staff helped her load the filly onto the Triple

Stripe gooseneck, set up with a box stall. Liv didn't drive the farm truck enough to have her phone connected to Bluetooth, so she located the local alternative radio station and listened to its selection of tunes and commercials for the solitary drive home, keeping an eye on the filly with the trailer cam.

Once she'd unloaded and led Chique into her stall in the office barn, Liv drew tranquilizer into a syringe, returning to inject the small dose before removing the filly's travelling gear. It didn't take long for the intravenous drug to take effect. She led Chique to the small paddock where Claire lingered with interest at the gate, and turned the younger filly out with her old friend.

Chique dropped her head and the two of them grazed, nose to nose. Liv extracted her phone, snapped a photo, and texted it to Nate.

Just Jay was the bright light in all this. When it came to Nate's career, it wasn't a bad thing to fly to Lexington, steal a win with the Triple Stripe colt in a Grade Two stake at Keeneland at the beginning of Breeders' Cup week; put his name more firmly in the consciousness of the American trainers. That was as close as they were going to get to the World Championship of Horse Racing this season.

In the eternal words of the sport: *maybe next year.*

CHAPTER FIVE

More than fine...

The ringtone jolted him into consciousness. He grappled for the phone, managed to hit snooze on the second poke, and rolled over.

This isn't what he did. He didn't hit snooze. He always got up with the alarm. He got up before the alarm. Just not this morning.

Downstairs, he could hear Chique's low rumble, echoed by Claire's sing-song. He usually fed them before leaving for the track, but this morning, Liv had beat him to it.

More than fine...

Twisting and sitting up, he stabbed at the screen, leaning back against the headboard. He pushed himself out of bed, got dressed.

More than fine...

This time he made sure he hit stop. *Sorry, boys, not feeling it.*

The big picture window was a rectangle of inky black. Maybe

he'd go back to bed after they left. Why not? Thursdays were dark; he might as well take advantage of this rare break. Guys booked off all the time for sketchier reasons. Why couldn't it be his turn?

The coffee maker gurgled when he pressed it into action, and he pulled two mugs and a glass out of the cupboard, pouring himself some juice while he waited for it to brew. After distributing coffee into the mugs, he added milk and sugar to one and gave it a stir, and left them on the counter as he shrugged into his jacket.

Three more weeks till the meet ended. He should be anticipating what came after that — the west coast, riding at Santa Anita — but California dreaming wasn't going to help this morning. He felt as hollow as the sound of his boots as he descended the wooden stairs.

Chique nickered at him, and he mumbled "Sorry," as he gave her merely a glance and opened the office door, balancing the mugs. He pushed it closed with his butt, the room's warmth doing nothing for his heart.

The oil painting of Chique's sire and dam — Just Lucky and Sotisse — grabbed his attention every time he walked in that room. It wasn't just a tribute to two great racehorses, but also to the man with them. Two and a half years, Geai had been gone, left standing between horses in a painting — and ever-present around the farm, in Nate's head, in Liv's. He didn't know if they'd quite achieved what Geai had hoped for them, and this winter wasn't going to do anything to change that. What he'd give to sit down with the old man right now for some encouragement. At least the colt they'd named for him — Just Jay, half-brother to Just Lucky — was a shining reminder of his memory.

His eyes dropped to find Liv watching him silently from behind the desk, the painting looming behind her. He set the sugar-enhanced coffee in front of her. The smile that drifted over her face twisted at his gut.

"Thanks," she said quietly, remaining focused on him instead of reaching for the mug. "Shouldn't you be on your way in?"

"You thought I'd leave without saying goodbye?"

A brief storm passed through her grey eyes before they fell to the papers on the surface in front of her. "The van's heading to Woodbine to pick up the rest of the load from here."

He knew that. She was missing the point. "They'll survive one morning without me." He slumped into the old overstuffed chair set at forty-five degrees to the desk and slurped some coffee — black because he didn't get indulgences like milk and sugar when he had to be sure to make weight. It was just a coincidence that it matched his headspace. "Thanks for feeding."

"I was here, figured I might as well." She fixed her eyes on her cup, steaming in front of her, and lifted it carefully to her lips.

"Isn't it time Chique had her portrait done?" He glanced from the curve of her fingers around the mug, back to the painting. Four years ago August, he'd sat here for the first time, sizing up this dark-haired, serious young woman as she scanned his resumé. *"I'm assuming you want to ride races."* First words out of her mouth, not counting the initial *Hi* with the handshake. Straight to the point.

"Claire too." Her smile was more convincing this time.

He hadn't cared to figure her out back then, too stuck in his own torment to acknowledge anything more than her demeanor and aesthetic. At least he didn't feel as low as he had then, but even though he was convinced now he'd left that mindset far behind, the current situation poked at a vague association. Cindy had pushed him away, because of his career. Now Liv was pushing him away for it too.

"Does Fester have a name yet?" he asked in a vain attempt to redirect his thoughts.

The way she reacted when he butchered the colt's barn name pecked further at his composure — the upturn of her lips, a subtle shake of her head as she sat straighter, tucking a loose strand of hair behind her ear. Again he had to wonder if he should change his mind, when she obviously wasn't changing hers. The fact that she was leaving now, with both Chique and Feste unlikely to resume training until January, said it all. She could have stayed behind with them, like she had with Claire that first winter; come down after Christmas. She could have stayed with him.

"*Téméraire.* We just got the name tag."

"Doesn't that mean 'reckless' or something? Kind of ironic for such a mild-mannered colt."

"Works with the pedigree, though." Liv placed the papers in a leather padfolio and stood up, zipping it shut. "Help me throw on some bandages?"

They functioned in the silence that had followed them around since that day in September— what had started as awkward had developed a character all its own. Liv would never comprehend why he would even consider not going. This is what he'd signed up for, getting involved with her. It was like they touched, then bounced back a distance from each other, always some peripheral force intervening.

"You want to get Chique?"

He nodded, and watched as she went to Feste, winding the chain over his sheepskin-trimmed halter, her face soft as she whispered to him. She never looked at Nate like that. Of course he would lose to a horse. Nate didn't know whether to laugh or cry at the irony. He could picture Emilie's amused face as she patted the back of a disgruntled Faye's hand. *"I hope you don't mind being second to a horse, sweetie."*

Nate led Chique out into the brisk November daybreak, the breeze lifting the filly's mane. Cory stood with the van drivers, hands deep in the pockets of her jeans, her short blonde hair curling around the edges of a red toque. Chique walked on without hesitation. *Damn it, filly. The least you could have done is stalled a bit.* He wasn't ready to let them go. Liv secured Feste across from the filly, and Nate followed her silently off the van. They watched the drivers dismantle the ramp, then climb into the cab with a wave. The transport rumbled slowly off. Nate trailed Liv and Cory to the Nissan.

"Have fun this winter, Cory," he said, and opened the passenger door for her while Liv waited on the other side.

Cory took that as an invitation, apparently, throwing her arms around his waist. "Thanks, Nate! Thanks for all the help! Good luck with the rest of the meet! And have a great time in California!"

He pushed her away and she ducked into the car. Too many exclamation points. He should be so excited. He shut in her cheer with a swing of the door, and shoved his hands into the pockets of his jacket as he returned to Liv.

"Guess this is it," she said.

"See you next year," he responded wryly.

"It sounds so far away when you put it like that."

"It is." There was so much he wanted to say, but he felt he'd lost his right to say anything. "Give me a call when you get down there, okay?"

"It's going to be strange without you around."

"Oh, come on." He laughed softly. "This is all part of your plan to keep Feste for yourself, isn't it?"

He reached out and brushed a strand of hair away from her face, his fingers lingering before he wrapped his arms around her and held her, not wanting to let go. Not for the first time, he felt like phoning Don, as soon as he returned to his apartment, calling the whole damn California thing off.

"Drive carefully," he said, kissing her cheek. He reached for the door handle, opening it, when he shouldn't be helping her leave. She hadn't moved yet.

Say something. Say something that will make this bearable.

Liv held his eyes, then blinked before folding herself into the packed vehicle. She glanced at him as she pulled on the seat belt. "Bye Miller."

She'd done it so easily. Maybe she was right not to prolong it. He watched her zip away to catch the van, and felt a chill as the wind hit the back of his neck. At least he thought it was the wind.

The barn was so deserted now, just reinforcing the encroaching emptiness he felt. He gathered the coffee cups, both of them barely touched, and locked the office behind him, trudging upstairs. He could wallow. Go back to bed. Watch Netflix all day. But something in him fought back, an idea taking shape as he dumped the cold brew and gave himself a warm cup. His phone camera, a tripod, the piano...he wasn't going to just fade away.

CHAPTER SIX

CHIQUE'S SNORT was loud and clear, the filly hanging her head over the fence of one of Payson's sandy paddocks. Liv ignored her, riding out on Feste, laughing at the filly's buck and squeal in protest of not being included.

Feste was sensible and bold, unfazed by things that would have set off his sister. Normally after sixty days the yearlings had a break until January, but hacking him about the grounds wouldn't hurt. In fact, it would be good for him. His swinging stride carried her down the laneway towards Route 76, small ears pricked with interest. Liv guided him left before reaching the office, to the trail that looped behind. *Over hill, over dale...* that's what Nate would have been singing, as they wandered in and out and up and down the gentle landscape.

Inspired by the training protocol they'd used for Claire two years ago — when Nate had talked her into doing things differently with the mare, who was a bad bleeder — Liv had dug out another of Geai's old books before she'd left: *Conditioning To Win*. It freaked her out to read how they'd trained yearlings back when the book had originally been published — breezing them so early, workloads that would bring PETA down on a trainer's head. Today's racehorses were treated like fragile birds, and one might think they were, because they sure seemed to break more easily. But Claire hadn't, not from training hard. It had been a loose horse that had taken her out. So maybe Feste wouldn't either. Liv would monitor his progress down to the nth, of course, but she was determined to build him into the strongest, soundest athlete she could. Chique's issues just convinced her of it, rather than scaring her off.

She let him jog on the level ground, past Payson's unique turf course, where she envisioned them doing most of their work in the next months. The sun was hot, humidity amplifying its effect, leaving the t-shirt under her safety vest drenched. Nate had texted her a photo of Ontario's first snowstorm earlier. *Poor Nate.*

Michel met them in front of the open shedrow. No asphalt apron here, just sand, and grass, and trees. And fire ants. Liv sidestepped one of the mounds on the way to leaving her tack on the rail, and returned to hold Feste for his bath.

It was too early to know what Feste might or might not be. It wasn't fair to have any expectations, so she was determined to just enjoy the process of bringing along another hopeful. And Chique? For the first time in years, Liv wasn't preoccupied with what was next. There was no pressure, no big races looming. She could worry about that in January, when the filly would hopefully be ready to start back. The theme for the winter was self-care, for all of them.

Nicole had stayed in Ontario to gallop for Roger, Jo grooming what was left, while Liv and Cory, Michel and Sue, handled things here in Florida. They alternated afternoon feeding duties, and Michel and Sue were on today, so after finishing with Feste and bringing his sister in from the heat, Liv corralled Cory — who didn't have a car, and was living with her — and headed for the coast.

She hadn't told Nate about the condo on the beach. It would have seemed too much like rubbing it in. A friend of her father's owned it, and it was going to be empty otherwise, so Jo was renting her place this winter, while Liv shared this paradise with Cory. Maybe next winter she'd share it with Nate.

It felt indulgent, stretching out on the sand and gazing up at the clear blue sky. She loved the ocean; never tired of its power as the waves washed up on the beach. It renewed her every time she came out here. It gave her clarity. It made her want to see if her father's friend would sell this place. She'd happily let the one in town go.

Two thousand miles had put distance between her and her doubts. Everything with Nate was going to be okay. This is how things needed to be. It wasn't a bad thing, taking a step back from the relationship. The way she felt about him scared her. He was ready for it all, and she'd felt herself being swept along, in danger of being swallowed whole; run off with like a rank horse.

It was too much, too soon. Speed kills — Thoroughbreds and relationships. It was best to slow everything down, let him go — figuratively, literally. But she really didn't feel she was letting him go. They were always connected, somehow.

"Aren't you going to open this?"

Cory's voice, as bright and energetic as the kid herself, pulled her back from the drowsy edges she'd been fading into. She'd forgotten about the mail Cory had grabbed from Payson's office. A little bubble pack, with the farm at home as the return address.

She hadn't recognized the block lettering spelling out her name over Payson's address. Cory dropped to the sand beside her, wrapping tanned arms around equally-tanned legs crossed at the ankles, her petite frame decked in a bikini top and bright pastel-patterned shorts. Cory didn't hide her curiosity. Who got snail mail anymore?

A data stick fell out as Liv unfolded the lined three-ring paper. Liv recovered it from her lap, two fingers closing around it as the others held the letter — because it was a letter — open. The writing was more familiar: half cursive, half printing, perfectly legible, a quick confidence to it.

Dear Liv,

You're probably on the beach right now, roasting in the sun while I freeze my ass off.

She had to laugh, because, well, here she was.

I kind of think I'd trade the stupid riding title for the beach at the moment.

Things are falling into place for California, as much as part of me wants it all to blow up so I can tell you I'm coming to Florida after all. Jeanne's contacted me about an apartment. Will's got a buddy who's going to look after the Mustang for me. Do some work on the poor old girl so she might live to see another year, and store it for me over the winter. I'm almost going to miss her as much as I miss you, but at least I knew better than to ask her to make the trip.

He loved that damn car. She felt a pang of guilt, thinking the car, at least, would have made the trip with him if he'd asked.

Will keeps saying we should do a show next year. Me going away doesn't help much with that plan either, but we'll see. Might be kind of fun. I'm taking my guitar to LA, at least. Don't think the piano will fit in my carryon.

"What's the stick for?" Cory, still watching, said.

"I don't know yet, and I'm not sure it's any of your business." She gave Cory a wry smile, and the kid took the hint and wandered down to the waves.

I know you think we're doing the right thing. I'm familiar with the "I don't want to hold you back" argument. It just hits kind of hard, because, well...I thought we were in this together. You, and me, and Chique. And I know it's just five more months. It's just that right now, five months feels like forever.

I'll go along with the agreement, but that doesn't mean I have to like it. And that doesn't mean I can't fight it, old school. I'm going to pretend I have to win you over all over again, because clearly I haven't done a good enough job.

Yours — really,

Nate.

PS — If you want more, send it back. And give the kids a kiss and a peppermint for me.

More? He must mean the stick.

She folded the letter, returning it and the flash drive to the envelope. Gathering her towel, she returned to the house and Liv opened her laptop on the kitchen counter. She keyed in her password, and plugged the stick into the USB port.

A couple of movie files. *Okay*. Double-click. And there he was, at the piano in his apartment, no preamble as he started to play.

Some guys did playlists. Nate — well, Nate did this. Nate recorded songs. For her.

Hearing him sing wasn't new, but it was something else all together with the piano. It was like the piano was meant for him, part of him, the notes melding with his voice.

The music resonated in a way that was both enthralling and uncomfortable, exposing feelings she was trying to keep tucked away. This was hard. Hard to fight. She'd been so convinced things were as they should be. Somehow this rubbed off the protective coating she'd applied over the conflict that remained below the surface.

It was too late to change things. She wouldn't be the one to derail such an important career move for him, if that's what he was looking for. She had come to terms with the deal and was determined to see it through until they were back in Ontario.

But she couldn't help it. She scribbled a note to herself, to find an envelope and send the stick back tomorrow, hoping it would get to him before he left for LA.

CHAPTER SEVEN

"Ready?" Roger asked.

Nate didn't answer, just nodded, and stepped forward to meet Jay, hopping aboard from the trainer's legup. *Ready to be done with this season, sure.*

He pulled down his goggles and tugged up his mask against the bitter northwest wind as Jo led them from the paddock. Driving wet snow pelted his helmet, and somehow the base layer he wore under his silks and breeches hadn't put him overweight.

Closing day just as it should be, miserable.

It was enough to make him feel sorry for those who had to stay here for the winter. At least he got to go somewhere warm, even if it was the wrong place. Tomorrow, both he and Jay would be on their way to sunny California. It better be sunny, anyway.

Triple Stripe always seemed to have a live horse in the Valedictory Stakes, a marathon of a finale at a mile and three quarters. The last two years it had been Sans Défaut. This year, Just Jay was stepping up.

It always attracted a full field, many of them seasoned campaigners who so rarely got to run at this kind of distance. Jay was the young upstart, but Roger knew how to prep a horse for this race, and Nate was confident he was ready.

All the horses broke with a sigh instead of the usual bang. It was a long, long race. Jay was clearly confused by the lack of urgency. And it was fair for the colt to slow slightly, the first time under the wire, but when Nate asked — *a whole 'nother time around, buddy* — Jay responded with renewed confidence. They stalked the speed, sweeping around the clubhouse turn tight to the rail, and when the frontrunner started to falter midway down the backstretch, Nate worked his colt clear. Jay settled nicely, leading the way into the turn. Jay was smart, and Jay had gears. This was fun.

At the head of the stretch he asked for one of those gears, and Jay opened up a couple of lengths. When no one came at him, he asked for a little more for insurance, and Jay gave it. Nate didn't know how far in front they were when at the end.

He and Jay were going to be good friends this winter; this budding bromance would have to be enough.

Will was driving him to the airport in the morning, so when it was finally over — the card of racing, the season — he drove into the city.

"Can I get you a drink?" Faye took Nate's coat, and sashayed to the kitchenette. A year ago that would have been for him, the way her hips moved, that coy glance over her shoulder. Maybe that was a little bit for him. A little *you had that, bud, and you gave it up, and where's your girlfriend, anyway? Oh yeah, she dropped you because you're going to be 2,000 miles apart this winter. Hope you survive that separation better than we did.*

He shook his head, then stopped lest she think that was for the beer she held out, which he absolutely wanted. Faye was in the category of *been there, done that, screwed it up royally*.

"Please. Thanks," he said, watching her twist off the cap easily before handing it to him. "Where's Will?"

"On his way home from work."

"Home? You say that like you live here."

"Do I? Hmm. Yet, I do not."

"Staying over is a little too cosy for me when you're around."

"If you drink enough, you won't care. But, details. Sorry not sorry. Guess you're going to have to suck it up tonight."

"So I am." He swigged a good third of the bottle. "Better be prepared."

Faye returned to the kitchenette, steam rising over a pot on the stove. "Hope you're hungry." She dumped dried pasta into the rolling water.

"I'm always hungry." While he didn't have a terrible time making weight, he still had to watch what he ate. "And it's not like I can go crazy. I am going to California to ride."

The door cracked open, Will entering. Faye set a timer, and did her sashay over to Will, tipping her head back for a kiss. Nate looked the other way, and missed Liv all the more.

Faye wandered to the fridge for another beer, cracking it and handing it to Will, then passed Nate a bowl of salad and waved him towards the small table that was usually stacked with papers and music. Nate didn't think giving him the greens was coincidence, and he let himself laugh as he wandered over and set it down.

"So, are you ready for California?" Faye asked, dishing out

the cooked pasta, now tossed with olive oil and garlic. "You know — besides wanting to get away from our weather."

Nate inhaled the steam rising off the fusilli before carefully loading his fork. She wasn't asking if he was packed. "Why wouldn't I be? I've wanted to get there for a long time. I almost went there in the first place, instead of coming to Ontario."

"You're not really sure about it right now though, are you?"

He met her eyes briefly. "I've got to do it. So maybe the timing sucks."

"Do you think you'll get to Florida?"

Nate shrugged. "I can't see Chique running down there, so it's not as if they need me."

"This has really got you down, hasn't it?" Faye set her fork next to her bowl. "You guys will survive. Besides, this is the best part, isn't it? All the silly maneuvering and second-guessing. You should enjoy it. Once you're actually together, that's when the hell begins."

"Hey!" Will interjected.

"I'm kidding." Faye smiled at him sweetly. Nate was happy they were happy.

He wasn't quite drunk enough to not care about sleeping on the couch, but he wasn't driving all the way back to his apartment. He still woke up at four-thirty, and dragged himself off the couch, folded the blankets and sheet and set them on the arm, and shuffled to the kitchen to pour himself some juice.

Liv would probably be at Payson by now, putting Chique out in the dark to give the filly as long as possible in the paddock while the horses trained. He opened the weather app on his phone, swiping left — he still had Indiantown in there. Hot and humid, chance of rain, like always. One further gave him Los Angeles.

Will looked wiped, but mustered a sleepy smile when Nate

handed him a cup of coffee. Nate, on the other hand, was buzzing.

"I can't eat this early," Will said. "Want to go?"

Nate nodded. "Sure. I can drive there. Give you a chance to wake up."

Will didn't fight him on that, tossing Nate his keys. He folded into the passenger seat when they reached the Camaro, which was just as old as Nate's Mustang.

"Faye's right, isn't she? You're not really sure about this."

Nate scowled at him before refocusing on the road. "You're dropping me off at the airport."

"We're not there yet."

"I'm doing this. If she wants space, I'm giving her space." A couple thousand miles' worth of it. She hadn't asked for it, in so many words, but he'd deduced that was part of it.

"Big of you. Very understanding."

"But I don't want to give her space, damn it. I want her with me always and forever, like that stupid song in *Napoleon Dynamite*."

"You're in deep, dude." Will chuckled.

It was painfully true. He had to stop thinking about it. "So what about you and Faye? You two seem disgustingly happy and shit."

"I'm going to ask her to come to Calgary with me for Christmas. Think it's too soon?"

Nate's eyes shifted over quickly. "I don't know. You're on your own with that one."

"Think you'll ever go back?"

And all of a sudden, this life of his, the one that seemed all shiny to an outsider looking in, showed a little more of its tarnish.

The farm in King City was appropriately covered in fresh snow, as if it had been special ordered for Liv. It was strange to be transported from the warmth of South Florida back to winter in Southern Ontario, but not nearly as strange as spending the holiday down there. Liv had only done that once, two years ago — officially her worst Christmas ever. But the memory made her think of Nate. New Year's Eve. A crazy night with a bottle of wine and an exchanging of woes. A first-class pity party, complete with dancing to a sad song. The kiss at midnight had been completely accidental. How different would things be now if she hadn't misread the entire evening and let it justify keeping him away? In a way though, this winter was about keeping him away. Again. Not in the dramatic, panicked manner of two years ago. This time she'd cited logic. It was a smoke screen.

"Thanks, Em." Faye peered approvingly at the label on the wine bottle Emilie had brought for their Boxing Day get-together at Northwest. "Mind you, it's the least you can do, deserting me like you are and running off to the Sunshine State with Liv."

"Are you really, Em?" Dean asked. "What about your Masters?"

"You're one to talk, brother," Faye chided. Dean had abandoned a Masters degree himself to take over training for his father's clients after their parents had passed away in a car accident.

"I will go back to it. I've changed educational paths so often, adding a few more months to finishing the journey won't matter." Emilie had changed majors several times in the course of obtaining her undergraduate degree before settling on the path that now saw her in a Masters program for physiotherapy. She handed a tin of homemade cookies to Dean.

"Forget all that, did you bake these?" Dean peeked into the canister.

"You know that's what Em does," Liv said. "Em bakes. I completely missed any fragment of the domestic gene."

"Clearly," Faye said.

Dean stayed for a drink, then disappeared with a handful of cookies, leaving the three women to catch up. The living room was cozy with its open fireplace, the house decorated with the same style and care Faye took with her own appearance. Light from the flames danced over the resident Golden, Gus — flat out, soaking up the heat, his greeting duties complete. Emilie parked herself cross-legged on the floor next to him, running one hand over his long coat, holding her wine glass with the other.

"Did you talk to Nate yesterday?" Faye asked, settling on the couch with Liv.

"We texted," Liv said, looking into her glass and swirling the red liquid around. "I figured I'd talk to him tonight. Opening day at Santa Anita and all that."

"You're hopeless. You let Nate Miller go, on his own, to California, then abandon him. If some gorgeous little blonde movie star snaps him up, you completely deserve it."

Emilie laughed. "You're one to talk."

Faye glared at her. "That's enough from you!"

Liv raised her eyebrows and looked from Emilie to Faye. "Is one of you going to fill me in?"

Faye refilled their wine glasses, then sighed. "Apparently Will going back to Calgary for Christmas was enough to derail me."

Emilie laughed. "Only because he asked her to go with him, and she couldn't deal with that."

"And you're being hard on me for letting Nate go to California?" Liv said. "At least my derailing was about careers, not lack of conviction."

"Is it, though?"

Faye was calling her out. She was good — or bad — that way, her best friend. Liv stared at the fire. Avoiding. Which was what she was doing with Nate, right?

"Really, Liv what's the deal? Why are you so dead set on not giving it a chance?" Faye persisted.

"After what he went through in Calgary, I'm not sure it's fair to let him think we can have what he wants. I couldn't do that to him." The quiet declaration was laced with sadness.

Faye's eyes flickered, like she was feigning indifference. "He never did tell me."

"It was kind of harsh. I can't blame him for leaving."

Faye's gaze shifted to Emilie. "I suppose you know, too. He tells you everything."

Emilie shook her head. "Not that."

Faye and Emilie were going to wait until Liv explained, that was obvious. Should she, though? It wasn't really her story to tell. But maybe Faye deserved to know.

"He asked his girlfriend to marry him and she said no, then turned around and married his brother, in a matter of months."

It landed as it had for Liv, when he'd shared it with her — like a brick.

"Poor Nate," Emilie said. "That should make you feel better, shouldn't it, Faye?"

"Not sure about that, Em. I already knew I was Rebound Girl. That confirms we never really had a chance." Faye looked at Liv closely. "But I can see how that information wouldn't help you any."

Liv ducked her eyes to the wine, her words almost a whisper. "I would hate to end up hurting him."

Faye had another long drink from her glass. "I think we both need to make resolutions. I will call Will and apologize for my little meltdown, beg his forgiveness, and hope he hasn't written me off." She smiled wanly. "See, I get that Will is much too good a guy to let get away. And you, sweetie, will let yourself believe you can have a relationship with Nate, because we know the problems are all in your head and it's this talking yourself out of it that's the biggest issue. Time to move forward." Faye raises her wine. "You in?"

Liv frowned. "Kind of late for that, isn't it?"

Emilie scowled. "Like Faye said, hopeless." She removed her hand from Gus's side, and the Golden stirred, a nudge with his nose drawing her back to the all-important task of petting him. "I think you're both insane. I'm not saying you should have gone to Calgary with Will, Faye, but you kind of overreacted, so you'd better fix that. And Liv, you and Nate are bigger than your precious independence. He had it bad for you long before even he would admit it — sorry Faye — and you're not oblivious anymore. We all want to believe in happy endings and Faye is right, it would be just wrong for you to throw that away. Take a deep breath and go with it. For all our sakes."

"So if it all falls apart, I've got that on my shoulders? Our collective hope for happy endings?" Liv smirked.

Emilie laughed. "I'm never going to suggest anyone has to have a relationship to be happy, but if I'm lucky enough for that kind of kindred spirit to fall into my life, I pray I have the common sense to grab him."

"Hear, hear," Faye said, grinning. "Nate's younger brother, remember."

"Wouldn't that be funny?" Emilie said.

"But far too easy. Shouldn't you have to go through hell like the rest of us?"

"The two of you just create your own hell," Emilie said, smiling with mock sweetness.

Liv let Faye refill her glass — Emilie declined, picking up her car keys to make her point, though they could walk home if they had to.

"Hey Liv!" It was Dean's voice, coming from another room. "Want to watch the race?"

Liv almost spilled her wine as she stood up, her eyes sweeping from Faye to Em, glowering. "I almost forgot thanks to you guys. Come on."

They crowded into Dean's office, his computer monitor full screen on Santa Anita as the horses came out on the track.

"Number six, Arosebyanyother, owned by Inspired Farm, trained by Don Philips, ridden by Nate Miller..."

It was just a glimpse, Nate ruffling the filly's mane with one hand while he held the lines in the other. Seeing him plucked a string in her heart — his familiar posture, the simple affectionate gesture for his mount. It fed her guilt. Did she lack the common sense Em talked about? She'd always thought herself so logical. But logic got in the way of love. *Love.* Where had that come from? And why did she feel like she had to choose between it and a career? Did they get to have both, in this world?

Arosebyanyother broke well and Nate settled her midpack, outside — out of trouble. The filly ran easily behind a pace that should set things up perfectly for her, given her come-from-behind form. Turning for home Nate picked her up and sent her, as calmly and cooly as he'd ridden the whole race. He merely waved his stick alongside her neck, the filly surging to the lead and beating her rivals handily.

He looked so good on a horse. But was that it? Were they just about the horses? Was there anything wrong with that, though? There would always be horses.

"I say this calls for more wine!" Faye declared.

Liv settled back on the couch with Faye. She'd call Nate later. A text wasn't enough, Faye was right. She had to make a better effort. She was the one who had put things on hold. Merely sending the flash drive back and forth over the miles didn't count.

She gave it enough time that he'd be done for the day, and sneaked into the kitchen, slipping on her coat and boots and stepping out into the sharp night air. Hit call, pressed the phone to her ear.

It just rang. Maybe he was out celebrating. An allowance race didn't usually merit anything special, but given it was his first win in California, maybe it was justified. Maybe that blonde California girl had materialized to help. As Faye had pointed out, it would serve her right. She didn't leave a message.

She went into the videos on her phone, and pulled up the latest one he'd sent, just to see him, to hear him, take solace in the sentiment. It was a cover of his favourite band, Switchfoot – *I Won't Let You Go*.

Liv had flown home, but spent most of the twenty-one hour drive back to Florida behind the wheel of Emilie's red Civic, her sister sleeping through the music that kept Nate jarringly on her own mind. A combination of caffeine, separation anxiety, and too much time to think kept her going.

It was late enough when they arrived that she drove straight to the condo, despite a strong urge to check in at the training centre. Emilie was tired, but that didn't stop her waking Cory. Liv passed out gratefully in her own room to the hushed whispers of the two younger women.

Cory and Emilie were dragging but happy in the morning, and Liv left them to find their own way to Payson. It would be good to have Em around. She set off in the dark in her own car, navigating the way inland.

"I'm back," she called as she headed directly for Chique's stall, grabbing a thermometer from the nearby wallbox.

Jo poked her head out of the feed room. "We vaccinated everybody yesterday, so they're all walking."

Chique flicked an ear at Liv's arrival, but didn't move.

"What's the matter, filly? Your vacs not agree with you?"

She took hold of the filly's halter, but Chique resisted. After inserting the thermometer, Liv ran her hands down either side of Chique's neck, checking for swelling, then down the filly's left leg, feeling one hoof, then the other. The heat that met her touch sent her heart racing.

Curling her fingers around the filly's pastern, a strong pulse leapt under the pads. The other pastern was the same. Hind hooves normal. Liv stumbled to her feet, phone already to her ear as she called the vet — who wouldn't even be on the grounds this time of morning.

She found Jo. "Chique's trying to founder."

Jo sent Michel to the track kitchen for ice. Liv dragged the tub from the tack room. Even in these days of modern veterinary advances, the first line of defence for acute laminitis remained frustratingly simple: cold therapy, in hopes of arresting the inflammation assaulting the sensitive tissues of the hoof before irreversible damage was done. When Doc Beckett arrived, he confirmed Liv's fears, and administered supportive medication and fluids. She felt ill, watching Chique's pain escalate, the filly sweating, shifting uncomfortably from side to side, rocking back on her hindquarters as she tried to relieve the pressure in front.

"Maybe we'll luck out. You caught it early," the vet said. "Get her started on that footbath."

Everything seemed to swirl around Liv. Michel dumped bags of ice into the tub. Jo dragged the hose over. They lifted one foot, placing it gently in the freezing bath, then the other. Chique trembled in the doorway of her stall, swaying slowly back and forth.

Liv was only vaguely aware the others had gone back to work. Sometime in the middle of it all Cory and Emilie had arrived, and they helped walk horses, muck stalls, turn yearlings out.

Nate. He needed to know.

She didn't bother to calculate what time it would be in LA; just fumbled to unlock her phone again, finding his name on her most recents, resting her finger on it to initiate the call. She willed him to pick up.

"Liv – what's wrong?" His voice was thick with sleep.

She couldn't speak.

"You're scaring me." His voice came again; clearer, more urgent, this time.

"It's Chique. She had a bad reaction to her vaccinations." It came out strangled, shaky. "She's got laminitis."

"I'm on my way."

"Nate, you can't – "

"The hell I can't. I'll call when I get a flight."

The line went dead, the phone remaining pressed to her ear. Chique still swayed, back and forth.

It was Emilie who was waiting for him at the Fort Lauderdale airport, standing on the fringes of the crowd welcoming his flight

— arms clutched around herself like she was cold in her t-shirt and shorts, brow creased as she scanned the arrivals. Fatigue lined her face and weighed down her shoulders. He scooped her up and squeezed her, her arms unhesitatingly returning the gesture.

"Sorry, Em. I should've rented a car."

She shrugged. "I needed something to do. Just help keep me awake, all right?"

"I can drive."

She didn't argue, handing him her keys and leading the way to the car.

"How's Liv?" he finally asked, pointing the Civic north on the Turnpike.

"How do you think?"

He could imagine.

He didn't care that he was driving too fast, pushing the little Honda through the falling night. Being in transit all day, it felt better to finally have some control over the speed of his journey.

Emilie stirred as he turned into Payson's familiar dirt drive, the place he'd spent the last three winters. The Triple Stripe barn was the only one lit up, Liv's Nissan parked out front. He pulled in beside it, leaving the keys in the ignition, climbing out.

Liv sat on an overturned bucket in front of Chique's stall. She rose in slow motion. She felt limp and powerless in his arms, her breath warm as she pressed her face against his neck. He pushed her back to look at her, but she ducked away, breaking his hold.

"You should go home and get some sleep, Em," she said. "Jo's taking over for me at midnight or so."

"Stay awake, Em," Nate cautioned. At least she'd napped on the drive. He turned to Chique and stroked her neck. The filly pressed her muzzle into his hand, but without her usual demands.

"She's loaded up with medication, so she's more comfortable, for now," Liv said. "A bad reaction, Nate. That's all it took. I can't believe it."

He caught the distress in her eyes before she slumped back onto the bucket, hands clasped over her knees, leaving him feeling even more useless. Feste pushed his head over his screen, and scratching the yearling's forehead seemed like the only productive thing Nate could do.

"How was your Christmas?" Liv asked out of the blue.

It seemed an oddly polite question. "Quiet would be an understatement," he responded.

"I should have called. Faye told me off for it."

"Did she." He laughed quietly. "I'm not sure I'll ever believe Faye is truly rooting for me."

Liv rose again, running her fingers through the water in Chique's footbath. "We should add more ice."

He nodded, and one at a time dumped in two of the partially-melted bags resting nearby. Liv picked up the plastic, pressing the empty bags into the old feed sac that hung on the rail for garbage. She touched Chique's nose and slipped into the stall.

Nate followed slowly, and slid down beside her in the straw, leaning back against the bank of bedding that provided cushioning from the cinder block wall. Every so often Chique's muscles trembled, her head hanging low over the crossbar, the tie attached to her halter only a formality. He wrapped his fingers around Liv's, and she squeezed back, resting her head on his shoulder.

"Happy Birthday to me," she murmured.

"Oh shit, Liv. I forgot."

"If you recall the other time we were together on my birthday, it's probably best forgotten."

He chuckled quietly. "That was a strange night."

"A bottle of wine would go down nicely right now."

"Promise tonight you won't run away if I kiss you?"

She looked up at him, and he wasn't going to tell himself it was wrong, when everything else about this winter was wrong. He tipped her chin up with his finger, and let his thumb graze her jaw as his lips met hers, lingering just long enough that when he pulled back, the ache in her eyes mirrored his own. It wasn't enough, but it would have to be, for now.

"I still hate New Year's." His hand drifted back to find hers. "At least we're broken up already."

"It's not like that."

"Isn't it?"

"I'm sorry, Nate. About all of it."

"Bygones," he said. Not that he was over it. "Just three more months, right?"

It might have been romantic — here together with the sounds of rustling hay nets, the occasional snuffle as a horse cleared his nostrils, someone else grunting in flat-out sleep in the stall behind them — if not for the distressed filly before them.

Liv was so still next to him, he thought she might be asleep. He glanced at the time. "Happy New Year," he said quietly. No champagne, no fireworks, no streamers.

A whinny rose above the ambient noise, and Liv stirred, climbing to her feet — breaking the moment.

"Jo," she said as headlights flashed into the yard.

Jo's eyes swept from Liv to Nate as he brushed straw from his jeans. "Get her out of here, Nate. I'll carry on. If anything changes, I'll call."

Liv insisted on driving, silence stretching like the lonely road in front of them until they began to reach civilization.

"Where are you going?" he asked when she drove past the familiar condo complex, where he'd lived just down from her the last two winters.

"You'll see."

They passed over the intracoastal, and he could tell they were near the ocean, the smell of saltwater hanging in the humid air. Liv pulled in beside Emilie's Civic, in front of a modern-looking detached house, right on the beach. He followed her to it, and she let them in.

"Wow," he said quietly, looking across a large room to the floor-to-ceiling windows opposite. He wandered over and stared into the darkness, just able to make out the ocean where it met the sand. "You've been keeping secrets."

When he turned, Liv was slumped on a stool at the island that dominated the kitchen, her head resting on her arms. The answers to his questions could wait.

"You should eat something. Any food here?" He drifted past her and took the liberty of opening the fridge.

"I don't think I could stomach anything, Miller."

"I see eggs. And cheese. An omelet, maybe."

She didn't move as he cooked, but lifted her head when he placed a plate in front of her. "Who knew."

He laughed. "It's not a five-course meal or anything. C'mon. Eat."

The other half of the omelet went down quickly – he hadn't eaten all day. Liv rose when she was finished, and took her plate to the sink.

"Want the grand tour?" she asked. "It won't take long. You've already seen the best part." She waved her arm at the big open room, and he followed her down the hall.

"Cory's room – now shared with Em," she said as they

passed the first door. "Bathroom." She pointed to the door on the right. "My room."

Liv went straight to the queen-sized bed and collapsed on top of the covers. He stopped, stuck in the doorway for a moment, then pulled his eyes from her. More floor-to-ceiling windows facing the ocean on the left, an ensuite on the right.

"Nice," he said, drawn to the windows. It was quiet enough he could hear the crashing waves. He glanced over his shoulder.

Liv had rolled onto her side, watching him. "You should get some sleep too. You might as well stay here. It's more comfortable than the couch."

He hesitated, not sure how much he wanted to test his self-control. He came over, pulling out a pillow and propping it against the headboard to sit with his legs resting on the bed next to her.

"Everything going okay in California?"

He shrugged. "Living the dream." The furrow in her brow was evidence his sarcasm wasn't lost on her.

"What's the problem?"

Besides the fact you're almost three thousand miles away? Success had come quickly and easily for him when he'd started his career in Ontario, and he hadn't missed a beat when he'd lost his apprentice allowance earlier this year. The west coast was making it clear it wasn't going to be as cooperative.

"Competition's tougher there," she said when he didn't respond.

"I just need faster horses to ride." If he hadn't lost most of his sense of humour, he would have laughed.

"I tried to call you Boxing Day, after you won on that filly."

"I saw. You didn't leave a message." Or call back. But he hadn't called her, either. "Don took Jeanne and me out for dinner."

She didn't respond, and he noticed her eyes were closed. Soon he could tell she was asleep. He tried not to think about how nice it would have been to spend the winter here, with her, condo on the beach – as if that's how it would have been. He reached out, and almost touched her before pulling back, getting off the bed. The living room sofa seemed a safer place to be.

When he woke he felt disoriented, sitting up abruptly. Lights were on in the kitchen, Emilie pouring herself a glass of juice.

"Hey, Nate. Get some sleep?"

"What time is it?" He didn't feel very rested, no surprise.

"Four-thirty. When did you guys get back?"

"I don't know. One o'clock or something."

"Any change with Chique?"

"No. Good or bad."

Emilie came over and sat beside him, sipping her juice.

"Where's Cory?" he asked.

"She worked Christmas, so she's off New Year's Day. Her mom came for a visit, so they're doing tourist stuff. She wasn't sure about going, but Liv made her. Not like there's much she could do that's not already being done."

Nate nodded, and rubbed at the ache behind his temples. "There more of that in the fridge?"

"Help yourself."

What he needed was coffee, but he poured himself a glass. "You guys really need to do some grocery shopping." They'd bought the good orange juice, at least.

"Give us a break. We've been away, then came back to a sick horse. It hasn't been a priority."

"I know." He wasn't hungry anyway.

Emilie's eyes followed him as he returned. "Guess you didn't expect to find yourself here this winter."

He shook head, wondering if she questioned the way he'd just dropped everything in Los Angeles and hopped on a plane to be here. For some reason he thought of Faye. Faye would never get that he would do such a thing for a horse, and would think it only had to do with Liv. Of course, it did have a lot to do with Liv. He wasn't sure the two could be separated; that one could exist without the other.

"So did you two talk at all?" Emilie asked.

He shook his head, resigned. "It's not the time. In a couple of days I'll be leaving. Gotta stick to the deal, right?"

"Why? Seriously, Nate...do you have to go back?"

"What are you saying, Em?"

"I don't know. It just seems like you should be here."

"You're not really helping. This is hard enough. Coming here, especially under these circumstances...of course I don't want to go back. But now Jay won a race out there, and Don wants to point him to the Santa Anita Handicap, and it would look really bad to bail. For what, really? Liv is tough. It's not going to make a difference to her if I'm here or not, once the smoke clears."

"Do you actually believe that?"

"She's given me no reason not to."

"Wow, Nate."

He glanced at her, not really surprised by her reaction. He was always the optimistic one, trying to think positive, no matter what. Somehow he'd lost that this winter.

Em glanced at the clock on the kitchen wall. "I'd better get going. You two take your time. The longer Liv rests, the better. You too, for that matter. Go back to sleep."

Instead he showered, then dressed in shorts and a clean shirt before slipping out the sliding door off the living room and wandering to the beach in bare feet. There was no hint of the sun that would rise in a few hours, just pinprick starlight scattered in the indigo sky, the rhythm of the waves as they crashed against the shore luring him.

There was no sense in rehashing anything on this visit — Chique was the priority here, not his personal angst. Of course if the threat Chique was dealing with was bringing Liv face to face with their collective mortality, and showing her the importance of hanging onto — whatever this was — he would take that, but she needed to express it, not leave him to guess.

CHAPTER EIGHT

Liv shed her clothes quickly — the ones she'd fallen asleep in — and showered, pulling on clean jeans and a fresh t-shirt and sweeping her damp hair into a ponytail. She was angry with herself for sleeping so long; she needed to get back to the barn.

She caught a glimpse of Nate through the window, a lone figure on the empty beach, and paused. He'd come without hesitating, despite everything. She pushed open the sliding door, and instead of rousing him to hurry back to Chique, stood silently beside him, following his gaze to where the sky transitioned from cerulean to pink to orange above the horizon.

"Hey," he said, glancing at her. "Get some rest?"

She nodded, noticing the fatigue etched on his face. "How about you?"

"Uh — a bit. I woke up before Emilie left."

"You could have stayed on the bed, you know."

He raised an eyebrow and looked at her sideways. She flushed — she could still be so naïve — and quickly resorted to the first plan. "Better get back and see how the big filly is doing. You coming?"

He laughed softly, following. Inside she picked up her keys, waiting while he brushed the sand off his feet and slipped on his shoes.

"We are going to grab some breakfast somewhere, right?" he said as he settled into the passenger seat. "And coffee. You still drink the stuff, don't you?"

"Sure." She didn't think she was hungry, but Nate seemed determined to make sure she ate. "I generally am able to take care of myself, you know."

"Does that mean I didn't need to come?"

He was grinning, but Liv felt he was baiting her, rather than making a joke.

"Well — need? I don't know. But — I'm glad. And — grateful — that you did."

He seemed entertained by her stuttering attempt to verbalize her feelings. "You're cute when you're flustered."

Liv gripped the steering wheel and looked straight ahead, frowning. Was she overreacting?

"Something to go okay with you?" She pulled up to a doughnut shop.

"You're calling the shots."

She almost commented on his attitude, whatever it was, wherever it came from. It wasn't just him, though. It was the cumulative effect of this winter so far, for both of them. She heard Nate sigh, but looked away as she turned off the ignition.

"I'm sorry, Liv. I don't mean to give you a hard time. I had to come, as much for myself as for you or the filly. I need to be here, and I didn't want you having to deal with this on your own. Whatever else is going on...we're a team, the three of us, right? I don't know what either of us would do if anything happened to her."

Liv looked at him for as long as she dared before uninvited tears welled in her eyes. She blinked them back, and quickly got out of the car. Nate followed slowly, and she sensed his dwindling morale — or maybe she was just projecting her own emotions onto him.

They bought extra food and coffee, Nate handing the woman behind the counter cash before Liv could pay. Liv thanked him quietly and picked up the doughnuts and bagels, leaving the tray of drinks for him.

By the time they got to Payson, most of the horses were turned out in the small paddocks behind the barns, and stalls had been mucked. Chique nickered softly.

"That's encouraging," Liv said. She let the filly push her muzzle into her open hands.

"She was certainly happier this morning when I got here than last night when I left," Emilie responded. "I told Jo to go home and get some sleep."

"Thanks, Em," Liv met Nate's eyes. "Good news, so far."

He nodded and turned his attention back to his coffee, which was finally cool enough to drink. "Bagels and doughnuts, Em. Breakfast of champions."

Emilie laughed. "No, that would be the orange juice and leftover fake champagne Jo was drinking at six AM," she said. "There's still some in the fridge, if you're interested."

Nate glanced at Liv, but Liv shook her head. "No thanks. But you go right ahead. What's left to do, Em?" She needed something to keep her occupied until Doc Beckett made his rounds.

"Looks like we need more ice," Nate said. "I'll go."

Liv handed him her keys, and pushed out a breath. Emilie's brow furrowed, and she looked like she was going to say something, but Liv started off towards the paddocks to check on

Feste. She didn't need one of Em's pep talks or lectures right now.

As soon as Liv started to take Chique out of the ice for the vet's assessment, she knew for sure the filly had improved. After his exam, Doc Beckett nodded.

"Keep up the ice bath for another twenty-four hours, and we'll continue with the medication. We'll do radiographs tomorrow."

Liv tried to take his guarded optimism for what it was, but Chique wasn't out of danger yet. Nate refreshed the ice, and helped Liv put filly back in the tub.

"How long can you stay, Nate?" Emilie asked, hovering.

"As long as I need to. Don knows what's going on, and I told my agent it was a family emergency. Nobody can tell me it wasn't." His gaze locked onto Liv. "Unless you want me to go."

It sounded like a challenge. If she wanted to be honest, it had been easier for her when he wasn't around. She'd had her emotions in check. Face to face, it fell apart. But she said, "No," simply, and held his eyes, wishing she could transmit feelings where words failed her.

Jo showed up as they fed lunch, and Liv let Nate and Emilie continue down the row, facing the assistant trainer with hands on hips. "You didn't need to come back so soon."

Jo waved her off. "Roger will be back tomorrow. I can take the day off then. Doc Beckett been by yet?"

Liv updated her on the vet's instructions. "How do you want to do this? I can do the night shift tonight if you want."

"You have to get on some horses tomorrow, so you need to sleep like a normal person. Come back at feed time, and stay the evening again. Take Miller to the beach this afternoon. He's looking a little pale."

"How about a grocery store on the way home?" Nate said.

Liv smirked. "Okay. But you're going to have to cook anything that doesn't come already prepared."

The supermarket was practically deserted, and Liv watched with curious amusement as Nate pushed the cart around, selecting items one by one. She threw in a few essentials — yogurt, some fruit. Back at the condo she grabbed an orange as Nate started putting things away.

"Make yourself at home, Miller," she said, walking to her room to change into a bathing suit. She could hear him laughing behind her.

Emilie was out on the sand already, lying face up on a towel, sunshine and contentment bathing her face. Liv settled beside her, and Em cracked open a squinting eye.

"Where's Nate?"

"Putting away groceries." Liv grinned. "I'm sure he'll be out shortly."

"It's a shame he has to go back so soon," Emilie said, both eyes narrowing on her. "He could come in handy around here."

Point taken.

Nate appeared in shorts, *sans* shirt. For once Liv had more of a tan than he did.

"Did you not find the man a towel, Liv? You really are a sad hostess. Here, Nate. You can have this one." Emilie scrambled up, tossing him her sunblock. "I'm going in the water."

He wasted no time dropping to the towel and lying back. "I've got to catch up on my sleep. Wake me up if I start to burn, okay?"

Liv let her eyes rove over him as his closed, his muscles lean under his light skin. She stopped herself from rescuing the lotion he'd ignored, the obvious possibility igniting her nerve endings. "Sure Miller. It's the least I can do in exchange for you making sure I don't starve."

She left him to doze, if that's what he was doing, and

watched Emilie for a while before leaning back herself, letting the sound of the waves soothe her. It was easy to fall asleep, her dreams light and meaningless.

"Hey, Liv. It's three o'clock."

The softness of Nate's voice in her ear lured her back, his breath on her neck. When she opened her eyes his face was poised just above hers, blond hair falling over clear blue eyes that locked on hers. He smiled, just a quirk of his lips, and pushed himself away.

Nate pulled down the ball cap he'd borrowed from Em — his rushed packing hadn't included one — and stretched his neck side to side. Sleeping on that couch was going to be the death of him, but even the couch was too close to Liv right now. He had to go back to California. He wasn't going to start something he couldn't finish. He wasn't going to screw this up. Their agreement, and all.

Feste galloped over Payson's turf course — ears forward, head down compliantly, striding out nicely. Nate remembered Chique at the same age, hauling him around with determination, eager to do more. So different, her full sibling; or maybe Liv was just better at keeping the young ones relaxed. She was definitely good at reserving calm for them when everything around her was upside down.

"He's looking good," Nate said as they walked back to the barn. "When are you going to breeze him?"

"When he tells me," Liv answered.

"He's so frigging polite, I don't think he's going to tell you anything."

The affection on her face dredged up feelings he'd agreed to put on ice. It was for the colt anyway, not for him.

Doc Beckett was on the shed when they returned, his assistant setting up the x-ray equipment in front of Chique's stall. Liv stopped Feste outside on the stretch of green.

"Cory! Where are you?"

"Here!" The kid's voice came in a soprano sing-song from behind the bridles hanging in the tack room doorway.

"Put your helmet and vest back on, and get on this colt to cool him out for me. We need the shed for Chique."

Cory didn't have to be asked twice. She bounced over, Feste not batting an eye at the kid's exuberance. Nate wished he felt an iota of that.

"Just take him on a little walkabout, then he can have a bath and some grass when you're done." Liv left Nate to leg the kid up, removing her own helmet and wiping her brow with an arm as she walked to the shed. Cory sauntered off on the dark bay colt, still grinning.

"Here, Liv, I'll hold her," he said when she pulled Chique out of the stall. She'd want to see the images as they popped up on the laptop; pictures that would determine Chique's future. Was he the only one obsessing over *their* future?

He watched distractedly, and the muscles in Liv's neck visibly relaxed as the views came up on the screen in succession. She glanced at him, the tension that had kept her lips in a resolute line easing, allowing a subtle upward curve.

"No sinking or rotation," Doc Beckett confirmed.

They'd managed to pre-empt irreversible damage, though careful management would continue. Nate steered Chique back into her stall, and Liv surprised him when he came out, wrapping herself around him. He pressed back, burying his face in her hair, breathing in the scent of her sweat like it was the sweetest smell on earth.

"I've got to go back." His words were muffled as he allowed himself to kiss the side of her head.

"I know."

Why had he thought — hoped — she would ask him to stay?

The airline was far too accommodating, finding him a flight that afternoon that would see him to LAX by evening. He wished he hadn't let his frustration get to him while he'd been here. He hadn't made the best of the little time they'd had together.

They reached Fort Lauderdale in plenty of time, but he couldn't deal with the thought of her waiting with him when he didn't know what more could be said. It would just inflame the wound in his chest.

"You don't need to come in," he said.

She didn't protest, pulling up to the curb outside the terminal. He met her behind the car as she opened up the back, and reached for his bag.

"Come out to LA for a few days. Once you're past worrying about Chique." It was a plea, out before he could stop it. But when would Liv ever stop worrying about Chique?

She searched his eyes, hers filled with conflict.

"Just a few days. No pressure. Maybe when Jay runs. Do that for your sad friend." He tried a grin, coming up short.

"Let me think about it."

She'd be reluctant to leave the filly again. An obscure set of circumstances had brought on Chique's laminitic attack, but from here on, the filly would be considered susceptible to another. He'd cling to the fact that Liv hadn't given him an outright no.

"I'll call to see how she's doing."

"Thanks, Nate."

"Family, right?"

She closed the space between them, but the awkwardness of their embrace made their limbs feel like wire instead of flesh; there was no comfort in it. Pulling away, he pressed the flash drive into her palm before scooping up his bag, and disappeared into the terminal.

"You need to go, Liv," Emilie said.

Liv kept her gaze fixed on the back of Feste's head.

"You need the break," Em continued, chatting as she posted on her own mount. "You've been stressing over that filly since it happened. I know, I get it, but you should really let yourself relax for a couple of days. Chique will be fine."

Emilie was right...as usual. Her little sister had somehow acquired all the interpersonal smarts she'd missed.

"Plus, you get to see Nate. Duh." Cory piped up from the two-year-old she jogged on Em's other side.

"Seriously," Emilie said. "Nate came all the way here when Chique was sick. You know how much this would mean to him."

"Plus, he's gorgeous," Cory warbled.

Liv had to laugh. No doubt Cory would be hopping on a plane without hesitation had she been in Liv's shoes. She probably would have followed him there in the first place. It was a relief to see Chique bounce back, but Liv still worried, every day, that she would get to the barn and find the filly in the corner, crippled and shaking again.

"She'll be fine, Liv," Emilie repeated. "You can do this."

"Who's going to get on Feste while I'm gone?"

"Oh! Me! Please? Liv!" Cory chirped.

She should have a fraction of Cory's enthusiasm. The kid put her to shame.

Liv had the beach more or less to herself that afternoon, Em and Cory off to Gulfstream to watch races. She'd added the most recent of Nate's songs to her phone, and the chorus played over and over in her head, even when she didn't have the earbuds in. He must have done this one in California, just him and his guitar — taking The Lumineers' *Ophelia* and changing it up.

Oh-oh-livia...

The sweetness of it squeezed her heart, but the last phrase of the chorus — which he hadn't altered and spoke, rather than sang — stopped it. Which one of them was the fool, really?

CHAPTER NINE

NATE GRINNED AT HER. That old grin; the one she hadn't seen, full on, since October.

"Some holiday, eh? You haven't even been here twenty-four hours, and Don's got you on the pony. Are you going to gallop a couple, too?"

"I'm not licensed in that capacity in this jurisdiction," Liv insisted, laughing. Not that she should technically be on the pony, either. Her credentials today were strictly that of *guest*. "How are you finding Don, really?"

"We get along fine. He's a lot like you. Wasn't much of an adjustment."

She rolled her eyes but had to smile as they reached the track. This felt right. So much better than when he'd come to Florida.

Nate and Jay left her at the on-gap, backing up, and she followed with her eyes until they jogged out of view — or she was distracted by the warm pink of the San Gabriel Mountains in the distance, she wasn't sure which. She refocused in time to find them on the busy racetrack, Nate holding the gleaming red colt to an easy gallop as they shimmered past. They would go once around, just a bit of light exercise to limber Jay up on the morning of his California debut.

"Those mountains are something, aren't they?" She glanced over her shoulder as they left the track.

Nate smirked. "Come to Calgary sometime, I'll show you real mountains."

Her eyebrows crept up. *Is that an invitation, Miller?* He rarely talked about his hometown; hadn't gone back since he'd left over four years ago. There was heartache there. Maybe he'd dealt with it now, but he still hadn't visited.

She put the pony in his stall when they returned to Don's barn, Nate setting the tack on the rail, leaving Jeanne and a hotwalker tending to Jay.

"I've gotta go," he said to Liv. "See you at the races?"

She nodded, then glanced at Don beside her as she watched Jeanne bathe the colt. "Looks like he's training great. He could be all right in there, eh?"

"He's got a shot," Don agreed. "But so does Paradise. A win would be nice."

Liv agreed. A welcome bit of good news, in a winter that had been sorely lacking.

The guest role was an odd one to play. Easier on the backside. Here, out front, in her sleeveless shift, unsettling. She watched the three-year-old filly Nate had won with on Boxing Day, moving up in class, come flying on the outside to catch the strong favourite at the wire. Next to her, Don looked over with his characteristic restrained smile.

"There's no question the kid can ride," he said. "He just needs a little better luck."

Liv controlled the twist of her lips. *Faster horses to ride.*

She followed the trainer trackside, remaining outside the winner's circle while the photo was taken. Nate seemed more satisfied than pleased by the effort, chatting with the groom as he pulled the tack off and gave the filly a pat on the neck.

"Lighten up a little," Liv said as he walked to the scales.

His smile was tepid. "One more before Jay."

It ended up being one more winner, a longshot for a small-time conditioner. Nate had controlled the pace, pulling away on the front end. She waited again on the fringes, feeling just a little bit paddock girl-esque as she scuffed her flats on the concrete apron.

"Looking good, Miller."

When he lifted his head, he grinned. "You'd better stick around. You seem to bring me luck."

"Since when are you about luck?"

"Maybe it's one of those things you don't believe in till it's disappeared."

"That might be profound if it wasn't so cynical." She crossed her arms, narrowing her gaze on him. "It seems so backwards for me to be trying to cheer you up."

"It is kind of sad." The grin resurfaced. "Let's see if we can make it a hat trick."

The San Pasqual Stakes, with Jay.

Nate wore the familiar red, white and blue Triple Stripe silks when he entered the small walking ring, going through the ritual of shaking her hand, then Don's. Don's instructions were merely a formality. Nate knew Jay as well as anyone.

"Good luck, Miller."

He suppressed a laugh before Don legged him up onto the chestnut colt.

They were the golden boys of the post parade, Jay's copper coat gleaming in the warm California sun, Nate's blonde hair hidden under his helmet. Once the race caller announced them — *"Just Jay, from Triple Stripe Stables, trained by Don Philips, ridden by Nate Miller"* — Nate broke him away from the pony to let the colt stretch out on a loose line, Jay bounding off powerfully.

Liv tightened her fingers on her binoculars, trailing them. When they came back to the gate, Jay had a dark sheen of sweat on his neck and a keen look in his eye. All eight horses loaded professionally.

A dark bay named Torrid broke from the one hole and shot to the lead, the field settling behind him. Nate parked Jay on the rail, and Jay rated comfortably for him, skipping easily over the track and waiting patiently for the race to unfold.

Torrid's fractions were quick — an honest pace that would set it up perfectly for the closers like Jay. On paper, the front-running gelding wasn't in the same class as the other five. Cheap speed. Not enough substance to go gate to wire at a mile and an eighth in this company.

Nate was biding his time, letting Jay gallop along the backstretch, maintaining his position on the rail. Torrid was already showing signs of fatigue. He only had to drift out a little to leave the hole that would give Jay a clear path to the wire, the perfect trip. They rounded the final turn and favoured Paradise moved up on the outside, his jock steering him a bit wider than seemed necessary, suggesting to Liv he expected Torrid to come out. The dark bay leader was giving everything he had, but he was tiring, unable to keep tight to the rail as they entered the stretch. Nate had Jay on the bit, ready.

Liv saw it — the awkward alteration in Torrid's stride — a split second before the gelding bobbled and went down, an involuntary gasp escaping from her throat. His rider toppled over his head, right in Jay's path. With no room to spare, Jay stumbled and went down with them, the rest of the field scrambling to avoid the spill.

Don didn't have to tell her to move. She was already rushing for the stairs, heart plunging from her throat to the pit of her stomach, the trainer close on her heels.

It was heartbreakingly obvious Torrid was in bad shape. Nate was up — thank God — holding Jay, a steadying hand on the trembling colt's neck as he watched the paramedics see to Torrid's unconscious rider. Liv left Don further behind, passing the trainer's assistant, Jeanne, and sprinting across the deep sand of the track.

She stopped short of Nate, sucking in erratic gulps of air to try and tame the adrenaline charging through her bloodstream. "You okay?"

Nate nodded, but his face was ashen.

"That horse isn't going to make it off the track." Don caught up, wiping his brow with a handkerchief while Jeanne took Jay's head, glancing at Torrid as the state veterinarian attended to him. "We'll get Jay a ride back to the barn and take a good look."

"We went right over top of him." Nate's voice quavered when he finally spoke, his attention more on the ambulance driving away with Torrid's rider than removing his saddle from Jay.

"There was nothing you could do," Liv said. "Go change and come back to the barn, okay?"

He nodded again, his eyes shifting to the tarps being erected around Torrid.

"Go," she prodded, and waited until he hitched a ride in a utility truck before jogging to join Jeanne in the van that would take Jay to the backside.

Somehow, Jay seemed to have escaped unscathed, but the relief Liv felt was deadened by her sorrow for Torrid's connections. Nate walked on the shed with hands jammed in the pockets of chinos, a dark grey jacket over an open-necked dress shirt. He nodded wordlessly as he passed the departing vet. When he was close enough, Liv noticed traces of dried sand on his cheek. Getting here had taken priority over a shower.

"What's the story?" He looked directly at Don.

"He didn't find anything obvious, but wasn't convinced there's nothing wrong. We'll look at him again in the morning."

"Any word on Cook?" Liv asked, hoping for an update on Torrid's rider.

Nate shook his head.

"Get some bandages on Jay, Jeanne," Don said. "If you find anything we missed, let me know."

Nate glanced at Liv, his jaw set, agitation in his blue eyes. "Drive you back to the hotel?"

"Yeah." She turned to Don and Jeanne. "My flight's pretty early tomorrow so I probably won't see you again, but keep me posted, okay?"

She followed Nate to an older-model Jeep, a cheap vehicle he'd picked up for the winter, waiting while he unlocked and opened the passenger door for her. Once he was in, his fingers closed tightly around the wheel.

"You sure you're all right?" Liv nudged.

He turned the key with an unconvincing dip of his chin. "I could use a drink."

They left menus untouched and words unsaid at the hotel bar. Liv watched him carefully as he took a deep draught of his beer, fingering the stem of her wine glass. His eyes locked onto the television at the end of the bar.

"What is it?" she asked.

"Something about the race. About Cook." He flagged down

the bartender, who had been closer to the screen. "What were they saying, did you hear?"

"Spill at Santa Anita this afternoon. One of the jockeys just died in hospital." He shook his head. "Crazy job." Then his expression changed, like he was noticing Nate's size. "Need another one?"

Nate drained his glass, setting it down resolutely and sliding it forward. "Please."

Liv sat in silence. Her presence and the knowledge she could relate to what he might be feeling was as much as he would expect, but it felt inadequate. It hadn't been her out there today. It had been over a year since she'd ridden a race. It didn't mean she'd left the risk behind — the metal rod in her thigh was a reminder that accidents happened during training too — but trading in her jock's license for a trainer's badge removed her a degree from the dangers of a profession she'd pushed him to pursue.

"What time is your flight?" he asked, going more slowly on the second beer, at least.

"Seven-thirty."

"I'll drive you. I think I'm going to book off tomorrow."

Liv looked at him sharply. Maybe she had no right to question a decision based on something more mental than physical, but if it got out, it would do nothing for his reputation around here — if people thought the accident had shaken his nerve. She was sure that wasn't the case, but many would make that interpretation. She didn't try to talk him out of it, though. She didn't feel in a good place right now to justify the argument.

He pushed his glass away. Half-empty, or half-full? "This isn't going to help anything. I should go."

"You sure?" She hesitated. "You could come up and hang for a bit." She didn't care what reaction the suggestion might draw. She wasn't sure being alone was the best thing for either of them at the moment.

His eyes were full of so many things, meeting hers briefly before he stood. Sadness. Regret. Appreciation?

"That's all right. But thanks." He reached into his pocket for a couple of bills. "What time should I pick you up? Five?"

Liv nodded, at a loss for something to say. He smiled faintly and touched her arm as he walked past.

There was luck and there was luck. Some days it just meant getting out alive.

Liv: *My flight's delayed a couple of hours. I'll get a cab.*

Nate: *Forget that. I'm already on my way. We can grab a coffee or something*. There was no way she was getting on a plane, back to Florida, without him seeing her again.

"Or something" ended up being a beach not far from LAX, coffees curled in their fingers. His was black, when he really craved what Liv had ordered. There was something comforting about the frothy warm milk of a cappuccino.

"Sip?" she said, proffering it, like she understood. Of course she understood.

He accepted the paper cup, closing his eyes as he savoured the fusion of creamy and bitter and thought about how her lips had touched the plastic lid. He hadn't kissed her since she'd come. Why hadn't he kissed her? Stupid agreement.

"Walk?" he suggested, relinquishing the cup, the flavours and warmth lingering. His seemed a poor alternative now.

Liv followed him to the sand. The dark waves of the Pacific appeared colder and more unruly than where the Atlantic met South Florida's shores. She shivered, gripping her cup between both hands. He slipped an arm around her shoulders, pulled her against him.

"So what will happen with Chique? Are you going to send her home?" he asked.

"I've offered to go back and manage the early runners at Woodbine for Rog."

"Feste too?"

"Of course, Feste too." She smiled, like it was ridiculous to think otherwise. "I'm going to start back riding."

"Really." It had been over a year since her accident. Chique's three-year-old campaign had provided a distraction, but with the filly's four-year-old season in question, it didn't surprise him she'd need something to occupy her. "So you are going to keep Feste for yourself. Can you train and ride too?"

"Maybe. We'll see." She sipped. "Sotisse had a filly this year."

"Just Lucky again?"

Liv nodded. "Another dark bay. I guess she's got a bit more white than Chique or Feste."

He didn't say anything; no reference to the next one in line, another one to keep them both going, something to look forward to in the midst of uncertainty. It was as if they were in suspended animation, strolling in another world, this beach so far removed from everything that was supposed to be.

He couldn't stand it, the small talk, and stopped abruptly, spinning in front of her. "This is crazy. This winter has been such a disaster. Chique...now Jay...what next? I want to tell you not to get on that plane. They say everything comes in threes, right?"

"Thanks for that." She laughed softly. "You've never been the superstitious one. Don't start now. One of us has to maintain some semblance of sanity."

"I'm not feeling so sane right now. That could have been me, yesterday. That could have been you. That's what we're a part of. I know it's not news, and I know we're not supposed to think about it except...what are we doing? Are we taking this for granted?"

The conviction in her gaze caught him off guard. "I'm not. Not anymore." Her voice was soft, sure. "And I know you never have. But you wouldn't like me much if you kept me away from that filly any longer."

"I'm not liking myself a whole lot right now, the way things are."

"And I'm supposed to fix that?"

His laugh was almost a sigh. "Yeah, I know. I just keep thinking something has to go right in the middle of all this; it may as well be us."

"We've got less than two months to go now. There's no point in second-guessing what's behind us — we'll both just drive ourselves crazy. What would we do, anyway? I still have to go back to Florida."

"I could go with you."

"Sure you could. And that might be great for us. But if you ever want to ride on this side of the border again, you need to show everyone that spill yesterday didn't rattle you — even though it did."

He didn't deny it — it wasn't as if his reaction wasn't obvious. At this point Liv might be the only one who knew, but if he didn't show up in that room later this morning, the first seeds of doubt would surface; initially amid his peers, then more significantly, among the trainers.

"Does it always come back to that?" he challenged. "What happened yesterday isn't going to keep me from ever getting on a horse again. It was just a blunt reminder that stuff happens so fast, and sometimes it seems we're just wasting time in a world where we might not have that luxury. I'm supposed to forget that and be worried about what everyone else thinks, to save my career?"

"Sometimes you have to. There's no guarantee things will work out between us."

He snorted. "That's what I love about you, always looking on the bright side."

"I never claimed to be an optimist."

"Maybe I'm just meant to be a Woodbine rider, Liv. Maybe I'm really not cut out for this."

"You don't believe that."

"Maybe I'm starting to. And what's wrong with that? I made a hell of a lot of money last season. What you're not saying is you'd think less of me if I abandoned this."

The way she paused — that had to be it. But —

"That's not it, really," she insisted. "I think you'd regret it. Running away."

Running away, like he'd run away from Calgary, five years ago. And had somehow continued to do, in some shape or form, since.

"But I'm so good at it," he retorted bitterly.

He broke away and left her behind, but she caught up, her hand sliding into the crook of his arm, hair blowing against his neck when she spoke, so quietly.

"Are you mad at me?"

He shook his head and laughed, then stopped and faced her, linking his arms behind her. She didn't push him away. "Only because you're so damn right."

"You do it to me all the time."

"What?"

"Read me."

"I'm not so sure about that."

"You do. It's aggravating."

"Well at least we know we're good at pissing each other off." He grinned.

"So, you're okay, then?" she said.

"I'll get through it." He brushed aside the hair that whipped across her face. "I know you've been working pretty hard to help keep my head above water. Thanks for that."

"Yeah, well, it's usually the other way around." Liv gave him a small smile. "It's hard to leave."

At the terminal, another curbside departure. Too many airports. Too many good-byes. This time, though, she kissed him, then held his face in her hands, arresting his eyes.

"Now call your agent. Salvage what you can of the morning. Then check into the room and ride this afternoon. That's the only way you're going to keep me from kicking your ass back at Woodbine. Right?"

All he could do was laugh, feeling like he'd been sent back into battle. But not before she'd said, like a shield maiden, she was going too.

CHAPTER TEN

The wind whipped, catching the quarter sheet covering chestnut haunches still sleek from more hospitable days at Payson Park. Happy Together skittered along the path from the training track, Liv holding the lines crossed in one gloved hand while she tugged the mask back over her nose, goggles protecting her eyes.

Was this dedication or stupidity, when she could have stayed in Florida till the middle of April with the rest of the Triple Stripe crew? Roger had been only too happy to let her have the job of prepping the handful of horses he'd decided would suit Woodbine's shorter early races. The main track wasn't even slated to open until next weekend.

She steered Happy onto the shed, her shoulders relaxing once she was out of the wind, and spotted Dean Taylor waiting with her groom Amy outside the filly's stall.

"Hey Dean," Liv said, smiling as she dropped her feet from the irons before ducking and directing the filly through the doorway.

"Welcome back," he said when she emerged with the tack,

extricating the damp saddle cloth and girth cover for her as she took the equipment to the tack room.

"Am I crazy, coming back this early?" She hung the muddy bridle on the tack hook before pulling the mask down around her neck and setting the saddle and pads on their rack.

"I wasn't going to say anything."

"Because you're here too?"

"Probably. You have time for lunch?"

Liv took off her helmet and re-did her ponytail before unzipping her muddy chaps, glancing at the clock on the wall. "Sure. I've got to clean tack and do up Feste, but I can meet you after that."

"Sounds good. See you there."

Once the tack and Feste were taken care of, she ducked into the office to run a brush through her hair. That was as close as she'd come to being presentable — not that Dean would care. The restaurant they frequented was popular with racetrackers, so it wasn't like the wait staff weren't used to it either. A dark cloud released a random flurry of snow as she climbed into the Nissan.

When she stepped into the front of the pub, Dean waved her over from a booth off to the side. "Is it too soon to ask if you'll come work some for me?" He eyed her over the menu.

"That's what riders are for."

"Not even tempted to dust off your tack?"

"Maybe." She hadn't made her decision public.

"One of them would win a race for you opening day."

Liv smiled. Dean always liked his horses. Sometimes he was right about them.

He looked past her, and Liv turned to follow his gaze. "Faye!"

"This must be a record. You only just got home, and I've

actually got you cornered." Faye slid onto the bench next to her and crushed her in a hug. "When does Nate get back?"

"I don't know. He's done okay this past while. Things kind of picked up for him."

Faye frowned. She was dying to ask more pointed questions, Liv was sure.

Her exchanges with Nate had been infrequent enough recently that Liv had begun to credit his fervor on the beach that morning more to his brush with death than impatience to see things between them progress. She missed him, wanted to see him, and now felt like she was the one waiting. That was a change; one she wasn't altogether comfortable with.

"So if Nate stays in California, who's going to ride your horses?" Dean interjected, then looked at his sister. "I was just trying to talk her into riding again."

"Are you thinking about it?" Faye asked.

Liv shrugged. "I need something to do, with Chique off. An unstarted two-year-old is a bit too eggs-in-one-basket."

"Normal people take up a hobby. How about crochet?"

Liv laughed, happy not to have to answer more questions about Nate.

"How's Chique?" Dean asked. "Do you think you'll bring her back?"

Liv shrugged. "That's up to her." And so far, the filly seemed quite content to spend her days hanging out with Claire in the paddock at the farm.

Dean picked up the bill before Liv could grab it when their server tented it on the table. "You can thank me by getting on my three-year-old for me tomorrow."

"Who is this horse?" she asked.

"Ride The Wave. Unraced, one of Catch The Joy's last foals. I'll even bring him over. Eight good?"

Liv rolled her eyes, but not without a smile. "Want to go in company? I can put Cory on Elemental." Cory had come back from Florida with Liv to start the final preparations for getting her apprentice license. The kid had worked hard over the winter, and even saved enough money to buy her own car.

"Sounds like a plan."

After paying the server Dean stood, but Faye kept Liv locked in the booth. "Dessert?" she said pointedly, her perfect eyebrows arched, then added low enough Dean wouldn't hear, "I require a more thorough update."

"See you in the morning, Liv." Dean pushed out his chin with a knowing smile, excusing himself.

"We had a deal, remember." Faye flagged down the server. "Can we have a piece of your cheesecake?"

With opening day a month away, Liv couldn't use the weight argument. She was Faye's prisoner, and just maybe voicing her concerns would help.

"So?" Faye said, fork poised over the cheesecake the server set between them, as if the sugar would extract words like a buffer solution extracted proteins.

"Not much to tell, Faye."

"You've got to give me more than that."

Liv sighed, and stabbed her own fork into the slice, deciding it was for fortitude, not extraction. "I told him, okay? I told him I was in. But since then, I can't help but wonder if he's lost his conviction."

"You don't really think that."

"I do. I really do. Like I gave him this whole big speech encouraging him to stay there, but now I just want him to come back. I hate this."

"I, on the other hand, love it. It's progress, sweetie."

"It's sad and pathetic, and so not me."

Faye's laugh was low, and maybe a little bittersweet. "I remember that feeling."

"Well, I don't like it. It's distracting. It's not like I'm in love."

Faye patted her hand, and pushed the cheesecake closer. "You keep telling yourself that."

With time to kill before feeding the track horses, Liv went to the farm. The sun tried to shine, the temperature a few degrees warmer than it had been that morning. Chique and Claire lifted their heads as Liv approached. Chique nickered, but went back to munching her hay — just one of the things that told Liv she was at peace with her current existence. Maybe that spark would never come back. Maybe Nate wouldn't either.

CHAPTER ELEVEN

OPENING DAY.

What better way to announce her return to the saddle than a victory? Dean had been right: the solid older campaigner he'd told her would win lived up to the trainer's assurance, prevailing by open lengths. Faye and Will were in the winner's circle, their happy-couple-ness something she'd never thought she'd wanted until half of her own went AWOL in LA.

How about another win? Elemental, in an allowance race with a field of Plate hopefuls pointing for the first prep of the season in three weeks. Saddled by Dean, as Roger was on the way back from Florida with the Triple Stripe string.

And why not close out the card by piloting Dean's Ride The Wave to break his maiden, initiating the buzz that the rangy colt was also being pointed to the Plate? She would have to give up that mount, though. Her obligation remained with her father's horse, Elemental.

Dean pulled Liv into him once she was on the ground. "Great way to start off the year."

"Thanks, Dean," she said, extricating herself from his hold.

"Too bad you can't ride him in the Plate. It would make a great winner's story if the girl next door rode my homebred colt."

"Sorry Dean. I don't write the rules." It would be a conflict of interest for her to ride anything else, if there was a Triple Stripe horse in the race. Dean was going to have to settle for the boy next door, she thought wryly.

Dave Johnson, who had been the top rider at Woodbine for several years until Nate had knocked him out of that spot last season, was the first to congratulate her back in the room.

"Impressive way to come out of retirement."

Retirement? Is that what it had been? She was twenty-seven. *How about we call it a sabbatical?* "Thanks Dave."

"So, where is Miller, anyway?"

Everyone was asking her the same question, assuming she should have the answer. Sometimes when she heard snippets of the latest gossip floating around, she felt the rest of the backstretch was more informed than she was.

"Still in California. Can't say I really blame him for staying as long as he can."

"Well, let me know if you need me for any of those horses."

"Thanks Dave, I will." At least with Johnson she didn't have to worry about any personal connotation — he was only interested in what was to his professional advantage. "But between me and Cory MacDonald, even Nate might find there's not much left over."

She left him with a smirk.

It was a long drive home when she was especially tired. She checked on Chique and Claire under Nate's empty apartment, ate a light dinner at the house, and fell asleep trying to read.

Nate hadn't sent her any more songs, but Poe's *Wild* played through her dream, reminding her of him — and that she was, most certainly, in limbo. The buzzing bored in like a jackhammer, prodding her awake — the song part of her consciousness now, her current ringtone for him. She fumbled, knocking the phone to the floor before her fingers found it, and swiped to answer, pressing it to her ear.

"Hey Miller." She tried to clear her head, hoping the lingering fuzziness made her sound casual, non-committal.

"Did I wake you up?"

She glanced at the time. "It's nine PM, Miller." It would be six in LA. "But that's okay. It's good to hear from you." And it was, so good. He could have called her in the middle of the night, she wouldn't have minded. She propped her pillow up against the headboard and leaned back, closing her eyes like it would help her see his face.

"You had a good day," he said.

"They probably thought they'd have it easy without you around."

"Way to straighten them out." He laughed, then was silent a beat. "Listen — I'm going to stay a few more weeks."

"I figured as much," she responded, her tone softer. "It's the right thing to do."

"Is it?"

"We don't need to go over this again, Nate. Besides, I'd just kick your ass in the standings up here."

He chuckled quietly. "Thanks. Just don't get too comfortable. I'll be taking my title back."

"We'll see." She smiled.

"So — " She felt his hesitation. "Are we still on the same page? You...me...when I get back?"

"We are," she said, with certainty. "Though if we're

supposed to be together, it does help if I know what you're up to. You know, so I can keep a step ahead of the rumours."

"Always so bloody practical," he said.

"Thanks for calling, Miller." She disconnected, holding the warmth of the phone between her hands because it was the closest thing to him right now.

The predawn sky was a little richer; the April air a little warmer — and Chique's yell for breakfast a little louder. A little more like the old Chique. Thank goodness for that. It grounded Liv, saving her from feeling her head was a bad romance novel.

"Is today the day?" she asked as she turned the filly out. Chique snorted into the darkness, clearing the surroundings of goblins, and settled to munch hay nose to nose with Claire. Not a yes, but not a no, either.

It was the first dark day of the meet — no racing — so after a morning of working horses, Liv did up Feste and drove to the farm, boots still on, helmet tossed on the passenger seat. She tapped the steering wheel to Panic! At the Disco's *Collar Full.* Just another song that made her think of Nate, and the Plate Party last year. Time to hit restart — for them, for Chique.

She brought Chique in, then grabbed Claire, officially in foal to Just Lucky for a February baby. When Liv approached with the tack, Chique snuffled the armful of brushes and equipment. Liv freed a hand to grasp the filly's halter, and snapped the wall tie to a side ring.

Feet picked, a quick brush, pads and quarter sheet and saddle in place, bridle on. Liv secured her helmet and led Chique out to an overturned muck bucket to mount. Claire whinnied from the barn, and Chique didn't even respond. A little more like *yes*.

Just a hack — past the training barns, in between the broodmare paddocks, into the woods; following the trail that wove through the trees. Chique's long-striding walk didn't wait for anyone, ears forward in expectation. It wasn't as if she didn't know this path could lead to the training track.

They came out by the stallion barns and Chique's head shot up — but neither the filly's sire, Just Lucky, nor Starway, the other stallion in residence, were turned out at the moment. Chique cast a look in the barn's direction, but carried on without hesitation. She knew where she wanted to go.

She slowed at the training oval's on-gap, and Liv closed her leg to nudge her past. With a huff, Chique powered on. When Liv dismounted back at the barn, the filly didn't seem to believe they were done.

And Liv smiled. Tomorrow they would do more.

Convenient of Nate to return on a Wednesday, the flight from California late so Liv could pick him up after the races. She was early, and wandered distractedly past greetings of varying degrees of affection, not sure where she was headed, trying to work out the tension she felt. She jogged up the escalator to Pearson International's shopping concourse with no particular destination in mind, needing only to keep moving.

She checked the monitor again: Nate's flight had landed, but it would be a while before he collected his luggage and cleared customs. Gradually she made her way back down to arrivals, and paced through the bodies gathered to meet the plane from Los Angeles.

So, here she was. Now that she wanted it — did he still feel the same? Were they really on the same page? Or had California changed things after all?

By the time she saw him, he was moving toward her, bags in each hand, guitar slung over his shoulder. He looked like a kid coming back from a surfing vacation — tanned, hair a bit long and a bit sun-bleached — instead of a guy who rode racehorses for a living. Liv stopped where she was, rooted as he approached, feeling all the uncertainty built from months apart.

He stopped in front of her, dropped his bags and met that uncertainty, maybe with a little of his own. Then he was surrounding her, his lips catching hers, hands roving up her back to mold her against him.

He drew away slightly with a shuddering breath. "The winter from hell is officially over."

Liv stopped short on the doorstep. "That's not the Mustang."

"No kidding. Are you coming, or what?"

Nate leaned over the top of what she had no trouble identifying as a 911 Porsche Carrera. It managed, for once, to pull her away from that shit-eating grin of his. Her eyes ran over its sleek lines, compact and sexy and a colour that would match the dusky blue sky in a few hours. It might not be brand new, but it was mint.

"Seriously, where's the Mustang?" She stepped slowly down to the circular drive in front of the house.

"Just get in."

He'd come in to the track with her that morning, got on a few despite his jetlag, and she'd dropped him off afterward — she'd thought to pick up the old car from storage. Slipping into the passenger seat, she couldn't help caressing the dash. *Definitely not the Mustang.*

"So, I hate to ask...is this yours? Or did you steal it from somewhere?"

Nate laughed and put it into gear. "Mine, as of a few hours ago. What do you think?"

"I think this winter went way better than you let on. You must be making too much money." The interior was immaculate — it had obviously been meticulously cared for. "Other than that, well, it's gorgeous, and about time you got rid of that Ford piece of — "

"Hey! No dissing the Mustang, remember? I still have it. Will's buddy is going to do a bit of work on it. I'm thinking it could be my winter car."

Liv snorted. "Because those cars are so good in snow. And when was the last time you spent winter up here, Miller?"

"When was the last time it didn't snow before I left?"

He put it in gear, the rumble of its engine musical as it crept around the circle and onto the main lane. That rumble was soon drowned out by actual music, when he cranked the equally impressive after-market stereo.

"And this?" she shouted over the loudness.

"Biffy Clyro, babe," he called back, grin at full wattage.

"Did you just call me *babe*?"

"Oops?"

She'd let him get away with it, this time. She reached forward and adjusted the volume enough to be able to carry a conversation without hearing loss. "What inspired this?"

He kept his eyes on the laneway. "It's like I said to you in California. You never know when it's gonna be your turn. So why not?"

"I don't know." Liv smirked. "Maybe because it probably cost enough to cover the down payment on a house?"

"I got a good deal. One of the older guys had it sitting in his barn. Sold it to me to help pay for renos to turn said barn into a home for his new wife. Can you imagine?"

"Still."

"Please don't tell me you're going to kick me out of that apartment now."

"I hope you're planning on having a good year, Miller."

"I'm planning on having a great year." His perfect teeth backed him up.

Cory beat his ass, student besting teacher, to win with her first mount. He couldn't whine about Roger giving her that one; the trainer had done the same for him two years ago. Cory worked hard, was well-liked; she deserved the support. At least he still got to ride in the race. Since Cory was on a Triple Stripe horse, Liv had to sit it out. Just as well, because she could lie in wait in the jock's room for the unsuspecting kid.

"We did a good job with her," Nate said, standing beside Liv as they watched a grinning, flour-doused Cory jostled by the swarm of fellow riders after her initiation.

"Not so bright of us, really." Liv grinned.

"We should start a school, maybe. Something to do when we retire."

"I just came out of so-called retirement, Miller. You planning yours already?"

He laughed. "Not as long as Chique's still running. Are you going to bring her back in, or what?"

Liv nodded, still watching Cory. "It's time."

CHAPTER TWELVE

NATE LEANED back in the overstuffed chair, feet propped on the edge of the desk in the office, the *Racing Form* in his lap. Liv, intent on paperwork, worked beneath the ever-present painting of Geai Doucet with Just Lucky and Sotisse. Geai had been right about a lot of things. It had taken some battles to get them to this point, but here they were. There were no more excuses; nothing left to get in the way.

He heard voices, and glanced up when Emilie pushed through the door. She had a weird look on her face. Then he saw who was behind her, and his heart seized. He staggered to his feet, the *Form* falling, his head spinning.

It seemed like Liv was moving in slow motion, coming around the opposite end of the desk, concern all over her face, like she must have put the pieces together. His resemblance to the man. The shock on his own face as he stared at the woman.

"Hi, Nate."

The timbre of her voice still resonated with every cell in his body. How, honestly? Liv stared at him now, waiting, her dark, determined reserve such a contrast to the invader's fair hair and warm features. He had to pull it together, because there was no escape. They had him cornered.

He offered a slight gesture with his arm, voice flat. "Liv, this is my brother Phil, and his wife Cindy." He paused, still stunned he was making this introduction. His eyes flashed to Liv. "This is Liv Lachance." He didn't add anything to it. "And I guess you've met Emilie — her sister."

Liv stepped forward to shake hands. Nate still couldn't move.

"Nice to meet you," Liv said politely, her face as guarded as ever. *I've heard so much about you,* her glance in his direction conveyed.

"What are you doing here?" Nate said bluntly.

Cindy's eyes flickered, from Phil, to Nate, to Liv. "Phil had business in Toronto. I decided to come along." She hesitated. "We thought we might have the chance to see you."

"You could have told me you were coming." It wasn't fair, their showing up like this. Ambushing him.

But if he'd known, he would have found some excuse to avoid them. When several provinces had separated them, he'd been sure he was past the feelings of betrayal and bitterness that had driven him east. Now that they were right in front of him, impinging on the new life he'd established, it all came rushing back. He didn't want them here.

Liv turned to him, a wave of sympathy crossing her face. "Why don't you take Cindy and Phil for a tour of the farm?"

Nate looked at her quickly. So much for compassion. *Great idea, thanks so much for the suggestion.* Not that she could really be expected to find him a way out.

"Yeah, okay," he muttered, gathering the *Form* from the floor and heading for the door. He needed to get outside, to try and find more oxygen. He glanced back at Liv, then Emilie, wishing one of them would come along to diffuse the tension. Clearly neither was offering.

It was bright out here, a clear spring day, nothing like the storm in his head. The nondescript rental sedan parked next to Liv's Nissan was out of place. It didn't belong. He looked over his shoulder at Cindy and Phil. They didn't belong either.

He inhaled deeply, swinging around to face them. "I'll drive you around. It's too far to walk." The weather was perfect for a stroll, but he wanted to get this over with. He pulled the keys out of his pocket and walked over to the Porsche, opening the passenger door.

"This is yours?" Phil said, eyebrows arching. "Nice, little brother."

"Yeah, imagine that," Nate said, not ready to play along, a sour taste at the back of his throat. Ironic he'd been the one to end up making that kind of money, though the new car was the only thing in his life that reflected it.

A shadow passed over Cindy's face as she ducked into the non-existent back. Nate turned away from Phil and walked to the driver's side, cursing himself for not going to Will's this afternoon.

He pulled the Porsche around and headed for the training area, forcing himself to matter-of-factly point out the buildings and tell the unwelcome visitors what went on around the farm at different times of the year. Driving slowly, they came to the mares and foals scattered in the two large paddocks on the right side of the lane. He shut off the car and got out, Phil and Cindy following.

"This isn't all of them," he explained. "Some of the mares are in Kentucky being bred. They stay there until they're confirmed forty-five days in foal."

"Mares with babies, too?" Cindy asked, and he knew she

was thinking that was a long trip for a foal — one typically only a couple of weeks old when they left.

He nodded. "They have the babies up here so the foals are eligible for restricted races like the Queen's Plate. There are some pretty good incentives for Canadian-bred and foaled horses. There are also incentives for Ontario-sired horses, so some of the mares stay in the province and go to local stallions. Two of the top stallions in Ontario are actually on this farm."

He leaned on the top railing, a few of the mares grazing not far away. Chique's baby sister peered curiously over Sotisse's grazing neck. The foal was built like Chique, but bigger; the same smudgy dark brown, save for a star that dripped down to a stripe and ended in a snip between her nostrils. After that, they were nothing alike. Chique would have been totally in his face by now. Of course he'd encouraged her attitude. Something about being the one to breathe life into her newborn lungs had forged a connection, or so he liked to tell himself.

A few of the other foals approached, and Nate watched them transform the troubled look on Cindy's face as they nuzzled fearlessly. Cindy had always been comfortable around the horses. She understood the all-encompassing nature of the business, had encouraged him, and he'd thought they'd had the perfect balance, but somehow it turned out what she wanted for him, she hadn't wanted for herself. Now he was faced with the other extreme, with Liv — these animals so much of everything she was, he still couldn't be sure there was room for anything else.

"I'll show you the stallions," he said, returning to the car and leaving them to catch up.

Driving around the woods, he wished he was running through the trails and not caught here with the past screaming at him. The Porsche came into the clearing and passed Geai's cottage. It wasn't Geai's anymore, of course.

Just Lucky was in the first paddock, and the compact bay stallion sauntered over with the same self-assurance he'd passed on to his first daughter.

Nate introduced them. "He won the Canadian Triple Crown ten years ago, then sired a Queen's Plate winner in his first crop. Chiquenaude," he said. "My claim to fame," he added quietly.

"Is she here on the farm?" Cindy asked.

Nate reached into his pocket and offered the stallion a peppermint, then pulled Cindy back carefully so she was out of reach should Just Lucky decide to take a characteristic nip. Touching her stirred a dull ache, liberally laced with what could have been.

"She just shipped into Woodbine." He was glad Chique wasn't here. He wanted to keep her from them; keep that part of the new life he'd made — one they'd never shared — to himself. "She had an acute case of laminitis this winter — it's a disease that affects the tissue in their hooves. Very painful, and potentially life-threatening. She got through it, but we were pretty worried about her." *We* could have meant all of them, from Roger and the Lachances on down, but it meant he and Liv. Chique, the thing that bound them together, stronger than blood. Blood ties, as his present company proved, were easily severed. "She's doing well now, but we don't know yet if she's going to make it back to the races."

Starway was next, and kept his distance on the other side of his paddock. "This guy has one of the top contenders for this year's Plate, Elemental."

"Do you ride him?" Phil asked.

"No, Liv does." Maybe she'd get her Plate winner this year — when once upon a time she'd planned to be the one riding Chique — though Ride The Wave was going to be a serious threat. It would be a little ironic if Nate took another victory in the classic from her — he'd inherited the ride on Dean's colt.

He left the dark bay and moved on to the next enclosure. "This is Just Jay." The role of tour guide was coming easily, words rolling off his tongue, distracting him from the torrent of emotions he was holding inside. "Hey, buddy!"

The colt's head shot up at Nate's familiar voice, and Jay charged across the paddock toward them. Nate passed Cindy a mint. "He's all right."

Phil kept a respectful distance as Jay touched Cindy's fingers, blowing softly, and inhaled the candy.

"He's hardly like a stallion."

"He's always been a real gentleman. Still technically a colt," Nate explained. "He was undefeated, winning four races in a row, then went to California for the winter. A horse fell in front of him in a race there and we went down over top of him. Jay ended up with a hairline fracture and was on stall rest for a couple of months. When he came home they put him here, so I'm guessing they plan to retire him, even though it's healed completely now."

"You were on him?" Phil asked. "You're okay?"

"Yeah. I walked away." He felt cocky and fearless as he said it. How different his life was from his lawyer brother. "The other guy wasn't so lucky." An image of the spill at Santa Anita hurtled through his mind.

"Is he okay now?" Cindy asked, hesitantly.

"No. He died in hospital that evening."

He couldn't make eye contact with either of them, touching Jay's smooth neck in the silence, recalling the moment when he and Liv had heard the news, sitting in the hotel bar. It was one of those instants where he'd felt everything change, so aware of the transience of this life. He had nothing to lose, really, and everything right now was reflecting that. Buying the car, riding like it was his last day on the planet, bringing home the winners again as a result. Coming to the conclusion that his place was here, beside Liv, whatever the outcome. It brought his anger toward both Phil and Cindy to the surface. He was tired of this little game. They didn't get to come disrupt it all.

"So what are you guys doing here, really? Is someone dying?" His tone was challenging, accusing, but if they were here to make amends, to put the past to rest, then they needed to get on with it and stop wasting his time.

"It's been five years, Nate. Isn't that long enough? Can't we get past this?" Cindy spoke, Phil silent. Phil, who Nate possibly held the most to blame. "You haven't been home once since you left. You know it's breaking your mother's heart."

Nate laughed, pushing past them. *What about my heart?* But the guilt he felt at the mention of his mother made him keep it to himself. He walked away toward the stallion barn, letting them to decide whether to come or not.

He felt a hand on his arm, Cindy appearing at his elbow. He flinched, but stopped short of pulling away.

"We have to talk, Nate. Please?"

Phil was ten feet behind her. Did she want to do this alone? Nate turned to face his brother, walked about halfway, and thought how good it might feel to throw a punch. He tossed Phil the keys to the Porsche instead.

"Take it for a spin."

Phil caught them and just nodded, forehead wrinkled above knitted brows. Nate started walking again, leaving Cindy to keep pace.

"So how are the kids?" he asked, with a sense of obligation, trying to suppress the accompanying bitterness. Twins, a niece and nephew he'd never met. "How old are they now?" He knew exactly how old they were, of course. Remembered the precise moment he'd gotten the text with the photo of their pinched, pink faces.

"Almost fourteen months." Cindy laughed in spite of the tension — that same sweet laugh. "How do you think they are, at that age?"

He let himself study her, despite the pain it caused. She looked the same as she had five years ago. Maybe her hair was slightly shorter, straight, a simple cut reaching just above her shoulders. Of course the last time he'd seen her she'd been wearing a white dress, that hair piled on top of her head, after the wedding where she'd married his traitor of a brother. He'd already had the Mustang packed, planning to disappear and get the hell out of Calgary once and for all. Cindy had caught him, tried to stop him — he was pretty drunk — but there was nothing left to say. At least nothing he wanted to hear.

What if she'd said yes to him, instead? He would have finished his degree, gotten a "real" job, been responsible. Maybe those would have been his twins.

"Neither of us meant to hurt you, Nate."

He couldn't help laughing, the sound of it choked, the taste of it acrid. "Really? You reject me, start seeing my brother, and within a couple of months you're going to marry him? And that's not supposed to destroy me?" He shook his head. "What the hell? How stupid was I? Were we even real?"

Cindy reached for his hands. He backed away, and couldn't look at her, her shining eyes killing him.

"You were going to give it up for me, this riding dream. I didn't want to be responsible for that, after always telling you you needed to follow it, even if it meant going against your father. This is what you were meant to do. I couldn't take it, this life. I'd be a wreck, wondering every day if you were coming back in one piece. And look at you. Awards and Queen's Plate and riding in California."

"So you were doing me a big favour. And Phil? What a sacrifice. He was always pissed at me for hooking up with you. I'm sure he was all too willing to sweep in and help with the plan. What a guy. How long had it been going on for, really? You know you didn't have to marry him to get rid of me. I was ready to leave anyway, after you ditched me."

It felt good to say out loud all the things he'd felt, and obviously still harboured. But her face made him falter, making him regret being so cruel when she was right. She'd had to break him to be sure he'd go. Some things had to be demolished so you could build something new.

"Don't ever doubt it was real," she pleaded. "I did love you —"

He wanted to hear her say *more than Phil*, and her hesitation made him hope it hung in her mind.

"But Phil was —"

Safe. He sighed, when he wanted to scream. "Yeah. I know. I get it."

He'd tried safe, following her lead, perhaps — with Faye. Safe hadn't worked out for him. He hadn't been allowed the easy way out.

"I won't apologize for it, Nate. We're happy."

"You settled."

"You would have been settling."

The comment knocked the wind out of him. He would never believe that marrying Cindy would have been settling.

"Look around." She swept a hand through the air. "Look at your career — that car. And you've found someone who's better for you than I could ever have been. She lives in your world, completely, not just as a terrified bystander."

"Liv?"

"I still talk to your mother, you know."

Nate rolled his eyes. Cindy and his mom had always gotten

along — his mother loved her like her own child. At least his mother had still ended up with a great daughter-in-law. It was only him who'd lost out.

"There's nothing set in stone there," he said, finally. "She's a lot of work," he added with a smirk. He could feel the sting of the punch Liv would have given him for such a smart-ass comment.

"Is she worth it?"

He met Cindy's eyes, and found he didn't hesitate. "I'm pretty sure she is."

"I'm not sure it's supposed to be easy."

"We were."

"Maybe that's just it. It was too easy."

She searched his eyes, reached out and touched his face. He closed his fingers around her hand, then drew her in. Maybe it was wrong, but it was necessary. Cindy didn't pull away.

He wasn't sure yet he could trust how he felt about Liv. Cindy couldn't know she was the one, but there was no going back. Liv was his forward.

"When do you have to leave?" he asked, keeping her close, reshaping her memory into something different from what it had been for the past five years.

"In the morning. Early. You need to come home and see your parents, and your little brother. Meet your niece and nephew."

"I know."

"Of course, I may never see Phil again. You did give him the keys to your Porsche."

Nate laughed as he released her and led her to the picnic table beside the stallion barn. "Yeah. Maybe that wasn't so bright."

He let her talk, about the people he'd known back home,

about his parents, about the twins. He didn't say much; spoke only when prompted. Phil would come back, return his car, take Cindy, and he would accept it all now, reminding himself a few hours ago he'd been content with his own life – excited, even. He would never be like Phil, working in an office, taking business trips. But Liv might never be the wife; there might never be kids; he might never have it all. He'd always wanted to believe it was there to be had, but now he wasn't sure. And he'd have to come to terms with that.

Finally they heard the Porsche, and wandered over to where Phil brought it to a halt. Cindy opened the door and peered in.

"Ready?" Phil said.

Cindy nodded, and slipped into the back again.

"You're looking a little too comfortable there," Nate said as he dropped into the passenger seat. Phil's gaze silently assessed him, reminding Nate so much of their father for a moment.

He didn't know what to say to Phil anymore but felt the need to put forth an effort, so he asked about their youngest brother Tim, though his mother always let him know what was happening. A few times Nate had even spoken with the kid.

"He misses you a lot."

"I guess Dad's happy, finally," Nate said. "He got his hockey player."

Phil laughed. "Yeah. You might not recognize the kid anymore. He's put on some serious muscle. And he's taller than me." Phil paused. "Dad's proud of you, Nate. He might have a hard time saying it to you – not that you'd give him a chance to try – but he is. You can stop thinking you're some kind of disappointment. You're anything but."

Nate looked ahead, dismissing the words as Phil drove. He had enough to sort through without starting on his father.

Liv paused next to her car as the Porsche approached. She couldn't just drive off. The interesting thing was, she didn't want to. She raised her eyebrows at Nate when he emerged from the passenger side. His brother was behind the wheel. Even she, who held fast to leaving others to things that didn't concern her, was curious. Or maybe it did concern her, because she was committed to this thing with Nate now, right?

"We need to be going," Phil said, coming around the car's sleek front to stand next to his wife. "I wish we could offer to take you both out for dinner, but I've got another meeting. There'll be another time."

Cindy reached for Nate, and it took Liv aback, protectiveness rising in her. But Nate seemed at ease, if not exactly cheerful.

"Promise me you'll come home soon," Cindy said.

"I will."

Phil held out the keys. When Nate reached for them, his brother pulled him in for a hug. Nate looked less convinced by this, a stiffness returning to his body, but he went along with it. Then he settled next to Liv, their arms almost touching, like he felt the solidarity she offered.

Phil held out his hand to her. When Cindy did the same, Liv took it politely but guardedly. She couldn't feel friendly towards this woman who had been so careless with Nate's heart — a heart that deserved better.

"Thank you," Cindy said.

Liv tried to read her brown eyes. Was there remorse there? An acknowledgement of what she'd done? "Why?"

"I think you know."

And maybe she did.

"Have a safe flight home," she said, Nate nodding in agreement without finding the words himself. She found his fingers and squeezed gently as they watched the rental car pull away. Nate was still watching when she shifted her gaze to him. "You okay?"

His eyes flashed to her. "It might be a while before I can answer that accurately. I'll buy you a drink if you let me, though," he said. "I think I need to decompress, and I could use the company."

Or maybe the supervision. She nodded. "Sure."

"I'll drive?"

She laughed with unexpected lightness. "Obviously."

Yesterday still felt like a crazy dream. There had been something powerful about that moment when Liv had faced Cindy; what had been confronted by what would be; the past relinquishing to the future. Liv had stood by him, a silent constant, a steady heartbeat when his own had been raging. It had blown him away, made him determined to find the good in the past, incorporate those bits into who he was now, and let go of the crap that was holding him back.

Holding him back from what? He hadn't thought there was anything, until the visit.

At the pub, Liv hadn't pushed him to tell her about it. They'd talked about everything but, as if the afternoon's events had never occurred. He wasn't in denial — he knew better than to try and flee from it all again — but he still had to process it. Words didn't heal as much as time did.

Endorphins helped, a hard run at the farm, alone, after the distraction of a busy morning at the track. In his apartment he sucked back half a bottle of water then headed for the shower, grabbing his phone from where he'd tossed it. He absently checked the screen. He resented being so tied to it sometimes, but that was how it was. Texts from his agent were his career's lifeblood.

Voicemail was rarer.

He started listening to the message, cutting it short when he heard his mother's voice, the wobble in it making him disconnect and find the most recent call. She picked up too quickly. Her *Hello?* was small and unfamiliar.

"Mom, what's wrong?"

Her answer sent him into shock. He barely remembered calling Liv after hanging up, but there she was at his door. She reached for him and he clung to her, burying his face in her hair as he tried to deaden out the drone in his ears.

"Sit down. Tell me what happened." She gently guided him to the couch, and the grip of her hands around his was like a guyline, keeping him from blowing away in a gale-force wind.

"They were driving home from the airport." He started slowly, his brain fighting the formation of words because the scenario he sought to describe was too absurd to be real. "The roads were bad — freezing rain." That wasn't unusual for Calgary, even at the beginning of May. "A transport going the other way lost control, crossed the median...no contest. They were probably killed instantly." Better for them than a lingering death; not so for those left behind.

"Guess this is it, then. I have to go." He didn't recognize his own voice. He'd promised Cindy, but never thought it would be like this. This wouldn't be the family reunion his mother had in mind.

"Do you want me to come?"

Nate lifted his head, forcing his eyes to focus, her offer touching the darkness. "You'd do that?"

"Of course."

It was that simple to her. He never would have asked,

knowing the position she was putting herself in. Their restart was just new, yet she was willing to throw herself in the middle of his first trip home since his frantic departure, for the funeral of the ex-girlfriend he'd thought was his soulmate — someone he'd hoped to marry — and where he could no longer avoid the father he'd endlessly battled on the direction of his life. Though it seemed contrary to Liv's nature, he'd begun to realize it was essential to what they were. It didn't matter what was or wasn't going on between them; some things were bigger than that.

"I can book the flight if you want," she said quietly.

"That's all right. I'll do it."

First he went to the kitchen, pulled the bottle of vodka out of the cupboard, and retrieved a jug of orange juice from the fridge. He dropped ice cubes into a couple of glasses, added juice to the liquor. The one he kept for himself was noticeably pale.

Liv accepted the glass from him, though she merely watched as half of his disappeared.

"You sure you don't want me to call the airline?" she asked again, the corners of her mouth drawn into a frown, her dark brows knitted.

He shook his head, finished the drink with another gulp, and glanced around for his phone — but hesitated before picking it up, like it was still radioactive with the devastating news. Finally he opened it, tapped and clicked and scrolled. YYZ to YYC, two seats — return.

Liv sidled closer, tucking a leg underneath her, her fingers reaching for his free hand. He curled his around them, tried to extract comfort.

"Do you want me to stay?"

Her grey eyes seemed almost blue in their earnestness. He did want that, more than anything, but the vodka was starting to have its sought-after anesthetic effect, and he worried in his impaired state he'd do something stupid; undermine this new level of trust.

"I'll be all right. But thank you."

She leaned in and brushed her lips to his, and he almost changed his mind. They could just sit on the couch all night; it could be harmless.

"Are you sure you're okay?"

He sighed, not feeling any more sure than she looked. "Yeah."

"I'll pick you up in the morning?"

He nodded feebly, and she left her glass on the coffee table, still half-full. It wouldn't go to waste. He followed her to the door, hands in the pockets of his nylon pants, vaguely aware they were still damp from his run.

"You never know, do you?" he said, meeting her eyes. The buzz from the vodka mingled freely with his anguish, but did nothing to dissolve it.

CHAPTER THIRTEEN

Nate gazed out the plane's window, transfixed by the clearness of the atmosphere above the carpet of vapour. Liv felt for what he must be going through, but was at a loss as to how to help him. Her only experience with death had been Geai, and all she had gleaned from that was that life does go on, but sometimes only after you crash. And sometimes you have to let someone else help you out. She'd been slow to learn that, but Nate had been her person. That's what made the decision to come an easy one, despite what she knew lay in store.

She'd never felt jealous of Cindy — even before meeting the woman, Cindy had seemed like a ghost. There would be comparisons made to the beloved daughter-in-law. Liv wasn't the open, warm-hearted girl that Cindy had been — not that any of those traits had done Nate any favours. Or maybe they had; maybe what Cindy had done was a greater expression of love than Liv was willing to give her credit for.

Nate touched her on the arm, returning from wherever he'd been in his mind, on that distant horizon line where the sky met the layer of clouds.

"It won't be much longer now. Do you want to sit by the window? I've seen it before."

There was no disdain in his voice – like he didn't resent the place, just the circumstances that had driven him away, and those that were bringing him back. She nodded, and they traded spots before the seatbelt light came on.

Liv looked out, putting the complications out of her head, anticipating the terrain as the plane began its descent. The land below was much flatter than she'd expected, and definitely less populated than what surrounded the airports in Toronto, New York City, Fort Lauderdale, or LA. There were still vast squares of farmland here. No sign of the Rockies, much to her disappointment.

Her nerves crept up as they landed, mocking her spontaneity. Maybe it hadn't been so smart, coming along, though Nate assured her his mother knew the details of their relationship. But mothers could see through things, past appearances to the more obscure and abstract kept beneath the surface. Nate didn't make his mother out to be someone anyone would be afraid of, but Liv wasn't sure how she would view the still-ambiguous nature of this bond between them.

He was on his feet as soon as the seatbelt light was off, reaching to the overhead compartment to retrieve their carry-ons, even though it would be some time before they could disembark.

She was usually a fast walker, but she matched Nate's uncharacteristically subdued pace through the terminal. He was dragging – he couldn't be looking forward to this reunion. The only experience she could relate it to was when she'd come skulking back to Ontario after letting her career fall apart in New York, but Nate really had no reason to be embarrassed or ashamed, except for leaving it so long.

She wasn't used to seeing him so serious, his face set like he was ready for a clash as he searched the crowd awaiting the arrivals. Then it softened, and he let his bags fall to the ground as he went forward and enfolded a small woman, dark blonde hair laced with grey, tired eyes weeping.

Liv stayed by Nate's luggage, tentatively putting down her own. Behind the woman stood a young man, dark hair, taller than Nate. He assessed her steadily, waiting just as she did, until Nate gently pulled away from his mother and threw his arms around him.

Nate took a step back, scanning cautiously. "Where's Dad?"

His mother answered. "He had to go into work briefly. He should be back by the time we get home."

Nate reached an arm toward Liv, encouraging her forward. "This is my mom. And my younger brother, Tim."

"Liv," the woman said, brushing away the hand she extended to pull her into a hug like she was family.

"I'm so sorry, Mrs. Miller," Liv said. "But I'm glad to meet you."

"Connie, please," the woman said, pushing a smile through persistent tears. "It was so kind of you to come."

Tim settled for the handshake before offering to take her bags.

Tim drove, heading west, his mother in the passenger seat next to him quietly asking about the flight and the weather in Toronto. Nate stared out the window. Liv could finally see the mountains, rising solemnly in the distance.

At the house Connie immediately busied herself, putting on a kettle and pulling plates from cupboards. "Would you like some tea? Something to eat? You must be hungry."

Nate smiled and glanced at Liv. "That's okay, Mom. Why don't you come and sit down?"

Connie scowled. "You're not riding this afternoon; you can

eat something." She laid out some fruit and Nate grabbed an orange and started peeling it while his mother set out cups. "You can sleep in the spare room, Liv. Tim took over the basement after you boys left, so Nate, you can stay down there with him."

She looked distressed for a moment...*you boys.* Nate went to her, his embrace fierce. How much he must have missed her, restricting himself to only phone calls these last years. At one point he must have been close to his family; a piece of himself he'd left behind. Maybe cutting himself off had been more damaging than he'd let himself believe.

The click of the door was followed by a scramble of nails on tile, a whirl of energetic Golden Retrievers converging on the small space. Nate let go of his mother and laughed, the two Goldens circling his legs before bounding over to Liv at the table.

She leaned over and stroked their broad heads — a male and a bitch — and found herself speaking to them softly in French. Nate smiled at her before footsteps distracted him, his body turning rigid when someone appeared in the doorway.

It wasn't hard for Liv to figure out who the man was. The set of the shoulders and line of his jaw were the same, and she could imagine Nate's hair being that muted grey-blond in another twenty-five years. He was taller, though not as tall as Tim, and his face was considerably more serious — but the features were so similar. The man glanced at her first, then Nate.

"Welcome back."

The voice didn't sound particularly welcoming, but it seemed more neutral than judgmental. Nate met the man's regard, then walked back behind the kitchen table. The grim look on his face made him look even more like his father.

"Dad, this is my friend Liv." Nate's eyes flashed to hers.

"My dad. Reid." He seemed to be withholding other sentiments that came to mind.

Liv rose as Reid Miller came toward her, hand outstretched. The Goldens scattered, the only happy ones left in the kitchen, tails wagging in defiance of the tension. The exchange was firm, businesslike. Unlike his wife, Liv thought Reid Miller's eyes were speculating, questioning her presence. Connie watched anxiously from behind her husband. That was it for the conversation, though. Nate wasn't offering anything more, and Reid turned to his wife and started talking about the funeral arrangements. Nate focused on the dogs, probably resisting the temptation to bolt, even though he'd want to hear what was happening.Then his phone rang, and he snatched it from the table, answering.

"Hey man." He paused, listening. "Will's coming on a later flight. Maybe we can get together after I pick him up."

Hearing Will was also returning for the funeral further cemented things from Nate's past for Liv. They'd grown up together, in this neighbourhood. Will and the racing industry in Ontario had been Nate's only destination when he'd departed. At least he'd had somewhere to go when he'd arrived in Toronto. He'd seemed so together when he'd come for the interview at the farm; there had been no indication of the hell he'd been through. Liv had always considered Nate one to keep his feelings close to the surface, but such a good chunk of his history he'd left buried deep.

After he disconnected, he pushed himself to his feet. "I'll show you your room." He slid past his parents, avoiding his mother's face.

Liv followed him, remaining by the door when he set her luggage by the bed. She scanned the walls. Hockey trophies of all sizes crowded shelves, and the same large win photo of Chique's Queen's Plate that graced the Triple Stripe office at

Woodbine hung next to the bed — much to Liv's surprise. She felt him watching her, and wondered what he was thinking; how it made him feel, seeing some acknowledgment of his success. Maybe this room was low traffic, but they weren't stashed in a closet somewhere like he might have expected.

"Was this your room?" she asked, just to break the silence, edging her way in.

"Once. When Phil moved out in his second year of university I took over his space in the basement. Typical teenager, right?" His hands were in his pockets, looking from the trophies to the win picture before turning back to her. "Are you tired?"

"A little," she admitted, the time difference catching up with her, and she waited for him to tell her what was going on for the rest of the day. Another position she wasn't used to being in. Her time was usually so tightly self-regulated that the current state didn't help her feel any less out of place.

"I told Will I'd pick him up at the airport. Then I guess tonight I'd better be at the visitation."

Liv nodded, slowly. "Is it all right with you if I skip that?" That would be far too awkward.

"Yeah, of course," he said, his face softening. "It's just great to have you here."

The kid had offered to drive, but Nate didn't want to just sit there. He'd already had enough of that, and it wasn't doing him any good. If he could block out everything in his head, deal with it later, maybe he could get through this.

His mom's sedan was a step down — or five — from the Porsche, but probably just as well he didn't have that much power underfoot right now. He didn't want to think about where along this highway the accident had taken place. Better not to know. Didn't want to think about the niece and nephew he had yet to meet, who would grow up without their mother and father. Didn't want to get into anything with his own father while he was here, because it would just upset his mother more.

He switched his attention to Tim. His little brother hadn't changed that much, as far as he could tell — sure he was taller, and he'd filled out a lot. But he still didn't say much, still waiting for Nate to ask the questions.

"How's the hockey going?" Nate asked.

"Good."

Nate grinned, knowing — thanks to his mother — the kid was being modest. He was the leading goal-scorer on his team, but Nate could relate to the reservation. It wouldn't merit an answer of 'great' until he made it to the NHL.

"Still going to school part-time?"

"Yeah. I wanted to work, but Mom and Dad insisted."

"Probably smart."

"That's real great, coming from you." Now Tim threw him a wry smile.

"Yeah well...I've been pretty lucky." And should probably be saving more money in case that luck runs out, instead of spending it on expensive sports cars. He didn't tell Tim about the Porsche. He kept thinking about throwing the keys to Phil, like that was his last real memory of his older brother. It seemed symbolic, though of what, he wasn't sure. Giving in? Giving up? *You win*...though right now it wasn't looking much like a victory.

"Hopefully I'll get drafted this year."

It was the first thing Tim had said without prompting. That would put an end to his studies...but their father wouldn't have an issue with that.

"So...girlfriend?" Nate continued.

Tim scowled. "I'm not gonna let a girl mess up my head when I'm trying to get my hockey career on track."

Nate laughed, looking ahead to the road. "You and Liv have a lot in common. The two of you could discuss the virtues of being single."

Tim looked confused. "So you guys aren't together?"

"Ah...well...sort of, maybe."

"Sounds like one of those 'it's complicated' things."

"No. Not really. It's just...not simple."

"Isn't that the same thing?"

"It's a long story."

"You're making a lot of sense. So why's she here?"

Nate smirked. Tim was asking all the hard questions, for someone who kept quiet. He hadn't realized how much his little brother was like Liv. Maybe that's why he'd been able to get along with her the way he did — he'd had practice without really even knowing it.

"We've gone through some stuff. Maybe I've been there for her a couple of times. We're not sleeping together —" How did he explain the layers of that reality? "— but it's kind of...deep."

"Sounds serious. Is there something you can take for that?"

Nate choked on a laugh. "Your day will come. You go ahead and get that career settled, then give me a call. I've already got the girl for you."

"Yeah, don't you be setting me up. That's bound to go badly. Sounds like you've got enough to deal with already, with your own love life."

"Smartass."

They'd timed it right, so they didn't have to park, picking Will up at the curb. Will opened the door and threw his bag on the back seat, climbing in after it.

"Hey, Tim, how's the hockey star?"

Tim brushed off the comment as Nate pulled the car into the traffic flow.

"So how'd it go?" Will asked, tapping Nate on the shoulder.

Nate shot him a dark look and returned his attention to the road.

"They didn't kill each other, if that's what you mean." Tim grinned.

Will laughed. "That's a good start. Where's Liv?"

"Back at the house," Nate said. "She's not coming tonight. Just as well. I guess we've got some stuff to do."

"You going to be all right for that, buddy?" Will asked.

Nate grimaced. "I'll manage. Ben said he'd see us there. It'll give us a good reason to leave early." He was silent for a moment. "You hungry?"

"Sure," Will said.

"They'll have food at the funeral home, won't they?" Tim interjected.

"They won't have alcohol." Will chuckled. "You'd better plan on driving from here on in, Tim. I expect your brother needs to get on the drink program to get through this."

Nate shook his head. Not that it would surprise anyone if he showed up drunk. And part of him would really like to see his father's face. He wished now Liv had come, as if she would ground him to his new life so he wouldn't succumb to the failures of the old. He'd told her when she'd hit a low after Geai's death that alcohol didn't help. He needed to heed his own advice.

"I think I need to show everybody here I can deal with stuff sober," he stated. "I'm pretty sure the last time they all saw me I left them with a memorable impression that suggested otherwise."

"All right," Will said. "We'll just go get drunk after, then."

The visitation was busy enough he didn't have to worry

about it being obvious he still wasn't talking to his father. He stayed next to his mother, focusing his energy on being her support. A good son, to make up for the one who'd run away. He was grateful things were sombre enough that no one said anything to make him feel badly for falling off the face of the earth as far as Calgary was concerned. All the same, when the time came he was happy to have that excuse to go.

"We've got some stuff to sort out for tomorrow, Mom." He drew her into a hug, and felt her nod against his shoulder as she squeezed back.

Worry lingered in her eyes as the guys gathered behind him. Even his mother expected him to go off the rails. Ben held up the car keys.

"Drive carefully," she said. They weren't just words.

At the restaurant he asked the server for water. Will's eyes went wide, and Nate just shrugged. It wasn't that he didn't want to be numb. And he didn't need to get up early in the morning, or make weight tomorrow afternoon. It was his mother's face, and his own fear, that if he started, he wouldn't stop.

Ben brought him back to the task at hand. "So we haven't played together since Will deserted us seven years ago, but tomorrow we're going to get up in front of a church full of people?"

Nate was having trouble thinking of Cindy coming up with songs to play at her own funeral. With the twins now, and Phil being a lawyer, of course they'd have wills. Phil would have made sure all that was in place. But the songs...the songs were all Cindy. Songs she knew he knew. And somehow he had to get up there and sing them.

"I should probably have a will," he said, trying to deflect his own thoughts.

"Sure buddy," Will said. "You do have a kind of dangerous job. You'll leave me the car, though, right?"

"Only if you agree to play at *my* funeral. Maybe we could pick out the tunes tonight."

Will laughed, but it lacked humour.

The house was dark when he returned, and he crept quietly downstairs. There was a light on in the TV room — and Liv curled up on the couch, asleep with a book in her lap. Rita, the female Golden, snuggled next to her; Dexter, the male, on the floor beside her. He wanted to curl up with them and bury himself there.

Liv lifted her head, eyes flickering open as she straightened and closed the book. Rita didn't budge; Dexter's tail thumped once. Clearly she'd been well taken care of.

Her head tilted slightly. "You okay?"

Maybe the question came because he hadn't moved from the bottom of the stairs, the scene giving him flashbacks of time spent down here. He shook them loose and walked over, leaning down, like his kiss was a breathalyzer to prove he was fine.

"Don't let my father catch that dog on the couch." He plopped down on the opposite end, his fingers weaving through the thick Golden coat to give Rita a scratch. "What are you doing awake?"

"I wasn't really awake." She smirked. "I slept for a while earlier. I'm all messed up between that and the time difference. How'd it go?"

"All right. A lot of people I hadn't seen for years. It's like a weird social thing, isn't it? Then Will and I met with our old band mate, Ben. We're going to play some songs tomorrow."

Her eyebrows crept up, a slight crease forming between them.

"Just another performance, right?" *Ride the horse you're on.* He shrugged, dropping his eyes to where Dexter's head now rested on his foot. "Cindy had stuff written out..." He faltered.

"She was just like that. Always planning everything. Except me. I don't think she planned on me."

"I'm not sure anyone plans on you, Miller."

There was no response for that, the feeling it left him with one he couldn't pin down and put in a box. An admission on her part that he had managed to break through her well-constructed walls. *She's stingy with words,* he'd said to the old farm manager, Geai, when he'd first questioned her trusting him with Chique. She certainly didn't share feelings freely. And this, the two of them, certainly hadn't been part of any of her plans.

But now he felt he had to step back, when it would be easy to press forward, to take comfort there. It wouldn't be fair to her, after all this time, to use her to fight his memories — of that time, of this room; to put her in that position, competing with history. The irony was painful, after the long winter in limbo.

One thing he could count on — she wouldn't question it, wouldn't challenge the physical line they still maintained, her personal and emotional space something she didn't seem in any hurry to give up. They were still like a couple of well-behaved church kids. Crazy or endearing, he didn't know.

She finally broke the silence that had settled, extricating her legs from the sixty pounds of retriever that had held her captive. "Tomorrow's going to be a long day."

Leaning over, she kissed him, the touch of her lips light. The weight in her grey eyes was anything but. When she didn't quite pull away, he almost...almost...

Listening to her footsteps as she ascended, he hoped he was exhausted enough to fall asleep, because he was tired of thinking, and remembering, and trying to figure out what losing the past would mean for the future.

Nate's voice never faltered, fingers unfailingly striking the right keys, the three members of this unplanned reunion managing to sound like they did this every day. Liv could feel his pain though; his need to believe there was a reason behind it all. She swiped at her damp cheeks with the sleeve of her dress, and felt Connie press a tissue in her palm, squeezing, her own eyes shining as she met Liv's.

There was no shortage of speculative looks in the basement of the church after the service, Nate wrapping his fingers around hers as they stood on the edge of the gathering. He introduced her simply as a friend to a flurry of faces and names she couldn't hope to remember. The way he moved around her suggested there was more to them; that reassurance in his eyes she'd come to rely on, his fingers on her back as he presented someone new. She went with it. Maybe she could be who and what they might think she was. Maybe she was becoming it.

He caught sight of something across the room, and touched her arm. "I'll be back in a sec, all right?"

Will appeared beside her like it had been staged so she wouldn't feel abandoned. Not that he filled the void Nate left, even though he was physically bigger. Nate weaved through bodies to a man and woman, each of them carrying a child Liv hadn't seen them upstairs.

"That's Cindy's sister Julie and her husband." Will paused. "And I'm guessing those are the twins."

It wasn't hard to figure out. Nate embraced the woman and looked totally natural greeting the children, Liv guiltily relieved he hadn't taken her over with him. She would have had no idea what to say. The thought of losing a sister was crushing, not to mention that of two kids who would never know their parents.

"You okay?"

Liv glanced at Will. Did she look that uncomfortable? Could he actually fathom how out of her element she felt?

"Come here a minute." He inclined his head to the side. "This is someone you should probably meet."

Will interrupted a middle-aged man who had the weathered look of someone who didn't usually wear a suit and tie. "This is Al Wilson."

The man grinned warmly, offering his hand. "Liv Lachance. I'm honoured."

Liv smiled modestly. "Great to finally meet you."

Al was the trainer, a family friend, who had given Nate his start with horses — the one to whom Nate had credited his broad range of skills, when most jockeys didn't learn a lot of horsemanship before being tossed onto a Thoroughbred. She was happy to finally have someone she could relate to in a sea of people who would never understand her way of life.

"Glad to see the kid finally got his license," Al said. "Would have been a shame for all that talent to go to waste."

"It took him long enough." Liv smiled again. "But maybe he knew what he was doing, taking his time. He's done a pretty impressive job of making the most of things since."

"You've been good to him."

"He's earned it."

There was more assessing going on, given the mild look on Al Wilson's face. Then he looked over Liv's shoulder, his features lighting up. "And there he is. Good to see you, kid. Wish it hadn't taken something like this to inspire a visit."

Seeing the trainer threatened to chip away at the mask Nate was working hard to maintain. He recovered, deflecting the combination of praise and chiding with an ease Liv had seen time and again.

"How are you doing?" Liv asked after Al excused himself with the usual pleasantries.

"I could use a drink, or five, but thanks for asking," he responded, letting his weariness show.

They returned to the house before the others, Nate leading the way into the dining room, loosening his tie as he went. He opened the door to a hutch, peering in, and pulled out a bottle and a couple of tumblers, then looked at her.

"Want one?"

Liv looked dubiously over his shoulder. "That depends. What is it?"

"My father's scotch."

"No thanks," Liv said, eying him before going into the living room, open off the dining area. She hadn't been in here, and glanced around before sitting on the chesterfield. Nate came over and sat next to her, resting his arm on the back of the sofa and swallowing a healthy dose from the glass he'd poured. He looked as if he wasn't sure if he liked it, but it served the purpose.

"Is that your Eclipse Award?" Liv said.

Nate glanced at the bronze statue resting on a table near the window — the trophy that had been given to him as leading apprentice in North America in his first year of riding. "I guess it is," he said, laughing softly. "I figured it would be a doorstop or something."

"Thought about it."

Reid Miller stood in the doorway, Connie scowling behind him. It sounded so much like something Nate would say, Liv had to smother a grin.

"I'm taking the dogs for a run. Thought you might want to come along."

Reid was looking directly at Nate, and Liv couldn't help studying him as well, gauging his reaction. He stared back at his father, his prolonged hesitation making Liv think he was going to say no.

"Okay." He glanced at her. "That all right with you?"

Liv nodded quickly. "Yeah, of course."

"I'll need to change." Nate walked over to the dining room, draining the glass, and set it on the table with his eyes on Reid before disappearing downstairs.

Connie poured a measure of whiskey for herself, Liv trying to control the lift of her eyebrows as the older woman settled into the spot Nate had vacated.

"It was very kind of you to come with him, Liv. He's very lucky to have a friend like you."

After a day where she'd felt stuck for words, even more than usual, Liv didn't hesitate as she looked into Connie's care-worn face. "I've always thought I was the lucky one."

Nate watched the dogs play, grabbing fallen branches and carrying them with wagging tails like the self-respecting Golden Retrievers they were. The walk to the park had been silent, and he'd found himself wishing that was good enough. He had nothing left, but this hadn't been an invitation he could refuse, not today. His mother deserved to have what was left of her family somewhat cohesive. It was unlikely he and his father would ever be close, but it could be a whole lot better than it was right now. Bygones.

Dexter came bounding over with his stick and a goofy Golden grin. Nate asked for it quietly, the dog releasing, sitting expectantly. When he sent it tumbling through the air, Dexter bounded off in hot pursuit with Rita on his heels.

"Sounds like Tim's doing great." He couldn't leave the silence, if anything was going to be resolved here. That seemed like a safe place to start. "Do you think he'll get drafted this year?"

"I'd be pretty surprised if he doesn't."

Stops and starts. This was either going to be a long walk, or a really short one.

"What's really going on with the girl?"

There was a trace of a smirk on his father's face, which was more than Nate had seen since he'd been back...and for a long time before he'd left.

"She's a friend, Dad."

Because first and foremost, she was. And wasn't that the best way for things to be?

"You like her, don't you?"

Nate sighed. "I do." That wasn't news, but he was aware his feelings were a whole lot more intense than that.

Reid shook his head. "You always pick the good ones, kid. Beauty and brains."

There was no use trying to explain the nature of his relationship with Liv to his father — like there was no "picking" her; it was a slow evolution over which he had no control. All he could do was see where it carried them, and hope it ended differently than his relationships had in the past.

"I know I was hard on you. It took a lot of guts to leave the way you did. I respect that."

Nate choked on a laugh. So they were going there. "Guts? I ran away with my tail between my legs."

"You did the right thing."

"Then how come you never let me feel that way?" He looked ahead to where the dogs were invested in some intriguing scent, finding he wasn't really angry anymore, just strangely reflective. "I couldn't do anything right as far as you were concerned. You know it was completely ridiculous to think I was going to play professional hockey, right?" He'd figured that one out himself, at about sixteen, two years after he'd started galloping for Al Wilson. No way was he ever going to have the size and weight needed to play the game at that level, but it just so happened those shortfalls came in handy for riding racehorses.

"I'm sorry about that. It's too bad, you were good. You're good at a lot of things." Reid paused. "And you went with something I admit I couldn't get my head around. I think you've made your point. You're the best in the country at what you do."

Nate grinned. "I don't know about that. Liv will probably kick my ass going head to head with me this year."

"That'll keep you humble. Probably not a bad thing."

Nate looked at him sideways. "Thanks. Anyone that can do that for you?"

His father laughed. "Yeah. You. That's why I kept that big old bronze door stop you sent us." He stopped and turned to Nate, his hands in the pockets of his jacket. "That was a pretty special thing you did today, standing up and singing like that."

"You thought Cindy and I were all wrong."

"And I was right. But that doesn't mean I don't appreciate what it took to do that."

He had to take the good with the bad, when it came to truth, and his father. It would be too much to have Reid become suddenly outspoken in his support. And now his mother would be happy. They were talking again — no small feat.

His mother was making dinner when they returned, Liv sitting behind the kitchen counter seeming almost at ease in her company. Both women looked up, as if they were expecting blood and broken teeth. Nate went to his mother and kissed her on the cheek, then wandered around the counter. He met Liv's eyes, and almost kissed her too.

The disturbed sleep pattern of the last couple of days wasn't doing anything for his brain right now. He was beyond tired with fatigue more than physical. At least it seemed to have plateaued.

He poured himself a glass of juice in the kitchen and sat at the table. Nothing had really changed with the décor, though he imagined his departure five years ago had created a disturbance. His return might have given some balance, had it not been for the tragedy that had brought him here.

Liv appeared in the doorway — no surprise she would be afflicted with the same disruption of time, if not the full impact of the trauma — but it was like she was his totem, the thing that grounded him in this haze, reminded him that only part of this was reality. And as necessary as it had been to come, as grateful as he was to have held his mother, and set right the past with his father, her presence made him want to go home. It was official now. This wasn't home.

"Sleep okay?" he asked.

"Better than the night before, anyway."

Nate leaned on the table, hands folded as she joined him. "We should drive up to the Rockies."

Liv looked skeptical, but intrigued. "Do we have time for that?"

"Sure. If we leave now." Their flight wasn't until the afternoon. They could get to Banff and back. "I told you you needed to see real mountains."

He left a note on the fridge, and they headed out in the dark with his mother's car. The landscape emerged as the sun rose, foothills giving way to immense rock faces, blasted to create the highway. Liv was silent, peering at the vast peaks stretching to the heavens, catching the early light.

Nate didn't stop until they got to Banff. They found a coffee shop open but not much else, and walked down the quiet sidewalk with steaming cups, looking in shop windows. Every other storefront sold stereotypical Canadian souvenirs — plush moose toys, Mounties, beavers, red and white flags.

"This might be as close as I've ever come to being a tourist." Liv looked at him sideways, lips twisting up at the ends.

"In your own country, no less."

He held out his hand, and she took it, shyly. She could hop on a plane for him without a thought, but this simple gesture was a stretch, even so far away from their regular lives that it was unlikely anyone would recognize them.

"Let's go somewhere we can see the mountains better," he said, leading her back to where they'd left the car.

He ended up stopping on the side of the road because neither of them was dressed for a hike. They leaned against the car and looked up at the surrounding grandeur, ignoring the vehicles whizzing past.

"It's incredible." There was reverence in her voice. "Prehistoric, like we're close to the beginning of time."

Eternal, almost. Close to forever.

"I didn't spend much time out here, other than skiing in the winter. Seems ridiculous to have something so amazing so near, and not take advantage of it." He probably left his eyes on her too long, his mind running parallels to this, to them. "But somehow it seems part of me, you know? I think if I lived out here now, I'd have to come up here all the time. As if it's where everything would make sense."

And maybe it did right now. And maybe she was why.

CHAPTER FOURTEEN

Elemental was the early Queen's Plate favourite. The Triple Stripe hopeful had two stake wins to his credit this season with Liv aboard, and looked to solidify his position this weekend in the Plate Trial. Dean was still on the fence about which race to enter his colt in — the Trial, or an allowance race, at the same distance, on the same day.

Faye, in jeans and a simple blouse, flashed Nate a smile as she set cappuccinos in front of him and her brother. She looked good no matter what she wore, hair and makeup always flawless. No wayward smears from a well-meaning horse on Faye; she didn't get close enough for that to ever happen.

"Have you made a decision yet?" Nate nudged Dean with his foot as he sipped some of the froth, and pondered whether he could indulge in a butter tart too. The little café had the best ones in this part of Ontario, something that hadn't changed when Faye had taken over running it last summer.

Dean doodled absently in the margin of a condition book. "Roger's entering Elemental in the Trial, I assume?"

"Yes."

"What do you think?"

"In three weeks, your colt will beat Elemental. On Sunday, I'm not so sure."

"That's quite the prediction. I hope this thing you've got going with Liv isn't affecting your judgment."

Dean's smirk was probably harmless, but Nate faltered a moment. Where was that coming from? "Absolutely not."

"Better not be, because I won't think twice about putting someone else on him if I'm the least bit suspicious."

Nate laughed, maybe too abruptly. "I'd love to win the Plate two years in a row — why would I mess that up? Your colt has a great shot. If we face Elemental Sunday, it might take more out of him than you want to be giving up right now — and that could affect his chances in three weeks. Give him an easy win instead. It builds his confidence, and sets him up perfectly. That's what I'd do, anyway. Whatever you decide, just name me on him."

He did find it difficult being in competition with Liv, but he wasn't about to say that out loud. She was unfailingly businesslike, and extremely fair when it came to the Triple Stripe horses, so that wasn't the issue. He had to go out there and forget who he was riding against, which wasn't always simple, knowing how easily one of them could get hurt. Their little rivalry did have a certain appeal, however...

The jangle of the bell on the door distracted him from that thought as Will shuffled in. Will leaned down to meet Faye's upturned face, heat there even in their simple kiss. A little reminder of what Nate wasn't getting. Or even asking for.

"Liv pulled in behind me." Will settled into a chair.

Emilie swirled in, and Nate caught Liv's eye and smiled when she appeared after her sister. Her quiet manner was a contrast to Em's energy, her fingers tucked into the loose jeans she'd had on for a morning of galloping and bathing and grooming. A dusting of alfalfa leaves still clung to her shirt, her hair loosely pulled back. She looked every bit as good as Faye. No, better.

"I've got news," Emilie said, her smile bright. "I'm helping revive the Plate Ball. And all of you are coming for moral support."

Faye laughed and clapped her hands. "Oh, can I help too?"

Liv scowled. "I put on formal wear for the Sovereigns, Em. I've met my quota for the year."

"You're going." Emilie pointed at her, then at Nate. "You're making sure, right?"

Nate grinned. "I got this, Em." He rose, making his way to Liv, and took her hand, going down on one knee. She stared at him, eyebrows knitted in what might possibly be horror. "Will you go to the prom with me, Olivia?"

"Please get up."

She tried to pull him, but he wouldn't budge. "Only once you answer me."

Faye drummed her fingers against the counter. "We're all waiting. Be grateful we're not videoing this, sweetie."

"We might, if you don't hurry up," Emilie quipped.

Liv looked at the ceiling, then dropped her eyes back to Nate with a smirk. "Yes, okay. I hate you all."

He popped up and kissed her quickly. "You coming, Dean?"

"To the prom? I think not."

"You can be my date, Dean," Emilie said.

"Save her the pain of going with whatever sack she might otherwise drag along," Faye quipped.

"Just come, Dean. It's for a good cause." Em was pretty convincing, with that sweet smile. "The money's going to New Chapter." Em was always coming up with fresh ways to raise funds for the local Thoroughbred aftercare organization.

Dean's scribbles became darker. "Some of us have horses to train for the actual race."

"Some of us have horses to ride, but they're not letting me out of it." Liv's arms were crossed, but she unfolded them and pressed her hands together. "Please, Dean. In solidarity."

He pushed himself up and grumbled, "Fine. Tell me how to buy a ticket, Em. I'll see you all later. I'm going for a bike ride."

Nate was starting to give her that look each day after galloping Chique: *let's get on with it.* He was right. After two weeks of training over the Woodbine oval, the filly was ready for faster work. She worried Chique might not be the same as she had been before the laminitis...but it was time to find out.

"Easy, Miller, right?"

"Yeah, boss, we can baby her a while longer. I'm okay with that." He grinned as he got tied on. "Don't worry. I'll take care of her."

Liv led Paz out of his stall, noticing Jo starting to walk out to the track with Roger, and decided not to underestimate the importance of moral support.

Nate made the usual casual conversation as they backed up on the outer rail, but Liv barely heard him, her senses analyzing everything about the filly. Chique's jog was businesslike and untroubled, and Liv hoped it was maturity she was seeing, not a decrease in the drive that had made the filly so competitive — and challenging.

Nate looked over as he stood easily in the irons. "I'm talking to myself, aren't I?"

Liv frowned sheepishly. "Sorry."

When they turned in and faced the infield, Chique stood alertly, ears forward, nostrils flared. That was the look.

Nate pulled down his goggles and let the filly start off, Liv keeping Paz close. Chique bounced, shaking her head and travelling sideways for a few steps before Nate straightened her and channeled her energy forward. The filly knew exactly what was going on.

Paz tossed his nose in the air when she pulled him up on the backstretch. She watched them gallop around until the tote board obscured her view, then picked them up again as they rounded the clubhouse turn. Chique galloped strongly, ears flickering back to Nate — asking, waiting. When he let her drop to the rail she switched leads, accelerating as they reached the half-mile pole. Liv hit the stopwatch and let Paz move enough to follow their progress.

Chique powered around the turn, eating up the first quarter before Nate gave her more of what she wanted. Another clean lead change as they straightened into the stretch, then steadily on to the wire. Liv stopped the watch and glanced down.

She spotted them through traffic again on the backside, Chique's ears pricked as Nate eased her away from the middle of the track, slowing to a jog. He parked Chique beside the pony gelding, running a hand under her tousled mane.

"She's grown up," he said.

"Just as long as you're sure that's all it is." Liv made a face. "That was slow for her."

"Well, that's what you asked for." He laughed as they started towards the gap. "Relax, Liv. Give her time. Don't forget what she's been through."

"You don't have to remind me." Sharpness crept into her tone, and she immediately regretted snapping at him. "Sorry."

He laughed again. "And this is only the beginning. Good thing I'm used to it already."

Roger and Jo beat them back to the barn, Jo ready with the

filly's halter. It was warm enough for a bath, and Nate set the tack on the rail before returning to hold Chique while Liv put Paz away.

"See? She's not even blowing," Nate said when Liv came out to stand with Roger. "She's fine."

As if to reaffirm the statement, Chique's neck snaked, teeth grinding, and Nate grinned as he ducked out of her way. The black tail sprayed them all with soapy water, and Jo had to grab it to keep from being lashed in the face.

"Seems her old self to me." Jo grimaced.

Roger crossed his arms. "That was fine. Just what you wanted."

"I know, I know," Liv said.

Nate relinquished the shank to the hotwalker. "I think we'll probably get the filly back to the races, Rog, but I'm not convinced we can hold Liv here together."

Liv pressed her lips into a line. "Don't you have somewhere to be?"

"No, actually I'm done for the morning." That grin of his teased her. "I was thinking I'd make a run to the kitchen. Can I get you anything?"

He didn't wait for her answer. Roger chuckled beside her.

"He's right, you know. About the filly, I mean. She looked good out there. He had a stranglehold on her. And the two-year-old is training great. You need to ride more races or something to keep yourself occupied, so you're not fretting so much. Then maybe you'll see how well things are really going."

She caught his eye as they walked onto the shed.

"You'll be all right. He's a good guy."

Liv ducked into Feste's stall and tied him to the back wall. That much was true — the colt was prepping like the racehorse he was supposed to be. With the winter's long, slow miles under him, the speed work was coming easily. She'd actually let herself start looking for a race. Chique stressed her constantly, but she was excited about Feste. He was trying on the sensible shoes Claire had left behind, while Chique danced to her own tune in knee-high spiky red boots.

"Looks like she's cooling out fine."

Nate leaned on the doorframe, holding out a bottle of apple juice. Had he run to the kitchen? Liv finished picking and painting Feste's feet before she came forward to accept it.

"All right. I get it."

She rested her shoulder on the cool cinder-block wall, aware of how close he was, and how that was okay. Regardless of the fact that they were no secret, she'd been clinging to a sense of propriety, her precious professionalism, but since they'd returned from Calgary it had started to seem less important.

He hadn't talked about the trip since they'd come back. He was different. Older, in the way that dealing with death couldn't help but age a person. More committed, which shouldn't have been possible, because he'd always been rock-solid, with his job. With her.

"Don't worry, we'll get her there," he said.

She laughed, surprised for once he hadn't pinpointed exactly what she'd been thinking.

She went to Feste, rubbing the star on his forehead, then looked sideways to Nate. "Can you breeze him tomorrow?"

He smirked, but there was a kink in one of his eyebrows. "I thought you might be keeping him for yourself."

Feste lipped at her fingers, and she tugged his upper lip gently. "I'm just asking you to breeze him."

"No you're not."

She met his eyes. "I did think about it. Keeping him. But when it comes down to it...I think all along I was planning to give him to you."

"Chique, Ride The Wave, now Feste...keep giving me your best horses, you're going to gift yourself out of a Plate."

"I am so beating your ass with Elemental this year."

"You keep dreaming." He grinned, held her eyes for a moment, and walked away.

"Well. You're not messing around," Nate said when Liv told him her plans for Feste's first race.

"You know how good he is."

"Oh I'm not questioning, just thinking I'm the one who's usually all high on the kids." His grin flashed. "Nice to see some confidence."

There was no sense denying it with this colt. Besides, the early two-year-old races were all short, so it would just be like another work...even if it was a stake race.

Her phone buzzed in her back pocket, and she pulled it out, glancing at the screen.

"Problem?" Nate asked.

She hadn't exactly hidden her scowl. She shook her head. "No. I've just – gotta go. See you tomorrow?"

She left him standing in the middle of the shed with a puzzled look on his face.

She'd forgotten about the Plate Ball until Faye asked her what she was wearing, and insisted a shopping trip was in order. Why had she agreed to this? Wasn't there enough to worry about in her life right now without making a big deal out of what should really just be an inconvenient social obligation?

"You gotta play the game a little," Faye insisted. "We need to make sure he's picking his jaw up off the floor when he sees you."

"Why?" Liv said, exasperated.

"It's all about power, sweetie." Faye's lips spread into that smug smile of hers.

"Oh come on. We're friends. I'm not getting into that."

"That's cute, but you really need to turn things up a notch or the two or you aren't going to get anywhere. He's probably scared to make any kind of move, so you've got to give him a little bit of an opening. Though we both know you'd never throw yourself at him."

"Yeah. Okay. I know better than to take advice from you."

"Just trying to help out," Faye said. "But you still need the dress."

"Téméraire..."

The colt began to dance beneath Nate as the announcer called an Anglophone's approximation of his official name. Liv wasn't watching this one in the room. It wasn't just that she was tired of the good-natured jibes, the "What are you doing letting Miller ride that colt?" She needed to be here, out front, binoculars clutched in a vise-grip next to Roger.

Nate left the pony behind to warm up, Feste's ground-covering stride a contrast to the easy gallops of the other entrants. The colt was the only first-time starter in the race, but he wasn't being overlooked. The position of favourite fluctuated between him and Way Too Normal, winner of the first two-year-old stake of the season. Reunited briefly with Paz and Nicole behind the gate, Feste loaded without incident.

Liv's hands trembled. Suddenly, she was terrified.

Terrified he'd hurt himself.

Terrified he'd run up the track.

Terrified he'd turn out to be everything he was supposed to be.

The gates crashed open, and Feste matched strides with Way Too Normal, gunning for the lead. Liv didn't want to look at the teletimer. Didn't really need to, to know they were flying — but her dark bay colt moved effortlessly, Nate quiet on his back. The two leaders opened up on the rest of the field, sizzling into the turn. Not that the others wouldn't catch up, if these two hit a brick wall mid-stretch, sustaining such a rapid pace.

Feste wouldn't. She knew how fit he was.

But Way Too Normal did — reaching his limit, going backwards. Nate calmly picked Feste up and urged him on by. Then steadily ran away from the rest of them, so it didn't matter who was coming on at the end.

Liv shook her head as Nate galloped the colt out. No flash, no drama — nothing like Chique — but Feste had set a track record just the same. Pure, uncomplicated talent.

This colt could be better than Chique. This colt could be everything.

CHAPTER FIFTEEN

FAYE HADN'T CONSIDERED the high school formal a rite of passage the way some teenage girls did – she'd been more into going for the sport of seeing who wore what and came with whom. Liv hadn't shared her friend's fascination, refusing any attempts Faye had made to drag her along.

Now it seemed it had all caught up to her, with this whole Plate Ball ordeal.

Nate's mock promposal at the café that day had been a joke, right? Because this *was* just a professional obligation. It was in support of Thoroughbred aftercare, something both of them supported wholeheartedly.

So why was she so nervous? This was Nate. And neither of them was eighteen. They both had to make an appearance, so why not go together?

Well, of course there was the fact they were riding the top two Plate contenders. Elemental had easily won the Trial, and later the same day, Nate accompanied Ride The Wave to an impressive victory in an allowance race, matching Elemental's time. The Northwest colt was definitely going to be the one to beat — and Nate was being very close-mouthed about his mount. He had to be careful, especially if Dean, of all people, had voiced concern about his riding against her and a Triple Stripe horse, but Liv knew any loyalty dissolved out on the racetrack.

But tonight? They were old news. Surely the gossips would find something more interesting to talk about. Any occasion where the track community gathered had the potential for good stories. Someone would get drunk and do something stupid; somebody would leave with someone different from whom they came with. She and Nate would observe the indiscretions, pick at food, avoid alcohol; maybe he'd drag her out for a dance, but it wouldn't be them inspiring tales.

But it was their first public appearance, socially. And the dress...

The dress was exquisite. Faye had talked her out of her default navy or black, and into this sleek, deep aqua strapless gown that reached the floor with a subtle flare, a satiny shawl for later in case it got cool. Emilie had done her hair, sweeping it into an elegant updo, though Liv had drawn the line at makeup, because she'd no doubt smear it by mistake. How did people not do that all the time?

The pendant around her neck — the one Geai had given her, with the tiny painting of a horse that looked just like Claire, and, okay, a nun — would centre her. She'd scoffed at that nun, but it had become her way of keeping Geai close. And as much as this thing with Nate still managed to catch her off guard, Geai would have loved it. If he was looking down from somewhere, he had a big old smile on his face.

The doorbell made her jump, reverberating through the house, which was empty except for her. Her parents had left earlier, Em before that, because she was involved in organizing the event.

She stood in the foyer with her hand on the knob, eyes closed; made herself breathe. *Stop overthinking this.*

Then there he was on the front step, grinning, of course, one hand tucked behind his back. "Sorry I'm late."

"You're not."

It wasn't as if she'd never seen the tux, but...*well.* Standing there, all flawlessly turned out, he threw an irregular beat into her pulse, sending a current through her veins. Faye's so-called advice popped into her head: *we both know you'd never throw yourself at him.* But what if she did? That would get her out of this whole thing, of that much she was sure.

He pulled his arm from behind his back to present a single, long-stemmed, red rose. Most women would have melted, but Liv laughed as she accepted it, her tension easing just a titch.

"Wrong race, Miller," she said, immediately associating roses with the Kentucky Derby, then caught herself for being ungrateful. "Thank you. Come in for a minute?"

He sauntered after her to the kitchen as she found one of her mother's crystal vases for the delicate bud. When she turned with it, she glanced away from the look he was giving her, and brushed past him to the living room to set the vase on the coffee table.

I guess the dress worked.

She walked slowly up the two steps to the landing, making herself hold his gaze. "If you've changed your mind and don't want to go to this thing, I wouldn't complain." She didn't care how it sounded.

There was a definite beat before a laugh that was a little strained, the shift of his eyes telling her it wasn't her imagination. "That would attract more attention than showing up together will." He reached for her hand, pulling her slowly towards him. "We'd better get out of here. It would be a shame to miss it when we both look so good."

One touch. She could just reach a hand to his neck; kiss him, put an end to this silly idea. His eyes were on her mouth, fingers warm against hers. But he directed her to the door. She locked it behind them, and hesitated when he held out his arm.

"Why are you so worried?" Now he was laughing at her, looking, quite possibly, relieved that they'd made it out of the house.

His arm felt solid beneath his jacket as they descended the steps, which was a good thing, because she might as well have been wearing heels instead of ballet flats, as unsteady as she felt.

He stopped again at the bottom of the stairs. "Really, what's up?"

"This seems altogether too grown-up. You're making such a big deal."

"I'm not making a big deal. It'll be fun."

"Fun? Why is it that everyone but me seems to think these things are fun?"

"It'll be fun because you're with me." He rolled his eyes when she didn't lose the deer-in-the-headlights look. "Fine."

"Does this mean we don't have to go?"

"You need to stop saying that. We're going."

Then he dangled the keys in front of her with a tilt of his head. She snapped them up, leaving him standing there as she swept around the front of the Porsche. She definitely wasn't waiting for him to withdraw that opportunity.

He dashed to open the driver's side door for her, waiting as she slipped behind the wheel and tucked in the gown. Foot on the brake, depress the clutch, pop the stick into neutral. The engine purred at the turn of the key, and she almost purred with it.

"Well? Are you coming?"

Humour me, it'll be fun...that was the attitude, wasn't it? Of course, maybe this was all just an attempt to knock her off her stride for tomorrow — though two could play that game, and if the looks she kept catching meant anything, he was just as vulnerable.

He started singing along to the stereo, naturally. Van Morrison, *Moondance.* He always seemed to mix in some old stuff, but this song, and his voice, stirred everything inside her just a little more.

Liv glanced at him sideways, trying to get her head back in the game. "Did you curate this playlist specially for tonight, Miller?"

"Naw."

Right. The next song, *Hey Pretty,* was proof of his lie. The Poe was for her. And tonight? Oh yes, she got the gist of the song.

It was hard to resist the temptation to go faster when she reached the highway, though that only meant they would get there sooner. She needed to play the role for a few hours, make him happy. This was what most women would kill for. A sweet car, the enchanting music, a handsome, well-dressed escort. He should probably be driving, but that restyling of the fantasy might actually make it work for her. If it had to be, it might as well be like this.

The big white tent next to Woodbine's grandstand was already humming. Part of her was happy it wasn't in a fancy hotel ballroom, because that would have made it harder to keep her mindset of seeing this as a job. They worked on the backside in the morning. They worked on the front side in the afternoon. This was just more work. On the other hand, it was like a big fishbowl.

They gave up the Porsche to a valet, both of them looking longingly after it. Nate finally grabbed her elbow, steering her away and looping his arm through hers again.

"Ready for this?"

Liv squared her shoulders and sighed. "Okay. Let's get it over with."

"You're so good for my self-esteem."

"It's nothing personal, Miller." She grinned at him. *Play the game.* He could have this night. She would be that girl.

Eyes and whispers followed them when they walked in. Her imagination? She tried to feed off Nate's calm as her anxiety escalated again.

"Aha! Congratulations, Nate. You did it." Faye stood to welcome them when they found their table.

"I had to let her drive my car to get her here."

"Well then, I'm surprised you made it at all," Faye said.

Nate helped Liv into the chair next to her and she flashed him a look she hoped transmitted *don't stray too far*.

"Fashionably late for maximum impact." Faye leaned closer as Liv watched Nate drift over to Will. "How'd the dress go over? Fabulously, judging by the way my brother's looking at you."

Liv glanced at Dean on the fringes, towering over Emilie's bug rider date, Jordan Cooper. Dean's eyes dropped abruptly.

"Ooooh, I saw that." Emilie seemed to appear out of nowhere, all bright and flushed and pretty, like some alien thing Liv could never believe was related to her. "You are so right, Faye."

"Of course I'm right."

"Right about what?" Liv said, feeling lost, which was not all that unusual with Faye and Emilie.

"I think we need some drinks, don't you?" Faye spoke up, looking pointedly at Nate and Will.

They obediently excused themselves, Nate throwing Liv an apologetic look.

"You already know my brother's had a thing for you forever." Faye said, Emilie crowded in close beside her.

"Stop saying that," Liv scoffed. She'd never actually believed it. But the way Dean had averted his eyes...*just, please, no?* Why was she so bad at picking up on these things?

Faye continued her rambling. "I'd somehow forgotten how good Nate looks in a tux. If you don't make something of tonight I don't care, I'm leaving Will and going after him again. You've had your chance."

"Faye!" Emilie gasped.

"I'm kidding!"

"I did consider staying at the house and having my way with him," Liv quipped.

"Sure you did." Faye patted her arm. "I'm beginning to think you are hopeless."

Liv welcomed the wine Nate set in front of her as he settled next to her. So much for avoiding alcohol. His glass looked suspiciously like Perrier.

"Just so there's no question you know I'm driving home," he breathed in her ear.

The wine was going down too quickly; they needed to open up the buffet. She reached for Nate's glass as he eyed her appraisingly. Liv gave him her best attempt at a demure smile, taking a sip — yes, Perrier — and placing it back in front of him.

In reality the buffet was wasted on her, her salad merely picked over. Nate's plate didn't look much different. Faye couldn't even tempt her with cake. It was almost a relief when the music started up.

"I really wish we could have had you guys play," Emilie said, looking at Will. "I guess we'll have to wait until tomorrow." Will and the rest of the band would be setting up after the race for a repeat of last year's Plate Party performance — exact location to be determined.

Nate reached for Liv's hand. "Dance?"

"Do I have a choice?" She smiled as he lifted her to her feet. There was no point resisting, though when she got out there she realized she hadn't drunk nearly enough wine.

Nate found her eyes, locking them in, his palm on the small of her back anchoring her. "You really need to lighten up."

"Why did you want to do this, Miller?" she asked.

He didn't respond right away, not going with the obvious reply — the one she was trying to tell herself, that they had to be here.

"We're good at the day-to-day stuff. It works. And that's great. Last thing I want to do is mess that up. But...sometimes you just have to go out of your comfort zone. And I hope you don't think I've got any sort of agenda here. It's not like that." He met her gaze, and he didn't have to explain what he meant. "I never went to my high school formals. I guess I thought I was too good for that, with my older girlfriend, or that she'd think it was juvenile."

He hesitated, the not-quite-ghost of Cindy in his words, Liv feeling the sorrow waft over him. She moved her arm further up his shoulder, bringing them closer, feeling him inhale before continuing.

"I guess I'm a bit of a romantic, and I feel like I missed out. And you and I...we're around each other all the time. I wanted to do something...memorable. That probably sounds stupid, seeing as you find the whole thing tiring. But this is how it should be done."

"So you're asking me to buy into the fairytale?"

Nate laughed into her neck, heightening her awareness of every part of him. "Don't go all cynical on me, Liv. You'll ruin it."

The band drifted into the next song, and her laugh helped

release some of the tension. "So you stacked the band, too? You are too much, Miller."

Of course he sang it to her, with his adjusted lyrics. When she should have felt singled out, like a spotlight was on them — because everyone had to be hearing this; everyone had to know — suddenly it was as if the two of them were dancing alone, barefoot on a beach with the sand between their toes, ocean crashing in even time to the punchy notes of the piano.

"Oh-oh-livia..."

It wasn't exactly a slow song, and she didn't even care that he moved her around the floor, somehow keeping them from bumping into others as he crooned the lyrics in her ear. But unlike his video, this time his clear blue eyes were right in front of her, arresting her somewhere between terror and thrill. As the notes died away, he simply mouthed the final words, his lips hovering over hers, their bodies unmoving, still locked in their stance.

"May I cut in?"

The voice jolted Liv out of her trance. Nate looked stunned — but he stepped back and yielded to Dean's request, much to Liv's dismay. She took Dean's hand awkwardly, and watched as Nate stormed over to Emilie and scared away Jordan.

"What are you doing, Dean?" Liv asked, her voice quavering.

He didn't seem to know what to say, appearing as uneasy as she did. She was lost without Nate's fluidity to guide her. Nate stared daggers over Emilie's shoulder.

"Faye said it serves me right, keeping my mouth shut all this time," Dean said, finally.

All spring...they had spent so much time together, and she had thought nothing of it. "Don't, Dean. Please."

"I have to at least feel like I tried. But it's too late, isn't it?"

This is what she got for being lukewarm. For not — as Faye

so indelicately put it — throwing herself at Nate. It wasn't perfectly clear yet what she felt for him, but she had to find out, and Dean — Dean was supposed to be her friend, not another complication.

"Serves me right," Dean said again, when she didn't respond.

Liv ducked away, dodging couples as she rushed to their table. She gulped her unfinished wine, spinning as someone touched her back. Relief flooded her when she realized it was Nate.

"I'll get some more drinks," he said, his voice remarkably calm compared to the hysteria she felt.

"Don't you dare leave my side." She clutched his arm and glanced over his shoulder, finding Dean almost where she'd left him in the crowd.

"I'll be right back," Nate promised. "With more wine."

"I don't need wine."

"I think maybe I do."

Em appeared in the space he left, and pulled Liv to a chair. "Good thing Nate's riding Dean's horse in the Plate tomorrow. He has to behave."

"Who has to behave?" Faye swept up, Will trailing on the ends of her fingertips. "The guys go for drinks? Why don't you go find them, hon?"

Will rolled his eyes as he caught the dismissal.

"Just Nate," Emilie said. "I don't know where Dean went."

"So?" Faye leaned in further.

"Nate," Emilie said.

"What did he do? What did I miss?" She looked at Liv hopefully.

"Oh, no such luck," Emilie said. "Your brother cut in on him on the dance floor, and Nate just about lost his shit."

"Where the hell was I?" Faye stood back, tossing her arms

in the air. "Trust my brother to keep it to himself all these years, then pick tonight to make a statement. I'll straighten him out, don't worry."

"No, Faye. I know how hard that must've been for him," Liv said. "Don't make it any worse."

Faye shook her head. "This should make things more interesting, at least."

Liv didn't care to know what Faye meant. She didn't want interesting. She didn't need Dean revealing hidden emotions, or Nate feeling provoked when he was on Ride The Wave tomorrow.

He handed her a new glass when he returned, reaching forward and clinking not wine but another Perrier to it. His composure was unsettling.

"I thought you said this would be fun. This isn't fun," she hissed.

"I agree. I'm sorry, I was stuck," he said quietly. "You should probably be proud of me for not decking him."

"Or really disturbed that you thought about it?"

"Do you think we've fulfilled our duty and can get out of here now?"

"Can we? Please?"

He nodded, setting his glass aside and rising. "When I beat Liv tomorrow afternoon, I don't want any excuses that I kept her out late, so we're going to duck out of your party early, Em. Sorry." He hugged Emilie, and tapped Faye's elbow, then folded his fingers around Liv's to guide her out.

A full moon hung in a darkening sky that matched the dusky blue of the Porsche, and she was glad he was driving this time, everything spiralling in her mind. She listened to the lyrics of his chosen songs — words of promises and broken dreams — wishing she could know what he was thinking as his eyes remained fixed on the road. Probably resetting. Focusing on tomorrow. Because it's what they had to do, wasn't it? The Plate was too big a deal to let tonight's fiasco interfere.

They left the highway behind, skirting up the rural roads that led to the farm, until they were creeping under the familiar old maples that lined the lane. He turned off the engine in front of the house, and she waited as he walked around, because he would want that. He didn't meet her eyes when he took her hand, helped her out. Didn't touch her as they walked up the stairs, staying slightly behind her until she turned to face him. Then he was as close as he'd been that moment on the dance floor — before the spell had been broken.

It was easy to recast it, expand it, their lips entangling as she laced her fingers behind his neck and molded herself to him. She couldn't tell if the drumming she felt was his heart, or hers, or if they were just synchronized now.

She'd been naïve to think she could manipulate this thing between them to her liking, to control it like the volume on the Porsche's sound system. Had she actually expected them to continue as they'd been, with sweet caution like they really were teenagers? There was no safety here, no halfway, not anymore.

With measured breaths he drew back, while her own respiration was wildly erratic. His gaze drifted from her lips, to her hair, like he was committing her features to memory before settling unwaveringly on her eyes.

"I love you."

The words had been diffused in the song, separated from reality. His outright declaration robbed her lungs of their remaining air, the sincerity of them paralyzing. What a risk he was taking, saying them to her, the model of self-doubt, knowing full well she wouldn't reciprocate the sentiment. But it didn't seem to matter to him. Did he know her that well?

Well enough to understand — and accept — exactly who he was dealing with, and be willing to ride it out?

"Please don't freak out."

There was humour in his tone, but his eyes revealed his fear. She concentrated on re-establishing her breathing, regulating her pulse, though she still couldn't speak.

"I should go." His voice was soft, steady. "Unless you're all right with me camping out on your doorstep till morning. Just to make sure you don't run away in the middle of the night."

She had to laugh with him, her forehead resting against his, amazed and grateful for his ability to find levity. When his arms fell away, she would have grabbed him to fill the chasm he left, if she hadn't still been frozen.

"See you tomorrow." And he stepped away.

Tomorrow. Somehow she had to arrange her thought patterns to align that tomorrow with the one that included riding in her first Plate — against him.

Inside, she didn't bother to turn on the lights, the glow of the moon through the windows enough for her to see her way to the sunken living room. She dropped to the couch, curling her legs underneath her, and stared out the sliding doors to the pale light dancing off the surface of the pool. The subtle fragrance of the rose reached her from where it rested on the table in front of her.

The front door opened, and Emilie came in, starting slightly when Liv turned in her seat.

"Hey, Em."

Emilie came down and sat next to her. "How was your date? Are you going to tell me what happened?" She paused. "Should I just leave you alone?"

Liv sighed, and looked out the sliding doors again. What had happened? Nothing...and everything. She needed to articulate it, not hide from it.

"He said he loves me, Em."

It should have been good news, joyful news, but Emilie's initial silence was an indication she knew it wasn't that straightforward for Liv.

"Wow." Emilie hesitated again. "That's incredible, Liv. Unless you freaked out on him."

Liv laughed, remembering Nate's own plea. "Remarkably, no. Not yet, anyway." She paused, inhaling. "How can I ever possibly feel the way he does, Em? He's so sure. I still can't come close to knowing how to do that, without giving up too much of myself."

Emilie's expression was sympathetic. "I don't know, Liv. I haven't had to work through that yet myself. But it will sort itself out. He'll wait."

"I think he's been waiting a long time already."

"Don't do this to yourself, Liv. Just this once, try to live in the moment, okay?" Em patted her leg with a parting smile.

How did that work, living in the moment? How did she stop her brain from rushing forward, predicting disaster, where she didn't do him justice, where he finally got fed up and threw up his hands in surrender to her inadequacies?

It would be easier to accept if he had just been interested in getting her into bed, but with Nate, it went so much deeper.

CHAPTER SIXTEEN

Sure, going to the Plate Ball would be safe. Keep him out of trouble. He'd let himself forget that nothing would be safe with Liv. She was conflict, risk, emotional danger, and he had thrown himself into her abyss, fool that he was.

He didn't regret it, though. He didn't care if she never loved him back, as long as she didn't leave, or send him away. There was a term for that, wasn't there? Yeah. *Bat-shit crazy.*

Ironically, he was scheduled to work one for Dean Taylor at six AM. What the hell had that been, last night? On the one hand, Nate had to hand it to the guy — he hadn't thought Dean had it in him. On the other, he needed to back off. One thing: it had triggered his own impulse to leave Liv with no doubt where he stood. Maybe he should have left it at the kiss. It had been a hell of a kiss.

Dean's assistant was in the worker's stall, putting on the bridle.

"Hey Nikki. Where's Dean?"

"In the office. He'll be out in a sec. I'll throw you up and you can take her a couple turns, if that's okay."

That was perfect. Not that he expected Dean to do anything but give him instructions, especially within earshot of his staff, but it would be easier to be businesslike once he was on a horse.

Dean greeted him blandly and walked out beside the filly in silence. *Good.*

The worker helped get him back in the right frame of mind – one that would prepare him to ride in the Plate in eleven hours. Dean seemed pleased with how the filly had gone, nodding quietly and confirming Nate's estimation of time with the clockers. Nate joined him in the office after he got off the filly. He had a while before his next commitment, so there could be some discussion of race strategy.

"Last night everything you were hoping for, Miller?"

I guess we're not past that. "It was a nice evening, for the most part," he said carefully. "How about we talk about your Plate horse instead?"

"How can I be sure your mind is really on my colt?"

Nate had to control the tone of his laugh. "Because it's my job? And did you ever stop to think this might work to your advantage? I know her colt. I rode him last year. And I know Liv. I know how she's got to ride this race to have a shot, and it works out perfectly for us. Your colt is more versatile. Elemental has a ton of speed. She'll get him to relax – she's very good at that. She'll try to force a false pace, and we're going to need to stay close, to keep it honest, unless someone else does. Your colt can do that, and still win. That work for you?"

Dean nodded, slowly. He looked satisfied, if not happy.

"We're both professionals, Dean. Trust me, when we get out there this afternoon, we're not going to be thinking about last night." He rose, hoping to pre-empt any more off-topic discussion. "I'd better get going. I'll check in at the end of the morning."

He had another one to work before the break, then was due to get on Feste. Feste had come out of his race perfectly, sharper than before, and Liv had decided to breeze him this morning — a surprising move, so soon after the race, but she justified it by pointing out how easily the colt had won his debut. She hadn't yet decided what his next start would be.

The Woodbine backstretch always vibrated on Plate morning, but this time the hum of it burned his ears and churned his insides as he arrived at the Triple Stripe barn. It had all seemed so right in the moonlight, but the rising sun was uncovering all his doubts.

He touched Chique's nose briefly after her rumbling nicker announced his arrival, and the filly started her *tap-tap-tap* on the mat when he continued past.

Liv was in the stall with the colt, tacking up. Nate found the bridle hanging on the door and brought it in, trying to read Liv as she accepted it, but she was clearly set in work mode. He couldn't take it personally. He needed to be the same.

He watched her right hand curl around the bridge of the colt's nose to hold the bridle, left hand quickly slipping a thumb into the corner of the soft mouth and guiding the bit into place. He should just wait outside, because standing here next to her wasn't helping him feel professional.

She glanced at him and smiled — a very careful, neutral smile.

"I'll take him a turn," she said, finishing with the throatlatch and making sure the bit was sitting evenly before she crossed and tucked the lines under the seat of the saddle.

Nate followed them out of the stall and leaned back against the cool metal door, staring up at the rafters, trying to refocus on breezing horses.

"Where's Rog?" he asked when Liv stopped Feste in front of him. He shortened both irons and tightened the girth a hole.

"Ponying one on the training track. We don't need him with these two boys."

Liv didn't speak as they rode out to the track, which wasn't really unusual, and Nate tried to force himself to think about anything but how close he had held her last night, and how distant she felt right now. He responded to casual greetings as they went through the tunnel to the main track, and pulled down his goggles as they began to back the two-year-olds up.

Liv's colt was a leggy son of Starway named Astronomical, winner of his first two races and prepping for a stake. The two colts galloped around from the wire, and started out together at the five-eighths pole. Nate let Liv get ahead on the turn, Feste running easily at his stablemate's shoulder, anticipating further instructions. Chique at the same age would have been pulling his arms out, or just plain running off with him to get past the other horse.

He waited until they were inside the eighth pole to ask Feste, only needing a short chirp to send the colt on and effortlessly past Liv's mount.

They eased on the backstretch, and Nate slapped the dark brown neck as they turned in. "Just a little preview of this afternoon for you." He grinned at Liv.

"Really." But she didn't look offended, because how could she, after how Feste had worked?

"He's the one."

"Let's hope so."

Business as usual.

Liv glanced at him as they headed to the off gap. "So...last night..."

The drone in his ears came back, the rawness of his bold statement staring him down. But she was bringing it up. And that tempered all the misfiring neurons, diluted the adrenaline — her being brave in her own way, by facing it head on.

"I'm sorry. It was a lot. We'll talk, okay?"

"Okay."

"Lunch tomorrow?"

"All right."

"Loser buys."

Liv laughed. "You're assuming one of us is going to win?"

"Actually, I'm quite confident I'm going to beat your ass. I just hope you don't hold it against me."

He left her bathing Feste while he dashed off to get on his next worker. When they saw each other again, over there in the room, they would be back to being opponents, vying for the same prize. He was good now. Which was a relief, because if he screwed up this afternoon, his credibility would go out the window.

The way Liv looked at him as they strode out to the walking ring for the Plate said it all. There was no careful smile left over from last night, just a professional challenge from a skilled colleague; a warning that he'd better be on his game, or he'd be eating this morning's bravado.

Nate greeted Faye and Will with a cursory nod before turning to Dean. Not that there was anything new to say, just some awkwardness to wait through. He was glad when the riders up call finally came. Dean legged him up on Ride The Wave and Nikki led them away through the fashionably-dressed throng.

It was a big field — fourteen horses, lots of traffic. Elemental had the four hole, and Ride The Wave the seven. Neither of them had anything to complain about there. His colt warmed up perfectly, loaded quietly, broke flawlessly. *Textbook.* Nate smiled as Elemental surged to the lead, and no one went with him.

He would let Liv have her way up there for a while, though when it came to race-riding, she wasn't naïve enough to think he'd be ignorant of her plan. Ride The Wave sat fourth first time past the grandstand, three-wide and out of trouble.

Nate let the colt accelerate around the clubhouse turn, fighting overconfidence as things unfolded just as he'd predicted. Liv glanced over at him when Ride The Wave appeared at her elbow. She smiled — and just sat there.

So you're gonna be like that. He flashed a grin back.

Liv didn't offer to go faster; in fact, she almost imperceptibly slowed Elemental, forcing Nate to make a decision. This wasn't Chique he was on — he had to remember that. Ride The Wave was talented, but relatively inexperienced, and not in the same league as his Cheeky. Going on with the colt wasn't really an option — he might as well hand Elemental the race right there. He had to hope staying up here with the slow pace wouldn't leave his colt flat-footed when the time came to turn on the heat in the stretch. He continued to let Elemental lead the way, and wondered if anyone behind these pedestrian fractions would be able to fool both of them.

Elemental remained perfectly relaxed under Liv's hold as they entered the final turn, when Nate would have expected Liv to be increasing the tempo. *Damn.* Ride The Wave was bored now, and getting distracted, ears flickering ahead to the big white tent, loaded with screaming voices. Nate smacked him once with the whip to get his attention, and Ride The Wave switched to his proper lead and surged to the front.

Elemental didn't take up the chase. There was no way that colt was done; Liv had to be playing mind games with him. But...*don't look back.* Ride The Wave's ears flipped forward again at the swarm of bodies on the apron, and he started drifting out.

He was going to have to drag all the potential out of this green colt. When Elemental came back on along the rail, Nate swore Ride The Wave was waiting for him. Liv's whip remained quiet — *how could that even be, mid-stretch?* Elemental drew even and hooked Ride The Wave.

Now Liv was extracting everything from her colt, Elemental refusing to back off, fighting bitterly with Ride The Wave. Nate cracked the whip once, twice, on the bay's hindquarters before doing some willing of his own with hands and voice, counting on his colt's basic instinct now to run; prove he was stronger, more courageous than his foe.

At the wire though, there was none of the uncertainty that had followed in those moments last June when Chique had staggered through the final strides, exhausted by her Herculean performance. Nate glanced over at Liv, both of them standing in the irons as their colts coasted past the clubhouse.

Liv looked back at him, wryness forced through the disappointment in her smile as she stretched out an arm to bump his fist.

"Just remember everything comes in threes, Miller."

He laughed and knew exactly what she was talking about. Same time, same place, next year — with Feste.

Liv leaned against the cool of the metal door, Chique and Feste picking the alfalfa from the timothy in their haynets on either side. There were people on the lawn, a Plate party in progress even in defeat, Roger doling out beverages from his usual post by the ice bucket. She watched the Porsche pull up at the end of the barn, Nate emerging, cleaned up in that same old navy suit he always wore. He could probably afford a new one, now. He quite possibly owned that tux he'd worn last night. She couldn't sustain her gaze as he approached, visions of that moment on the doorstep flitting left and right behind her eyes.

"Congratulations, Miller."

There hadn't been opportunity to put her arms around him like this after the race. He'd been detained, swept up in the revelry, parading the winner in front of a sea of photographers, gold and purple blanket of flowers draped over his knees, instead of hers; Ride the Wave's withers instead of Elemental's. By the time he'd been free of the media after the presentations, she was ready to ride the last race. At least she'd won that.

He wasn't content with a hug, his lips finding hers. "You scared me," he said.

"What, out on the racetrack?" She smirked.

"Well, yeah, but just now, more so. Why'd you leave like that?"

She looked down, arms dropping back to her sides as she took a step away, turning towards Feste and Chique. Because she had. She'd driven past the Northwest barn first. Seen him there, with Dean, who seemed to have forgotten last night's drama now that the offending party had won him a Queen's Plate.

"I don't know. Too many people, maybe." She let Chique nuzzle her hands while Feste craned his neck over the screen next door. "It was more fun last year." She looked at him sideways, one corner of her mouth turning up.

"You owe me lunch, remember."

"I guess I do. Though you're the one who made all the money this afternoon."

"You did make it pretty interesting."

Chique nibbled her net, keeping one eye on both of them in case they came up with treats. A year ago they'd stood here after the filly's win. It had taken twelve months for things to shift again as powerfully as they had that evening.

"I don't know what happens next, Nate. I'm not going to run away...but I'm not where you are. The way things ended last night was probably inevitable...but it still knocked me sideways."

He was close now, his back to Feste, a hand reaching to Chique by proxy maybe, like he was afraid to touch her in case she did bolt.

"I'm sorry. I mean...don't think I didn't mean it. And it's not like it just happened last night, like it just hit me, that I'm in love with you." He hesitated, the intensity of his gaze too much for her to take full-on, so she watched his hand instead, Chique's lips rubbing insistently like she could conjure up the peppermint he couldn't possibly have forgotten. "The timing was probably wrong. I let Dean get to me. But with everything that's happened this year...I was banking we'd come far enough you wouldn't panic on me, and would at least give me a chance to remind you nothing's changed."

"Everything's changed," she insisted, eyes matching the force of his, direct enough to keep him from countering. "But I know all the effort now has to be mine. And I am prepared to make an effort."

"Sometimes you have a way of making what might otherwise be touching sound so clinical." He slid his free arm around her waist to kiss her gently.

She drew in a breath, fingering the lapel of his jacket. Chique bumped her elbow like she was saying, *would you get on with it girl, so someone can get me a candy?*

"I think I get it now, what you've been saying all along. I know how much I've stalled about the two of us, but you know me, Miller. I'll never stop overthinking. There will always be some excuse. And then some disaster will happen, and this, *us*...it'll be gone too."

"You kind of live in a world of impending doom, don't you? I'm officially worried now."

Chique snorted in resignation, burying her muzzle in her haynet. *If you're going to continue to put this poor man through hell, I'll be over here when you're done.* He did look genuinely scared, prompting Liv to forge ahead.

"I want to take both Chique and Feste to Saratoga. I might be throwing Chique back into the thick of things, but there's a nice little turf stake there for her. The same day there's one going three-quarters for Feste. If he turns out to be everything you keep saying he is, we'll consider sticking around for the Hopeful."

He exhaled, a look of wonder taking over his face. "Wow. Okay."

"You know Don always ships some horses from Belmont with Jeanne. She has a house there — you might remember that." She frowned, wading through that memory. She could certainly say Nate had seen her at her worst. She hoped her best was yet to come. "We could stay with her."

"We?"

"Well, you could just fly down for the races, if you want."

"You're serious."

"You'd have your own room," she said, lips twisting.

"I don't know what to say. You're sure?"

"You can think about it. You might be giving up the riding title at Woodbine if you come." The jock's community at Woodbine was competitive enough that someone — like Cory, who was on her way to establishing herself as the season's hot apprentice — could rack up a lead in the standings that would be hard to top.

"Is this a test? Like, am I supposed to be thinking of my

career here?" He grinned. "Give up the title at Woodbine...but ride at the Spa with you? I think I'd be crazy to turn that down. I'm assuming we'll both have to get to the Fort for a rematch of today in the Prince of Wales, but...hey, here's to Saratoga."

He raised an imaginary glass, and she obliged by meeting it with one of her own, their knuckles touching.

"What's the matter?" she asked.

"I'm just waiting for the catch."

"No catch. Leave the paranoia to me. I've got plenty enough for both of us."

"You could work on that, you know." He used it as another excuse to brush her lips with his. "Come on. I can hear the band starting up over at Dean's. They might need me. I'm a much better singer than Will."

CHAPTER SEVENTEEN

"We made it, baby."

Nate grinned at Chique once she was settled, putting a hand on either side of her muzzle and planting a kiss between her nostrils. Feste took in the tranquil rows of viridian barns and terra verte trees with his usual class, helping himself to a drink from his bucket to test out the local water before tearing into his haynet.

Nate touched Chique on the nose before sauntering over to Liv and Jeanne. "I'm not going to want to leave."

"Welcome to Saratoga," Jeanne said. "No one ever wants to leave."

"You keep absorbing that atmosphere, Miller." Liv took one more look at Feste and Chique to convince herself they were fine. "I'm heading to the house for a shower."

"Right behind you," he said, but he wasn't. Not yet. He was going to give her a head start, and do just as she said: soak this up.

Jeanne crossed her arms and leaned against the rail. "So, you and Liv. How's that going?"

His lips twisted in a crooked smile. "Very cautiously."

"The winter didn't knock any sense into you, I guess. A little more complicated now that she's back riding. A whole lot of juggling there."

"Nothing I haven't already been dealing with in my career so far."

Back when he'd first started galloping at Woodbine and working daily with Liv, he'd told himself it was a bad idea, but he'd gone and done it anyway – gotten involved.

"Married to Triple Stripe, eh?"

He choked on a laugh. Liv wasn't ready to wrap her head around love, let alone the future. Wait – Jeanne was talking about the job. *Easy, Miller.*

"You sure don't like to pick easy spots, do you, Nate?"

"You're the first one to put it that way."

"Well, you let me know if I'm cramping your style around the house. I can make myself scarce."

He was kind of counting on her being an inadvertent chaperone, but he didn't say it out loud, pulling his keys from his pocket. Chique rumbled. *Yeah, of course I've got mints for you and your brother in there too.* "You need help feeding this afternoon or anything? I could come back."

"You're a rider, Nate. We let the grooms do their jobs around here. Go."

He vaguely remembered the way to the house – and more clearly remembered the time he'd been there, uninvited. A different picture greeted him this time when he pushed through the door from the garage that opened into the living room.

Liv, wearing shorts and a loose t-shirt, damp hair falling around her shoulders, standing by the counter with not a wine bottle in sight.

"Are you proud I left of my own accord?" she asked with a wry smile.

He grinned, kicking off his shoes and leaving his bag by the door to step up into the kitchen. "Right. You just didn't wait for Jeanne to chase you away like she did me. I know what she's like now too, you know. California doesn't make her any softer."

She didn't move away when he put his hands on her waist, resisting the temptation to slide them under her shirt, seek the smooth skin over the muscles of her back. He could think of a lot of things he wanted to do, but just kissed her and put his arms around her, breathing her in as she nestled against him — which was pretty incredible by itself.

"Do you think we'll pull it off?" he murmured into her neck.

She didn't try to deflect his question, or ask if he was talking about them, or success with Chique and Feste. "Guess we'll have to find out."

This was about more than the next week, or however long those two horses kept them in Saratoga. Complicated. Everyone kept saying it was complicated. But he was determined that it wouldn't be, if he was careful.

Nate didn't wait for a leg up, hopping lightly onto Chique in the middle of the shedrow.

"That's still the reigning Canadian Horse of the Year there, Miller," Liv called, settling into the tack on Feste after Jeanne had helped put her there.

"And she's still fifteen hands with shoes on." He knotted his lines and tucked his feet into the irons, slapping Chique on the neck as she began her march.

Liv had to smile. The two of them were still her idea of hashtag *relationshipgoals*.

"I'd say 'lead the way,' but she seems to have other ideas," he quipped once they were off the shed, Chique passing her brother like she knew where they were going.

"Have you broken it to her that she doesn't get to gallop today?"

With that reminder, he dropped his irons a few holes for security. Just because they only intended to let the pair stretch their legs with a walk around the grounds didn't mean Chique would be on board with that plan.

The equine traffic crossing Union Avenue this time of morning was heavier than that of the cars on the road, security monitoring and directing as needed. Chique assessed her surroundings alertly, unsure enough of where she was that she had to listen to Nate and keep an eye on Feste. The colt strode out boldly. Chique shuddered with a sigh, and dropped her head level with his.

"He's no fun, is he?" Nate tweaked the top of her crest, and Chique lifted her neck into his touch, shaking her head and dancing. Of course Nate couldn't just let her chill.

There was a timelessness to the Saratoga backstretch, the ritual one largely unchanged in the last hundred years. Grooms bathed their charges; hotwalkers turned left around the walking rings with steaming horses, stopping every few circuits to allow sips from water pails set on overturned buckets. Sheds were dressed up with hanging planters, hand-washed white flannel bandages hung alongside to dry.

The gallopers on the Oklahoma training track captured Chique's attention, her head flying up again. The filly started to jig, bumping into Feste.

"Tomorrow, filly," Liv promised.

They crossed back over Union Avenue, following the horse

path around the outside of the main track, the shade of the trees scattering the morning light over the horses' coats. Liv glanced at Nate, then Chique, then Feste. There was hope here. So much good.

"Let's let them have a little jog around Clare Court. Her reward for not tossing you."

He laughed, scrubbing Chique under her twisty mane until she was on her toes again. "There's still time for that."

Clare Court reminded Liv a little of Woodbine's "field," just with more trees, and nestled within the heart of the backstretch instead of on the outskirts. The steady cadence of their horses' hoofbeats — Chique being remarkably compliant — added to the peace she felt, the sense of all being right in her world, at last.

Chique seemed satisfied when they pulled up, walking home full of happy snorts. Both horses would work over the track on Wednesday, a final old-school blowout before race day Saturday.

"I didn't think you were going to come back." Jeanne met them in front of the barn, Chique's halter in hand.

"Where did you think we'd go?" Nate quipped. "Isn't this the happiest place on earth?"

"I thought that was Disney."

"Same thing really, right? All the magic; where dreams come true."

He dropped to the ground, and threw a glance over his shoulder, catching Liv's eyes with a grin that made her believe.

In the haze of early mist that hung over the main track, Liv closed her fingers possessively around the strip of leather that connected her to Chique. The filly was sharp, there was no question. She didn't have to say anything to Nate for him to know he needed to be careful, not exploit that readiness. She probably didn't need to take him to the pole, but she did, of course, controlling whatever she could for as long as she could.

Chique shot away from the pony, dropping to the rail, but she was a different horse now, with maturity befitting the big sister. He didn't have to maintain a stranglehold to keep her pace steady as she swept into the stretch, though he didn't dare open his mouth, or she would have been gone. With his slight release inside the last sixteenth, Chique took advantage, seamlessly lengthening her stride. It would be the bullet – fastest three-eighths of the day – he was sure.

Liv didn't speak when they met up again on the backside, so if she thought it was too fast, he didn't know. It wasn't as if he could take it back now anyway. Chique had needed that; that last bit of speed to tighten the screws just so. Now she was ready for her comeback.

Next was Feste. *Just go easy.* Nate had never needed the pony to break the colt off before, but yeah, no point reminding Liv of that. When she freed them, he crouched, Feste putting down twelve-second furlongs as naturally as breathing. Just a kiss, and the colt would give him an explosive burst reminiscent of his sister, but that could wait till Saturday.

He didn't let Liv stay silent this time. "Okay?"

She nodded. "They can both gallop a little tomorrow, though. No days off, or we'll be rebuilding that barn."

Nate ran a hand over the colt's dark neck, the humidity an added layer on Feste's slick coat, damp after the effort, though he was barely breathing hard.

Liv's seriousness had started to rub off on him. One thing, it made it easier to stick to his resolve not to push the physical side of their relationship. That, and pounding the pavement in his running shoes for a few miles after dinner – alone.

Restless. Liv couldn't keep her nerves where she needed them, too many thoughts about the next day's card flying around her brain to focus properly on this one.

She didn't know. Didn't know if being here was the right thing for Chique. Starting back at Woodbine would have been much easier. Feste, though, deserved to be here. Tomorrow he would prove it.

She was having a terrible afternoon. Her best ride was in the last, but Nate came out of nowhere with a longshot to nail her at the wire. Now that it was over, at least, her mind was free to run wild.

She stood beside him in the jock's room to watch the replay.

"Sorry, boss." A mid-afternoon downpour had left the track muddy, the outline of goggles creating a mask of clean around his eyes, his teeth looking especially white against the dirt spattered on his face.

"That's okay, Miller. Just keep that momentum going for tomorrow, all right?"

"Absolutely."

His confidence sparked boldness in her, and she thumbed some sand off his lips and kissed him. The way it wiped off his grin, changing it into something between amazement and shock, made the background chorus of whistles worth it.

"See you back at the house," she said, pulling off her helmet and kerchief and dragging the elastic out of her hair as she headed to the women's change room to shower.

She dressed dutifully in a navy print skirt and white silk tank top, brushing her hair back into its ponytail because drying it was too much work. It felt like a chore sometimes to maintain a professional image — one of those things Geai had insisted was important — especially on a night like tonight when she couldn't get out of here fast enough.

The grounds had quickly emptied out, only stragglers and clean-up crew remaining. A few tailgaters packing up their chairs and coolers noticed as she scooted under the administrative building's overhang, and she signed a couple of autographs. She didn't mind it so much anymore, was used to it, but just the same, was relieved to reach the refuge of her car. She and Nate probably could have shared the driving most days, but in some way, arriving and leaving in her own vehicle preserved some vestige of her independence. Silly maybe. Important, still.

Baked fish and a salad — honestly, it was like she was learning to cook. Nate usually made dinner for all three of them, and while she knew part of the reason he did so was because he had to be more careful about his diet than she did, she felt guilty always leaving it to him. And tonight, she needed something to do while she waited.

Table set, a couple of wine glasses on the counter...the bottle he'd promised to pick up would help take the edge off. She hoped he came home with it soon.

Home. It kind of made her shudder. Preparing this meal, however basic, was altogether too domestic for her. But...she was making an effort. And she wanted to, because he had said things, big things, and while it was still all scary, she didn't want it — him — to go away.

The door from the garage creaked when it opened, and Nate dropped his jacket over the back of a chair and set the bottle of red on the counter next to the glasses — then kissed her, the astonished look she'd left him with in the jock's room toned down to amusement.

"This looks dangerous. Where's Jeanne?" He reached into a drawer for the corkscrew.

"Don came up this afternoon, so she's having dinner with him and one of the owners."

A glass *now* was more important than letting it breathe, so Liv picked up the open bottle and poured. She didn't wait for him as she took a sip.

"Cheers." He crossed his arms with a smirk.

"Sorry." Liv looked sheepishly over the glass, but took another swallow.

"Are you really that worried about tomorrow?" He picked up his own glass and carried the bottle to the table.

"Apparently." She wasn't riding tomorrow, and needed to sleep tonight. The wine would help. It was straightforward.

"They're both doing great. It'll be fine."

Always reassuring, and always right. Was it pathetic she needed that? It was probably better to latch onto his positivity than the alcohol.

Liv forced herself to follow the unrelated discussion, every now and then shrinking from a look that let her know he wasn't fooled by her feigned attention, that his nattering was his way of calming her like he would a young horse She made the second glass of wine last, proud that there was still some left in the bottle when Nate started to clear the table.

"Thanks for dinner," he said, filling the dishwasher while she was content to watch. "I'm going to get out of this suit."

Maybe dressing as she had had taken effort, but changing seemed like more so now, when she'd probably be in bed in an hour. Liv eyed the bottle, and emptied what was left into her glass. The wine had done enough she didn't feel inspired to pick up the novel sitting on the coffee table. She turned on some music instead, settling on the couch, letting the melody lull her.

Nate returned with his running shorts on, carrying his t-shirt. Liv would no longer claim immunity to the clear cut of his muscles under smooth, lightly tanned skin, no fat getting in the way of their definition. He left the t-shirt on the armrest and came around behind the couch.

"Not something else you're good at, Miller," she murmured, letting her eyes close as his thumbs worked her traps, so tight they'd been close to seizing up.

He may have intended for it to be relaxing, but it triggered an element of intimacy she knew he'd been avoiding. She dropped her chin and tried to separate herself from it, then thought, why? Faye seemed to be able to remain detached when it came to sex, why couldn't she? It was, after all, just basic biological impulse, wasn't it? She had a rational, logical mind that thrived on science. It was the psychological aspect that messed people up.

He stopped and leaned over to kiss her softly on the neck, then reached for his t-shirt. Liv snatched the shirt away from him, dropping it on the floor, and curled her fingers around his wrist. She needed a distraction from thinking about tomorrow; maybe attempting her first seduction was a worthwhile one.

If she dissolved the physical barrier and proved it was just an evolutionary, hormone-driven exchange — leaving the emotion out of it — she'd be further ahead. Still in control. Power, Faye would call it.

Faye's voice niggled. *We both know you'd never throw yourself at him.*

Faye knew nothing.

But while Faye might have scoffed at Liv's lack of confidence, she'd also played the role of big sister and made sure Liv was prepared for the possibility. Saratoga, together...anything could happen, right? No excuse there.

Nate grinned as Liv dragged him down. It wasn't as if they'd never made out before, so he was allowed to be unsuspecting. His hands went to her waist as she slid closer, arms slipping to his bare shoulders. He tasted like minty toothpaste as she kissed him, while her own mouth was no doubt reminiscent of wine and fish — *ugh*. He didn't seem to mind.

She made herself aware of the strength of his back, feeling him flinch as her hands drifted to his obliques and returned to his shoulders. Those shoulders and arms were capable of containing the energy of a speed-driven Thoroughbred — holding it, guiding it, extracting every ounce of effort from it — but so were hers. When she laced her fingers through the softness of his short hair, he deepened the kiss, and she told herself not to back off, to enjoy rather than fear the unknown. *Mind over matter*. The music faded into the background, a soundtrack to someone else's story, aiding her ability to feel displaced.

He pulled her on top of him, like he'd picked up on the control thing and was willing to give that to her. All of a sudden her newfound assertiveness started slipping away — *what am I doing*? She tried to hide it when his eyes locked onto hers, battling with her uncertainty as he slid the elastic from her ponytail, her hair falling loose, still damp, into her face. She closed her eyes, concentrating on what should be instinct. She could be someone else, someone who fingered his collarbone, ran a hand over his chest, smiled as she admired the firmness of his abdomen beneath her palm. She could name each muscle group — keep it scientific, a study of the human form. His hand grazed the back of her thigh beneath her skirt and she fought the flight response, still so close to the surface, hoping he would misinterpret the tension in her body for arousal — not that it was completely absent by any stretch, but the conflicting parts of her brain weren't totally in harmony. The tips of her fingers reached the edge of his shorts.

His hand snapped to her wrist, arresting it there, and she flew to the end of the couch, feeling caught like a naughty child, as he rolled off. He was on his feet before she blinked – pacing like a caged animal, silent and not particularly friendly.

When words finally came, his voice was strained, the heel of his hand pressing into his forehead. "What is this, Liv? This isn't you. You need to stop letting Faye Taylor get in your head."

Flush crept up, heating her cheeks. He couldn't know her that well. Except he did. He'd seen right through her.

"I don't want this, not right now. You don't need to be anyone else. I love you. Damn it, I want to marry you." He glanced away. "You're going to have to figure out if you feel the same." He scooped up his t-shirt and pulled it over his head, all but diving for the door. "I've gotta get out of here."

Her heart found a new tempo, testing the boundary of her chest.

This was not how this was supposed to go.

He was dripping, the humidity so close he'd broken a sweat in the first strides – though he hadn't been far from that anyway. His running shoes crunched furiously over the gravel on the road's shoulder, skittering a step when he hit a rock. This was stupid. He should turn around. It made no sense to get whacked by a car in the dark and end up dead in a ditch.

A flash of lightning lit up the darkening sky, the crack of thunder on its tail a little too close for comfort. When the rain caught up, it came in sheets, soaking him to the skin.

True to form, he had overreacted to the night's bizarre development and thrown it all out there. Hey, love? Why not marriage? If anything could make Liv run, it was that.

He should have just gone with it. It wouldn't have been hard. He'd have put money on her backing off. Her defences would've kicked in before they got anywhere crucial. But it moved the line, changed the boundary, set the stage for next time — if there was a next time.

What if he backpedaled? Eased off on his initial conviction? That would be so much easier. No one waited anymore. It's not like he had before.

But his history stuck its tongue out at him. Sleeping with someone just seemed to scare them off. So this time, he was holding out, like some kind of twenty-first century freak.

Jeanne was sitting at the kitchen table and looked at him strangely when he came in, saturated. Liv was gone.

"Nice evening?" Jeanne asked.

He laughed abruptly. *Chaperone. Right.* "Yeah. You're fired."

It wasn't really sleep, the state from which he grappled to regain consciousness — more like someone was holding him just below the surface, not letting him come up for air. He crawled groggily out of bed. He had to catch Liv before she left. He should have knocked on her door last night, just to say something...something that might make him feel better.

No such luck. The house was empty, the Porsche the only car left in the driveway. This day...this day was already too long.

Chique stood tacked up on the wall when he got there. He cocked an eyebrow — he'd just assumed both runners would walk — but willed it back to neutral when Liv emerged from the tack room with a bridle.

She faltered — just a step — then dropped her eyes to the sandy shed, brushing past him into the stall. The air he sucked in to catch his breath was full of her, the memory of her on top of him flooding his senses, sending them haywire. He ducked in behind her, reaching for her arm before she made it to Chique's head.

"Listen, Liv, I'm sorry."

"You didn't do anything wrong." Her tone was flat as she broke free of his grasp, unsnapping Chique from the wall, slipping the lines over the filly's head.

"I did. I need to explain."

Her hands worked quickly, unbuckling the halter, looping it over her arm while she slipped in the bit and settled the headstall behind Chique's ears.

"We have to start talking, Liv."

"Not right now we don't. We can do that later."

"It's always going to be like that, isn't it?"

She stared him down, uncompromising.

He sighed. "Yeah. Of course. Later." He knew that. It was always later. After the Triple Crown. After the winter apart. Just when he'd thought they were finally working on *now*.

"You can get on her around the shed." She turned the filly toward the door, chasing him out. "I'll walk Feste."

Wow. He hadn't seen that...*veneer*...in a long time.

It was Jeanne who met him in front of the stall with Chique once he had his helmet and boots on. "Is one of you going to tell me what's going on?"

"Just throw me up."

Chique jigged down the shed once he was on, Nate letting his legs dangle while he snugged up the girth and knotted the lines. She seemed confused when he didn't direct her out to the track. They just kept going around and around, like the thoughts in his brain.

It was early yet, so he let her play, loose-lined, sometimes racing just shy of a canter with her head snaking all the while. It wasn't very long before the grooms working on the shed got angry with him, and he reeled her in and convinced her to behave. He tucked his feet into the irons and tried his best to think about anything but what was foremost on his mind, his energy wired into Chique's. He should be concentrating on this afternoon, Feste's race, Chique's post-laminitis comeback. Of course Liv was stressed. It wasn't as if he didn't understand that.

She was still walking Feste when he emerged from Chique's stall with the tack in his arms, the filly annoyed he hadn't left her with a flake of hay.

"I'll be back before I head over," he said.

Liv at least stopped in front of him, nodding. "All right."

That was it, nothing more. Getting away from her right now would be good. He had to get his focus back to riding. Screwing up those two races this afternoon would just compound the disaster.

Feste looked fabulous — the drizzle didn't do anything to diminish his lustre. He paraded confidently beside the stable pony, alert but relaxed. Nate reached across to stroke his sleek, dark, neck, and Liv pressed her eyes closed, trying to silence the words that swirled inside her head. Last night's declaration had made the Plate Ball seem like grade school.

Later. It was Feste's moment.

She let herself feel a touch of pride, even as the announcer botched Feste's French registered name: *Téméraire*. It was an accomplishment to get a Canadian-bred, especially a two-year-old, here. She wasn't alone in thinking he was the best colt in this field of very nice juveniles — the odds board reflected her opinion.

The horses broke off into their warm-ups, Nate taking

Feste alone around the clubhouse turn, the starting gate waiting in the chute, six furlongs from the wire. Heavy dark clouds threatened more rain, but Liv hoped it would hold off until after Chique's race. Feste wouldn't care, but his princess sister might not appreciate it.

The start was clean, and Feste broke on top, Nate letting him stay in front, taking a gentle hold and settling the colt just out from the rail where the track would be firmest. Feste responded perfectly, showing sensibility Liv wasn't entirely sure Chique would ever develop.

Liv glanced at the tote board – for an off track, Feste was setting quick fractions. She wasn't concerned. After his morning times, splits like this were within the colt's ability. Longstreet crept up on his outside, staying close. *Enjoy it while it lasts*. Feste had gears.

Another colt gave chase, to the right of Longstreet – second choice, Market That. Nate let Feste maintain his pace, but wouldn't be coerced into going any faster. Neither rival offered to go by. The next tier bunched behind the three leaders.

Rounding the final turn, Nate still sat relaxed, the other two riders getting into their colts. Market That started to crowd, running a little green. Nate glanced over. Longstreet didn't like the pressure, his head going up, legs climbing. Feste's ears flicked forward, but the colt was only acknowledging the filled grandstand – something new and notable, but not enough to alter his course.

Then he swerved, connecting with the rail, tumbling into the mud like the ground had given way beneath him, Nate tossed over his head. The close-packed field was sent into a frenzy. Someone toppled and crashed over Feste; another leapt wildly. The rest somehow managed to avoid the pile.

Liv couldn't breathe.

Don had his phone pressed to his ear, dragging her with him, a frightened child terrified of what she'd find at the three-eighths pole. The crowd crushed on all sides, straining to see what was happening, oblivious to her dread. Their collective murmurs made her feel like she was in the middle of a hive, the drone of it filling her ears, its density suffocating her.

All the parts were in play before they reached the scene. Horse ambulance. Human ambulance. Tarp. Don made no attempt to stop her as she pushed past to her fallen colt.

The state veterinarian's words came from far away, only fragments making it through. *Can't be sure...aortic rupture... post mortem...*

Nate, unmoving, on a backboard.

There was nothing in her stomach – she hadn't been able to eat all day – and the force of her contracting diaphragm doubled her over. Don grabbed her as her legs buckled.

"Liv. You've got to go check into the room."

"What?" Her voice was reedy and foreign as she tried to straighten.

"Unless you want to pick someone else to ride Chique. Go. You don't need to watch this. There's nothing you can do. Chique still has to run."

She stared at him, then the slam of the ambulance doors jolted her back to – *Nate*. "No – wait."

Don grasped her forearms.

"Liv! Go. He's alive, all right? They say he's stable. By the time they get him to the hospital and actually know something, you'll be done with Chique. I'll call the stewards."

"I can't." All the times Nate had joked the only way she would get the mount on Chique was if he ended up in hospital. She didn't want it, not like this.

"Go!"

He sounded so callous. She didn't care anymore. It didn't

matter if Chique ran, with or without her. But in a world that had spiraled so completely out of control in the last ten minutes, she needed a direction, and Don's words were the only thing on offer.

Mutters of sympathy met her in the room, but she tuned them out, shutting herself away in the women's area. She scanned the *Form* mechanically – not to size up the opposition, but to see who was available through exclusion. There were other, very capable riders who would jump at the opportunity to ride the filly, and given Liv's current state, would do a better job.

Nate's name kept leaping out.

She left the paper face down, because the cover article announced Chique's return, a photo of Nate on her, winning the Mile – a race that carried more merit than the Plate on this side of the border.

It had to be her. Nate would never let her hear the end of it, would he? Nate, who loved her, wanted to marry her. She'd had no response for him last night, and refused to discuss it this morning, convinced it would wait. Her reluctance seemed so shallow now.

Breeches and stockings and paper-thin boots. Her hand froze on the red, white, and navy colours – the traditional ones, the silk-silks, while the day-to-day nylon ones were...where? Muddied from the spill, cast aside as the medics worked on Nate: assessing damage, attaching monitors, starting initial treatment.

A knock on the door jolted her back. It was time. She smoothed a clean kerchief over her hair, positioned her helmet, picked up her whip. Tried to shut out the noise in her head, because that's what she did. She was a professional, and that demanded she block out anything that might affect her ability to give her mount her best. Even this, impossible, thing.

When she stepped off the scale and handed her tack back to the valet, Ricky Acosta met her eyes, when no one else had dared, like he had been appointed spokesperson.

"Good luck, Liv."

His face was sincere, but luck had run out on her. The bullets had struck: one killed, one maimed. She needed more than luck. *Just let Nate be all right, and keep us safe.* Whether it was an attempt at positive thought, or a prayer, she didn't know.

The drizzle had turned to a more persistent downfall when the riders filed out to the paddock. Jeanne kept Chique under the shelter of the saddling stall, the groom playing with the filly's bit to keep her attention. The fat white shadow roll seemed fluorescent in the dimness as Chique swung her head, antsy at being asked to stand still. It took a moment for Liv to register that Don wasn't there. Jeanne must have put on the tack.

She refused to look at Liv at first. Both of them were adopting roles they hadn't planned on — Jeanne stepping in to saddle, Liv picking up the last mount she had ever really wanted.

"The turf is soft." Jeanne finally spoke, stating the obvious in an attempt to address the task at hand. She peered up at the dark sky as the rain came harder. It was a relief when the call for riders up came.

The downpour quickly soaked her in the post parade, and even though it was still warm out, Liv shuddered, chilled. She told the pony rider to let them go, and sent the filly off on her own. Chique didn't test her, galloping strongly but remaining manageable. They pulled up on the backside and turned in, both of them staring over the infield. Liv closed her eyes. Breathing in. Breathing out.

The pony met them to file onto the turf course, leading them up behind the gate and handing them off to the starter's assistant. Once they were in position, it was just her, Chique, and the lawn before them.

Chique flew out, Liv leaving her alone, waiting for feedback. The grass had give, but not too much. Chique, quick and catlike, skipped over it.

The others let her have the lead. Liv didn't have any illusions she'd get away with anything. No one was feeling sorry for her out here; any sympathy had been left in the jock's room. She shortened the filly's stride, conserving, but didn't expect to be left up here, dictating the pace, for long.

It was easy now to forget everything else — Chique absorbed it all. Liv hadn't felt anything like it since Claire. It was different in the mornings, even at speed — there was always something retained, held back, saved for the afternoon. While Chique was not in full flight, this was faster, freer, than any dawn trial. The best was reserved for the real test, when horses were matched against each other, and money and pride were at stake.

Around the clubhouse turn and coasting into the backstretch, they were still alone in front. Did the others think this pace, though slow, was enough in these conditions? Were they taking their chances, expecting the filly to tire? Or were the bigger, heavier horses just having more trouble than her compact filly? Maybe she was going to get a bit of luck today after all.

Chique powered through the final turn, relishing the inner course's tighter oval with something like authority — building momentum with strength Liv lacked. At the head of the stretch, the filly was in command with more left to give.

Grief hit Liv like a brick wall as they reached the spot where the accident had occurred, numbing her temporarily, leaving her deaf to the popping whips and riders' cries behind her. Chique pulled her past, rescuing her, and she left all of it in a little box somewhere in the corner of her chest.

Her hands and voice came to life, asking now, picking Chique up to keep her stride active when it might want to tire. The filly responded, ears laced back. Inside the eighth pole, twelve more seconds....

Beyond the awareness of Chique's exertion — each breath as she drew air into her lungs, oxygen into her bloodstream, blood to her heart — Liv was conscious of another horse. Like a train rushing up behind them, the rhythmic puffs of someone else, coming on. Chique pinned her ears and dug in, and Liv threw herself into the cause. She didn't look back. It didn't matter who it was.

The filly was dwarfed as her foe drew alongside, but Liv looked only at the green between Chique's ears and the pole that marked the finish. Another stride, another breath. Block out the dark image beside them, press on.

But somehow everything, every effort, all Chique's courage, wasn't enough today. A flash of light at the wire lit up for the photo the stewards would examine to determine the result, but Liv could have told them now, had they asked her. She stood in the irons, and for a strange moment felt as if she might fall, tumbling to the marshy turf beneath them. How easy that would be, if it could be like a dream where she never hit the ground. Maybe then she would wake up and find that's all this had been. She would go to the barn and find Feste waiting for her; Nate would show up and for once she would acknowledge they should talk *now,* because later might never be.

Liv galloped Chique back on the main track to the front of the grandstand. The groom and Jeanne were waiting, and Liv half-collapsed when her boots met the slop, falling against the filly. Chique sidestepped, agitated, as Liv's fingers fumbled to release the overgirth, then fought the billet under the saddle's skirt to unbuckle the girth.

Jeanne grabbed her arm. "Get out of here, Liv. Go to the hospital. You don't need to come back to the barn. We'll take care of Chique."

Or, she could just run away.

The version of Saratoga she'd climbed back from, those darkest of days when she'd fallen so far, and had done just that — run away — it closed back in on her now. They would take care of Chique, because she couldn't. What made anyone think she could do anything for Nate?

She had to get a grip. She had to go to the hospital, face what she might find there.

For better or worse.

That's what he was asking for.

She didn't shower, slipping back into her dress, the chill staying with her. Carrying an umbrella was more about hiding than shelter as she skirted through the crowd, finding her car under the staid old trees, leaves limp from the weight of the rain.

In the hospital parking lot she left the umbrella behind, letting the drops fall on her face, and drew her hands back over her braided hair to smooth it, but it was pointless. There was no hiding her distress. Just a moment, and she would go in. Geai's medallion felt heavy around her neck, not offering its intended comfort. *Ste-Anne, protector from storms.*

The triage nurse looked up as she approached, probably appearing like a prospective patient with her drawn and pale features, disheveled dress, arms hugged around her midriff.

"There was a rider — a jockey — brought in." She didn't expect they'd had any others. "Nate Miller."

The nurse nodded. "You are?"

"Girlfriend."

The knit of the nurse's eyebrows seemed to judge her — rightly so, because wouldn't a proper girlfriend have followed the ambulance?

"I'll call the doctor for you. You can have a seat."

It was a quiet emergency department, at least this evening: a mother and an uncomfortable child, another person holding a swollen wrist. The air conditioning made it freezing, a tremor beginning in her jaw that threatened to start her teeth chattering. She'd never thought to bring in her jacket. She wasn't thinking at all.

A doctor appeared only a matter of minutes later, scanning the room, catching her eye. It scared her that he'd responded so quickly.

She'd forgotten his name before he'd finished saying it, and his tight smile didn't reassure her as she pried her hand free from its grip on her elbow to shake the one he offered, his fingers much warmer and softer than her own. "Liv Lachance."

"I know who you are," he said.

She dismissed the comment, impatient. Apparently he was a racing fan, because why else would he know her? "What's going on with Nate?"

"What's your relationship? He's your boyfriend?"

Liv stopped herself from throwing her hands in the air. "Yes."

"What about family?"

"They're in western Canada," she snapped, exasperated. *Clearly I'm not enough.* "Are you going to tell me? I saw that spill. It was bad. He could have been killed."

"Then he got off lucky."

Getting out alive was the version of luck bestowed upon them today, but only in part, because Feste was dead.

She followed the doctor through doors, keeping up to his

long strides, not letting herself feel any optimism until she had all the information.

"He was conscious when he got here. No internal injuries. He's broken his left clavicle, and a couple of ribs."

She could hear the unspoken *but...*

"We're concerned because he's experiencing paralysis below the waist."

The spinning started, and she had to reach for a wall. The doctor stopped short, but he continued talking.

"We did x-rays, and there are no fractures. We're going to have to wait until the inflammation reduces before we know more. Maybe that will be all it takes. In the meantime, we'll do more tests. All good news, really."

Liv wasn't sure Nate would see any of it as good news.

"In here." The doctor motioned to a doorway. "Let me know if you have any other questions."

A curtain was drawn around the bed, and all she could do for a beat was stare at it, her pulse throbbing in her ears. She glanced up at the doctor.

"Thank you," she managed, but it was so wispy, if he hadn't nodded, she wouldn't have known it had even been audible.

Liv could tell Nate wasn't sleeping, even though he didn't acknowledge her. She went around the bed, into his line of sight, and pulled the chair there to the edge, but it hurt too much to hold his gaze when it finally zeroed on her. Because what could she say? With the pain and uncertainty he was dealing with, how could she deliver any more blows?

"Did you ride the filly?"

She could nod. By comparison, it was the easy question.

"How did she run? Is she okay?"

"She's okay." That was the only positive news she had. "She got beat, Nate. Caught at the wire. But no excuses. She was game all the way."

His stare burned into her temple. "You have to tell me."

She shook her head, pressing her face into her hands, sucking air through her fingers. If only she could cry, curl up beside him...but he was too fragile, and she had nothing left, not even tears.

Distance would get her through this. She set aside the emotion, drawing on the person who'd be on her way to being a veterinarian four years ago. "They think it was his heart. Aortic rupture."

"Was anyone else hurt?"

She gave a short shake of the head, biting her lower lip before it started to quiver.

"Did the doctor talk to you?" he asked, finally, his voice toneless.

"Yes."

"What if they're wrong, Liv? What if this is it?"

She shook her head more assertively, sitting up. "We'll get you back to Toronto. My father has a good friend who's a surgeon. He'll be able to recommend a specialist. They'll sort it out."

She hadn't panicked when he'd told her he loved her; hadn't really even panicked last night when he'd put a thick and heavy layer on that, but now, seeing him like this, her anxiety was barely contained.

"I'll call him now." The chair scraped over the floor as she jerked to her feet. "And your parents. I have to go back and check on Chique – I'll update you in the morning."

The pressure in her chest made breathing seem impossible. What a horrible, horrible person she was, that she couldn't get over her own distress to sit by him. A fresh and clear reminder that she was incapable of being for him what he had always been for her.

When she reached the parking lot she broke into a run,

drops streaming down her face when tears wouldn't. It wouldn't be much easier to go back to the track.

She walked to Chique's stall, past the empty one that waited, neatly bedded, for a colt who would never return. Chique rumbled in the darkness from behind her haynet.

Liv slipped in and put her arms around Chique's neck, pressing her face against the smooth, solid muscle of it. Chique pushed back, wrapping her head around Liv's torso, always in search of treats. How much could the filly sense of the day's devastation? Horses were such a highly social species. Racehorses spent so much time in relative isolation, their people a substitute for their own kind. The reverse was often just as true. This business was so all-encompassing, the horses were both co-warriors and friends.

She'd always thought equine bonds safer than human relationships, but today it was a toss-up, when her heart had been torn violently from her chest, scattered in pieces over the muddy racetrack.

CHAPTER EIGHTEEN

AND SO IT COULD HAPPEN, just like that. The life you knew, the one you told yourself you didn't take for granted — but did — could change, or disappear, for good. It was given, and it was taken away. Just like that.

Being back in Toronto didn't change anything. It was just bigger, and busier, with a world-class neurosurgeon and proper health care. He didn't let himself think about Liv. When he started to go there, things got dark in his head, fast. He would always be associated with the death of that beautiful, promising colt. There would be no redemption from that.

She had acted swiftly, facilitating the arrangements that had seen him transported to Ontario less than twenty-four hours after the injury, though he had yet to actually meet the specialist. On the outside, at least, Liv managed well in crisis — coolly taking charge to ensure the most favourable outcome — even if it was only a coping mechanism, her way of detaching herself. He envied her ability to separate herself from the barrage of feelings that had to be plaguing her, the same way they were him.

The door swung open, a cluster of lab coats gathering at the foot of his bed around whom he assumed to be the surgeon. Nate felt a bit better — at least it wasn't going to take all day to be seen by this guy. Liv slipped in behind them like she was late for rounds. She wouldn't have looked out of place in one of those white coats; hair pulled tightly back, smudgy shadows under weary eyes, her lips pressed together in grim focus. Nate, on the other hand, listened with about the same attention he'd give a TV medical drama. *How long till hockey starts up again?* All he wanted to hear was that they could fix him, and soon.

"I'll be back once we've got the results." The surgeon — Dr. Collier, he'd caught that much — nodded at Nate, and Liv ducked out of the way as he brusquely left the room with his entourage.

Liv glanced at Nate, a small, exasperated sound vibrating in her throat before she disappeared after them. He would have laughed if it weren't for his cracked ribs. Her reaction said it all — she was used to getting more consideration from the veterinarians she dealt with. He'd just sit back and let her do her thing — as if he had any choice.

She returned in a few minutes and sat next to the bed. "He wants to be a hundred percent sure there's no fracture, so he's ordered more diagnostics...but he still thinks it's probably just the inflammation causing pressure on some nerves."

"When are they going to do all this?"

"Hopefully this morning, but you know how hospitals are. Don't be holding your breath."

"Shouldn't it be just a little more urgent?"

"I'm sure if it was urgent, he'd be on it. If they decide they need to do surgery to release some of the pressure, they still want to wait till the inflammation's reduced. Time is a good thing here, Miller. You want to avoid surgery if you can."

"Did he mention surgery?"

Liv nodded.

"Were you going to tell me?"

"I just did, didn't I?" Her eyes flashed at him, not completely able to mask the hurt this time. *Nice job, Miller.* "I talked to your mother again last night when I got in. She's going to come."

There would be no stopping that, of course. His mother would be overwrought — it was probably killing her not to be here already. His father, on the other hand, would be grimly shaking his head in the background. *Great choice of occupation, son. Hell of a lot of good that Eclipse Award is doing you now.*

"Chique get back all right?" He made himself ask, to get away from the depressing subject of his condition — though it was all twisted together, a tumble of barbed wire that pierced his skin any way he tried to move.

"I haven't been in to see her yet."

That didn't fit. Nothing would take priority over Chique's welfare, for Liv — certainly not his sorry state. His first instinct was to make a smart-assed comment in his disbelief, but he managed to stop himself. "Don't you think you should have checked on her?"

"I followed the van from Saratoga and put her in the stall myself last night. All they have to do is walk her. I'm sure they'd call if something was wrong." She was back on her feet, halfway to the door, her gaze locked on the floor. "I'll call later to find out what's going on."

She hovered, eyes uneasily returning to him, maybe waiting for him to say something to stop her from leaving. But he just left it all there, in that messy mass of sidestepped emotions that simultaneously tied and distanced them.

He couldn't really blame her for wanting to bolt. Maybe she'd been right all along, and they weren't meant to be together, because if this was some kind of test, they were failing.

It was like the accident had left her heart paralyzed. There was no prospect of surgery to repair it, and she wasn't sure whether time would reduce that inflammation and bring the feeling back. There she was again, a horrible human, comparing her situation to Nate's. He was allowed to be a jerk, when she was being so remote.

She left the city, because she couldn't bear to go to the track. Seeing Chique would just remind her of Feste, his Woodbine stall emptier than the one at Saratoga, left that way out of respect. And there would be the inevitable questions about Nate. Jo and Em would make sure the filly was all right. There was nothing Liv could do to protect Chique. It didn't matter how right she tried to do everything, how much care she took. It could still blow apart, just as it had with Feste.

She didn't want to go home, either. She'd successfully avoided her mother, getting in late enough last night, and leaving early enough this morning, but that wouldn't last forever. She wasn't ready to endure her mother's concern, and again, the questions about Nate. Instead she found herself heading to Northwest.

There had been a time in recent memory she would have sought only solitude, today she needed Faye's ability to be no-nonsense but comforting without saying anything stupid. Of course, Faye would also drill her about what had gone on before the accident, and that would mean admitting what a fool she'd made of herself.

But Faye's vehicle wasn't there, only Dean's truck. It shouldn't be there, this time of day — he should still be at the track. Dean must've taken Faye's car into work to get it serviced for her.

The Porsche looked shiny and conspicuous next to Dean's dusty black pickup. She'd promised to drive the 911 back from Saratoga, leaving her own car behind, because heaven forbid anything should happen to the Porsche. She locked it in paranoia, even out here in the country.

The Taylor's Golden Retriever, Gus, bounded out the back door and across the deck, leaping off and shimmying up to her knees. She crouched and let him smother her face with his overly-enthusiastic tongue, burying her fingers in his thick ruff – a display of affection she could allow, when everything else was locked down. When she looked up, she saw Dean, towering from the first step with his hands in the pockets of his jeans, sad and awkward.

Liv shot to her feet, stepping backward. "I thought Faye might be here. I should go."

"Come on, Liv."

His tone stopped her mid-turn. Dean took the last step, reaching out slowly, and put his arms around her.

Liv let herself feel a shred of the grief and strain, setting aside, for now, the weirdness the night of the Plate Ball had inserted into a friendship she'd always valued. Maybe he held on too long, and she felt guilty for not stopping him, but she was so tired of pretending.

"Come in?" he asked.

She nodded, and followed him into the kitchen.

"Why are you home so early?" she asked. "Is everything okay?"

Dean opened the fridge and extracted a pitcher of orange juice.

"I had to be here for the vet – my manager had a couple of personal appointments today. Faye's having lunch with Will in the city. I think she was planning on going to the hospital. Thought she might see you there. You haven't talked to her?"

Liv shifted her attention to Gus, his big head resting conveniently on her knee. Faye was used to Liv being a bad friend, but not texting before showing up now seemed like a major oversight.

Dean splashed vodka over ice in glasses and topped them with juice, and planted one in front of Liv. Nate had served up the same drink after he'd told her about Cindy and Phil's accident, and she wondered if vodka and orange juice was a recommended tonic for times like this, or just something Nate and Dean held in common. She left the glass there. If she started drinking, there might be no end; the potential anesthetic effect was far too tempting.

"So...you holding up okay?"

The compassion in his voice made her eyes burn, and she bit her lower lip, reaching for the glass after all. She peered into the ice, but set it back down. "I don't really have much choice."

"How's Nate?"

She shrugged. "I'm sure he'll be a lot better when they sort him out. They're still doing tests."

"He'll be okay though, right?"

"That's what they expect."

She could talk about Nate, like a patient, careful not to let her confusion creep in. Nate had a right to be angry, and frustrated, but she would never have thought he would direct it at her.

"Do you think it's shaken him up at all?" Dean asked.

Liv choked back a laugh. "If you mean his confidence, no. I think as soon as he's walking and halfway right again, he's going to want to be back on a horse. Way before he should be. I get that. And I'll be glad of it. Or at least, remind me I should be, when the time comes, because right now, all this..." She finally took a swallow of the drink, the alcohol strong as it hit the back of her throat.

Dean hesitated. "The two of you, then. Is it for real?"

Liv looked at him critically, caught off guard by his timing and directness, his gaze a reminder that everything right now was wrong. She didn't want this from Dean. She needed her friend back. And now that she was wondering what was going on in Nate's head, she wished she could return to simple companionship. She'd been right about this romance stuff. It ruined everything.

"I don't know," she said. She'd thought it was. It was unraveling far too easily. "You and I were always the ones who wondered why everyone else put themselves through the hell of relationships."

Dean settled into the adjacent chair, sizing her up like he knew a challenge when he heard one. "So why Nate?"

Liv sighed, pulling at the thickness of Gus's soft ears. "I don't know what to tell you. And it took a long time. He was ridiculously persistent." The corners of her lips lifted, even if it seemed bittersweet now.

"That's what I get for keeping it to myself all this time."

She glanced at him, abandoning Gus to cup both hands around her glass. "I don't know anymore if there's any future to this thing with Nate. Maybe it was just a bad experiment on my part, a stupid attempt to be a normal person, and I'm really meant to be alone. And if that's the case — and I have absolutely no problem with that — I don't want to have lost two friends."

She held his eyes this time, saw the words hit home, as hard as they'd been to find.

"All right. I hear you." There was a trace of resignation on his face as he said it. "What are you going to do with Chique?"

She lifted the glass to her lips again and glanced away. It

was a relief to get away from the personal stuff, but thinking about Chique right now was hard. "I haven't even thought about it yet."

"With Nate out, I need someone for Ride The Wave in the Breeders'."

"Steve Gordon." She didn't want another of Nate's big horses. Chique was guilt enough.

"I heard about Elemental. You know The Wave. Come breeze him in a couple of days. Winning the Breeders' for me would go a long way toward easing the pain of you spurning me."

"Fine." Liv met his smirk with her own, standing. "Let me know when."

She couldn't say no — fighting it would just sound absurd. Liv and Elemental had turned the tables on Nate and Ride The Wave in the Prince of Wales, but Elemental had pulled up sore in his last breeze. Not that the mile and a half of the Breeders' would have been the best spot for him anyway.

It wasn't even noon, and she was lost. She drove back to the farm, past the house to the small barn, and pulled up outside the side paddock. Claire nickered and ambled over, her distinctive roundness evidence of the life growing inside her in undaunted defiance to the surrounding catastrophe. Liv had been looking forward to this foal, a baby out of her rock by Chique's sire, Just Lucky, but now...now she was afraid to look forward to anything.

She ducked through the fence rails and slipped her fingers over the bridge of the mare's nose, pressing her cheek to Claire's, and tried to synch their breathing. Closing her eyes, she felt the first tear trickle down her cheek but brushed it away, and left Claire with a kiss on the soft skin behind her nostril.

The interior of the barn was cool, the door to the office

unlocking with a click. She couldn't look at the painting of Geai this time, ducking under it to find the drawer with the spare key to Nate's apartment.

The air inside was still and stuffy, and she leaned against the door for a moment after closing it behind her, feeling like a trespasser. The piano was too silent, his guitar still in the back of the Porsche where she'd stashed his minimal belongings from Saratoga. She wandered around the room, taking quiet steps like she was afraid of disturbing something.

The photo of him with his two brothers and Cindy still rested on top of the piano, now accompanied by a smaller one that poked at her heart. It was from Florida, the winter Claire was three, when Nate and Michel had come to see her ride at Gulfstream, and the three of them had gone to eat afterward. It had been a joke, Nate dropping an arm over her shoulders, a shot Michel had snapped and posted on Instagram before she'd even known about it. A bit of fiction that had, in time, become reality. A reality that was breaking down.

His bedroom door was half-open, and she pressed it back, creeping in. He'd left it neat, bed made, a couple of books on the nightstand. She crawled onto the bed, pulling out a pillow, and curled up, hugging it to herself and inhaling. It smelled like the old Nate; the one she'd last seen that moment she'd reached for his hand and pulled him down to her, unaware that less than twenty-four hours later, life would never be the same.

Tests broke up the morning, but left him exhausted, which just added to his frustration. Lunch wasn't anything to get excited about. At least with the prospect of hospital food, he wouldn't have to worry about his weight. Not that he'd be riding any time soon.

Someone would be by to clear the picked-over meal tray – that seemed to be all he had to look forward to. Then Faye poked her head around the corner of the door. Nate laughed, and decided it was worth the stabbing pain in his ribs.

"Wow, I must be in bad shape for you to visit me."

"Ha ha," Faye said, wheeling the meal tray out of the way and chastely pecking him on the cheek. "I had lunch with Will, thought I might as well stop by."

"Where is he? My oldest friend can't even come see me in my darkest moment?"

"He had to go to work – couldn't get off. We weren't sure if we could visit this morning."

"Have you talked to Liv?"

Faye leaned her hip against the side of the bed, crossing her arms and looking down at him with a frown, picking up on the tension in his voice. "Just a text. She said she was going to have a nap and would catch up with me later. Which in true Liv form sounds all logical and healthy on the surface, but can't be trusted. I'm guessing she is not handling this."

"The two of us are like this massive black hole right now. It's just way too much grief in the same place. I can't take it."

"So, how were things going in Saratoga anyway? You know, before...this."

Nate squeezed his eyes shut, his mind going straight to that moment, Liv being all daring and sexy, a bit of fun that had gotten bent so entirely out of shape. "It was great," he said quietly. "It was just starting to feel like we were finally getting somewhere."

"What happened?" Faye knew him too well. She hadn't missed that he was withholding.

"I'm not telling you, Faye. She has to be the one."

"Something did happen, then."

"She needs to talk to someone. She sure as hell won't talk to me."

Faye rolled her eyes. "Sounds like you're being altogether too dramatic. I know what happened to the colt is terrible, but why should that change what was developing between the two of you?"

"Why? Because I'm stuck in this hospital bed with more questions than answers, and she's running around all dark and tormented, chasing after doctors. I never really got to find out what she actually feels about us, and now we have to deal with what happened to Feste, and Chique getting beat, and this. If she has any kind of feelings, you'd think now would be a good time to say something, right? Instead she's just distanced herself. You remember what happened after Geai died. She shut herself off. I'm afraid she's doing it again."

Faye's eyes dropped — she'd been a casualty of that too. "You guys really need to cut each other some slack. You have to give the smoke a chance to clear. No dire predictions or major decisions right now, okay?"

"You'll talk to her? Please?"

She sighed. "I'll try. But you know there's no guarantee she'll talk to me either, right?"

There wasn't, of course, but he was reaching for any sliver of hope right now.

Her eyes narrowed, one edge of her lips curving into a familiar smirk. "It is so wrong, me playing counselor on this, you know."

He tried to grab onto the humour, but couldn't dredge up even a grin. "I know. Thank you."

Liv woke with a start, sitting up abruptly, blinking sleep away from her eyes. *Where...?* It took a second. Nate's apartment. *Damn*, what time was it? She was supposed to call him. She felt around for her phone, finding it under the pillow. Seven o'clock. And...notifications. Why hadn't she woken up? Somehow it had switched to silent. She hadn't done that, had she? Some warped, semi-conscious slip of her finger? Stupid phone, not doing its job when she actually needed it to.

The first one was from her mother. *Spoke with Mrs Miller. Flight AC447 23:37. His father and brother are also coming. Your father says you can take the Jag to pick them up.*

Talk about worlds colliding. She'd left Nate's mom with both her cell, and the Lachance's landline for back up. Figures she'd called the home number. Nate was more open with his mother than she was with hers. The thought of Anne Lachance querying Connie Miller to fill in the holes of what she knew of the relationship between their children made Liv uneasy. Of course, it might not matter anymore.

Faye next. She'd been just leaving the hospital after visiting Nate. *CALL ME!* That was five hours ago.

She fired off a quick response as she stumbled to her feet. *Just woke up! Ugh. Have to get ready to drive to the airport. Tomorrow, promise.*

It felt too weird to phone Nate at the hospital this late, but she had to. She needed to be up-to-date on him before she saw his family. The call was brief, information gathering only, the spaces between words tight and filled with the unsaid.

Her lack of nerves was bizarre as she waited at the arrivals gate for the flight from Calgary — a definite change from the first time she'd met Nate's family. With the calls she'd exchanged with Connie Miller since the accident, a strange bond had formed. Ironic, now.

She saw Reid Miller first, the man's stern, reserved face not much different from the last time she'd seen him. She'd met the man under tragic circumstances, and the situation with Nate that had brought the family to Toronto was hardly favourable; it wouldn't be fair to judge him on her time around him so far. She hadn't told Nate that his father and brother were coming – she hoped he'd appreciate it, but it was quite possible he would not.

Connie, in contrast, greeted Liv with open arms, holding her so tightly Liv had to fight back tears.

"Thank you so much for coming to pick us up, Liv. You must be exhausted. We could have taken a taxi."

Liv just waved her off and reached for Connie's bag.

"How's he doing?" Reid asked as Liv led them to the parking lot.

Liv glanced over. Even his voice was similar to Nate's. "I think he's just anxious to get the surgery over with."

"So they're going to do surgery, then."

She'd forgotten they wouldn't know, which was silly, because she'd only learned herself when she'd phoned Nate. "Tomorrow afternoon."

"They think that will reverse the paralysis?"

She nodded. "The surgeon seems confident, but it's not entirely without risk. It would probably resolve on its own given time." She could relay the facts. She just couldn't look at Connie.

"But far be it from my son to wait," Reid said.

The sarcasm wasn't lost on Liv, but waiting had gotten her into all sorts of trouble, so she wasn't going to judge.

The next morning at the hospital, she stayed by the door — not the picture of the doting girlfriend — watching Connie sweep straight to her son's bedside.

"Wow, everyone came." Nate glanced past his mother to his brother Tim, with a fleeting smile at his father. "Guess the career move isn't looking so bright right about now, eh?"

"You're going to be okay though, right?" Tim said.

"Yeah, for sure," Nate responded with confidence Liv wasn't sure he felt. "Sorry I probably won't be able to show you around while you're here. What do you think of Toronto?"

"Not much. So far all I've seen is the airport, a hotel, the highway, and a hospital."

"Maybe Liv's sister and her friend can do something about that while you're here. Is Cory still around?"

He found Liv's eyes, making her wonder what was going on in his head — and wishing she had the courage and the tools to find out.

"She's in Fort Erie for a few days."

She absently listened to the conversation, flowers next to the bed that hadn't been there yesterday dredging up her guilt for not coming back last night. After settling the Millers in a hotel on the airport strip, when she should have gotten herself a room, she'd driven all the way back to the farm and crashed at Nate's again, because it seemed to be the only way to feel close to him right now. Like maybe she could get herself used to the idea of a lifetime of that — and hope that in time, when he was better, he'd still want her there.

She hung back as his family had their parting words before inching to his side, still lacking any fresh ideas of what to say.

"Thanks for looking after my family," he said.

"It's the least I can do."

"Doesn't seem that long ago it was the other way around." He tried to smile.

"I wish I was better at this part."

"Hey — it's okay."

He opened his hand, and she reached for it, pressing her eyes shut as she squeezed.

"I walked Chique again this morning. I'll get on her tomorrow." How quickly she defaulted to talking about work. "Everyone was asking about you."

She relayed all the messages from the backstretch, wishes for good luck and promises of prayers. It had been silly not to go in yesterday. The whole Woodbine community felt the impact of the accident, aftershocks vibrating through it.

He didn't look at her as she spoke, like he'd shut a part of himself off, and that scared her more than the impending surgery. "Please tell me you're going to get through this okay."

He met her eyes, reading her face, which for once was transparent, when his was anything but. "I'm sure you've got the surgeon on his toes. See you on the other side."

It felt like a dismissal. She should have kissed him, except it wasn't enough to erase everything that was wrong, so she shrank away.

Liv left the Millers in a waiting room. She didn't know where she was going, but she couldn't just sit this out. Through halls, skipping down stairs, until she reached the lobby. Her eyes darted around. Flower shop, gift shop, coffee shop. Doors, with fresh air — as fresh as big city air could be — on the other side. She loped toward them.

Then there was Faye, in her face, stopping her in her tracks.

"Hey, where are you going?"

Caught. "I just needed to get out for a while."

"He's in surgery?"

Liv nodded.

Faye pulled her into a hug. "He'll be okay. Before you know it, you'll be fighting to keep him off horses."

The twist of Liv's lips wasn't a good approximation of a smile, if Faye's expression was any indication.

"Is there somewhere we can go?" Faye glanced around, steering Liv away from the door. "It's ironic hospitals don't have bars in them, don't you think? You could use a drink." Only Faye would make such a warped observation. She continued, her perfect eyebrows peaking. "I'm sure there's a bar close by."

"I'm not leaving."

"You looked like you were a minute ago."

Liv sighed. "I know. I guess you showed up just in time."

"Funny, that. Coffee it is, then. At least it's Second Cup."

Just the feel of the hot beverage between her palms helped. Cappuccino was her comfort food. Faye led the way to a nearby bench and pulled her down.

"His parents here?" Faye asked.

"His brother too. They're upstairs."

"You need to tell me what's going on. Something happened in Saratoga, and Nate's not telling. What the hell is that about?"

Liv shot her a look, brow furrowed. "What did he say to you?"

"Well that's just it, nothing. He said it had to come from you."

"Not now, Faye. I've got enough in my head without rehashing that. Why are you here, anyway?"

"You're welcome." Faye laughed. "I thought you might appreciate the moral support. Would you rather I leave you and your head alone?"

Yes, actually.

"C'mon. Whatever it is, it's eating at him, and by the looks of it, you too."

What had she learned? There was never going to be a good time...though talking to Faye was just another reminder of how she'd failed to clear things up with Nate. She popped the lid off her drink and blew on it before slurping some of the foamed milk.

"It's all your fault, actually. You and your stupid advice. It was the night before – the accident." Her heart started to pound in her ears just thinking about it. "I was stressing out and needed to distract myself. I probably drank too much wine. And attempted to throw myself at him."

Faye tried to smother her laugh, unsuccessfully, and Liv flushed, scowling. *Some friend.*

"And this was a problem?"

"Apparently, because he pushed me away and left the house."

"You're leaving something out."

"So it's not bad enough he wanted no part of me?"

"Oh, I'm sure that wasn't the case. How far did it go?"

"I really don't want to talk about this, Faye."

"Of course you don't. Seriously, what are you leaving out?"

She glanced back at Faye, then sipped from her cup, not caring it was too hot to drink. The sting as it burned the top of her mouth seemed a fitting punishment for her actions across the board. "Maybe the part where he said something about marriage."

At least Faye didn't laugh at that. Liv stole a sideways peek.

She was smiling. "Now it all makes sense."

"Great. How so?"

Faye slipped an arm around Liv's shoulders, and Liv felt the tremor of her low laugh.

"I know you don't think of stuff the way you need to sometimes, so let me try and help you out. Nate is a little bizarre. He seems to be able to show restraint better than any guy I've ever known, but it obviously comes at a price. He has this kind of sweet, very old-fashioned ideal that's never really panned out for him, but I'm betting he's pretty determined it's going to with you. I'm sure he thought it was going to be easier, because he counted on you not showing any initiative. Except, apparently, you did. Hence his major overreaction." She laughed again. "It's priceless."

"I'm so glad you're amused," Liv grumbled. "But marriage, Faye. Even if he was overreacting, it was obviously on his mind."

"Oh come on, sweetie. This isn't news to any of us."

"So what am I supposed to do?"

"Next time he asks, say yes, damn it."

Liv almost spat out the mouthful of coffee she'd taken, and Faye thumped her on the back as she coughed.

"Breathe. Take some time to wrap your head around the idea. You might surprise yourself. But in the meantime, the two of you really need to talk."

True, but that was proving easier said than done.

"I should probably go back upstairs," Liv said, sighing. "You can meet the family."

"Oh, I don't know about that."

"Don't be ridiculous. Connie is sweet. They know Will too, remember. At the very least, you can do it for me."

"The in-laws, eh? Well, all right." Faye grinned.

The Millers were where Liv had left them. Connie and Faye hit it off immediately, and Liv found herself thinking it should have been Faye Nate had fallen in love with; Faye he wanted to marry. It would have been so much simpler that way.

Nate knew the answers to the questions the nurses asked. He knew who he was, and where he was. He had a question for them, too, but wasn't coherent enough to ask it yet. It was all a bit foggy, but not enough to obliterate what he most needed to know.

Next time he woke up he was back in his room, feeling a lot more with it. He made his own initial assessment. *Yes.* Sensation. He closed his eyes, whispered gratitude, then waited to hear a more complete report from the surgeon.

Liv slipped in the room, approaching slowly. She reached out and touched his fingers tentatively.

"Hey," he croaked, the word catching in his sore throat.

"So?" Her eyes searched his face.

"So far so good, I guess. You okay?"

She shrugged, and looked away, and he wished he could sit up and hold her.

"Can you get me out of here?" he joked.

She laughed, just a small one, but it was good to hear.

"Just promise me you'll take it easy. Don't rush anything."

"I seem to remember throwing you up on Paz not long after you fractured a femur."

"That was different. This is your spine. Something goes wrong..."

The surgeon had already drilled it home — there would be no forcing this recovery, and Liv would do her part to make sure. She had all the power, really, holding the weapon that would be most effective in extracting his compliance — Chique. The realization caught him unawares. When it came down to it, he was just like Liv. It was all about the job; all about a horse.

CHAPTER NINETEEN

Chique's ears worked like antennae, funneling information from her surroundings. A flick forward at the bad-actor up ahead, a pin and a wish to take up the chase when a worker dropped to the rail on her inside, surging by. Liv kept her hands set at the base of the filly's neck, silently telling her *no*.

They rolled around the turn, and the ears shot up again, Chique's lead change fluid. Liv let her gallop along, past the empty grandstand, under the wire, around the clubhouse turn. She wished she could let the filly go — it would help clear her mind of the clouded thoughts there.

Nate was being released from hospital today, the surgery a success, though his full recovery would take weeks. Yesterday after dropping off Reid and Tim at the airport, Liv had settled Connie into Nate's apartment — ending her little camp-out — but Connie had insisted Liv go alone to pick Nate up.

Being alone with Nate right now wasn't comfortable.

Chique dragged her into the backstretch before Liv reluctantly pulled her up, spotting Roger and Paz parked perpendicular to the outside rail. The filly snorted and tossed her head, the bright white shadow roll bouncing with it as Liv asked her to stand.

"She looks good," Roger said.

"She feels good."

Roger didn't take hold of the filly for the walk back. The days where Chique needed that were gone. Liv felt a pang in her chest, missing that Chique all of a sudden, because that old Chique was so tied to the old Nate — the *just relax and embrace the crazy* Nate. She was afraid the accident had erased the last traces of that version of him.

"Have you decided on a race for her?"

Liv shook her head, her eyes dropping to the twisty flop of Chique's mane. "Guess I should look at a condition book. The only reason I took her to Saratoga was because of Feste." Her voice tripped over the colt's name. She swallowed and continued. "I'm sure there's something for her here."

She needed to sit down and decide, now that Chique had made it successfully back to the races. But it was hard to do without Nate in the equation. He'd always been the glue that held their little team together. He hadn't asked about the filly since before his operation.

Jo met them in front of the barn. "I can do her up for you, if you want to go," she said, unbuckling the throatlatch as Liv dropped lightly to the asphalt.

She didn't, really. But she nodded, pulling off the tack. "Thanks, Jo."

When she arrived at the hospital, he was sitting on the edge of the bed in track pants and a worn t-shirt. She pulled clean black jeans and a short-sleeved shirt out of the plastic grocery bag she carried.

"Your mother sent them," she said, scrunching up the bag and shoving it in her pocket.

"She didn't come?"

Liv shook her head, but didn't explain.

He shrugged, and started to pull the t-shirt over his head with his good arm, flinching as it snagged on his right shoulder. Liv stepped in, gingerly easing it free, stopping herself from tracing the bruises on his torso, the grooves between his ribs that were a little too deep. Her fingers trembled, emotion flowing freely down her arms, being this close making all her nerves misfire. There was a little fire in his eyes, their pupils dark as he caught her quick glance. The tee fell to the floor and she groped for the shirt, trying not to look at him as she helped him into it. He started on the buttons, slowly. The lower ones he managed okay, but when he grimaced halfway up, she took over, resisting the temptation to close them all the way to the top to cover up as much as possible; get the memory of the feel of his skin under her palms out of her head.

"I'll come back in a couple of minutes," she said, and left him to figure out the jeans on his own, not before catching him smirking at her modesty. Yeah, fair. Not too long ago she'd been willing to rip his clothes off.

A nurse had a wheelchair ready — hospital policy, he had to go as far as the door in it. He hadn't bothered to tuck the shirt into his jeans, and reluctantly settled into the chair once an RN made sure he was wearing a sling on his right arm. The model patient act would probably last for about five minutes once he was in the car.

Many of the hospital staff interrupted on their way out. No surprise, really. Nate was a charmer, probably had the lot of them wrapped around his little finger. Liv had just forgotten, because he seemed so indifferent right now with her.

It felt strange to be driving him in his car, but now it was just one more strange thing on top of a mountain of weird. The last time — and first time — she'd been behind the wheel of the Porsche with him in the passenger seat was on their way to the Plate Ball. A lifetime ago.

The Bluetooth picked up her phone, because of course she'd added it to play music, but she felt self-conscious about it now, like she'd made herself too comfortable. He didn't attempt to change it, though. He didn't even poke through her playlist to find something to sing along to, like he would have in that other lifetime.

"Can we go by the track?" he asked as she merged into highway traffic.

"Sure," she said, glancing over, but he was looking straight ahead. She shouldn't have been surprised, but hadn't expected it, just the same.

She parked in front of the barn and watched him get out and head to the deserted shedrow with a careful stride that bore no resemblance to the confident, athletic one she was so familiar with. Liv followed as far as the doorway, but couldn't go any further.

He sauntered to Chique's stall, talking to the faces that poked out on his way, averting his eyes from the box that remained empty. Chique nickered multiple notes at the sound of his voice, and craned her head over her screen, her crazy forelock falling in disarray over one eye. The edges of Nate's lips turned up, but even his smile was reserved. He touched her muzzle with his good hand, then slipped in with her.

Liv closed her eyes, seeing the reunion like she was watching from the corner of the stall. Chique's head pressing into him, gently exploring hands that produced no treats, instead stroking her neck, pulling at her ears, straightening her forelock. None of it would alleviate the pain and emptiness.

He didn't stay long, Chique pushing her head out and

staring after him. He didn't look back, his gaze dragging the neatly-raked shed as he came closer. He tried to meet her eyes, but they faltered, and he kept walking to the car.

"We could go get something to eat if you're hungry." It wasn't anything close to what she should be saying, but it was all that came to mind. A place to start, when she really had no idea where to begin.

"No, I'm okay. Kinda tired I guess."

"All right," she said, and started the car, feeling guilty for being relieved.

Sitting on the couch with a beer in his hand and his mother in his kitchen was not how Nate thought he'd experience the Breeders' Stakes this year. But here he was.

"You're moping," his mother said, setting a plate of sliced veggies at his feet on the coffee table. To offset the beer, probably.

"So what am I supposed to do?"

"Go in there?"

He'd needed to see Chique on the way home from the hospital, to know she was still there, and to give him a reason to look ahead, do his rehab, so he could get back and ride her again. But being at the track, in the meantime, was not something he wanted to deal with. All the condolences, the questions, the encouragement — he didn't need any of it. And he certainly did not need to be there to watch this.

"It's not as if I'd be any use to anyone. I can't even walk hots with this collarbone." Though that's the way it went in this business. One day you were riding at Saratoga, the next you could be back on the end of a shank, turning left. You never quit, you just downgraded. It was like Hotel California, you could never really leave.

"Maybe you're right. Maybe time apart is what both of you need."

He shot her a dark look. It wasn't what he wanted to hear, but maybe it was true, and he needed physical distance to figure out what was most important. Liv...Chique...riding — in that order? He wasn't sure they could be separated. Remove one element, and the whole thing fell apart.

Ride The Wave was on his toes in the post parade, Liv's long braid and straight-backed posture making them a contrast to the bored stable pony and his slumping rider. The colt looked even bigger and stronger than Nate remembered, like he'd grown and filled out in the last three weeks since the Prince of Wales. And Liv looked good on him. But she looked good on everything.

Between a pedigree that suggested he'd love the mile and a half distance, and the absence of Elemental, Ride The Wave stood alone as favourite. Nate hadn't had much to offer Liv about riding the colt that she hadn't already sussed out, but at least they'd talked about that. He set the beer bottle on the table and balanced on the edge of the seat cushion once the field was loaded.

The colt broke alertly but heeded Liv as she asked him to moderate his enthusiasm — he wasn't a front-runner, as much as he thought he wanted to be at the moment. He rated perfectly for her, sitting just behind and outside of the two speed horses who battled for the lead as they charged into the clubhouse turn. She kept him tucked there all the way around, and broke him out midway down the long homestretch of the EP Taylor turf.

"Wow," he muttered as the colt blew by the pacesetters and pulled away with authority, showing none of the immaturity he'd gotten away with in the Plate, but paid for in the Prince of Wales. *Such a nice colt.* Dean would probably want to think about running in the Canadian International after that.

He tried not to calculate what his paycheque would have been for that ride. The paycheque that was Liv's instead. Better her than someone else. He might have to talk her into marrying him for the financial support.

"Then there's that," he said, jutting his chin at the screen before sweeping up the bottle again and draining what was left.

His mother glanced at him, then the television, where Dean fucking Taylor crushed Liv in an embrace and planted a kiss on the top of her helmet.

The Porsche was gone. Liv checked on Claire before going up to the apartment, where Connie opened the door.

"So you let him have the car keys?" Liv smirked.

"Oh, he just went for a little drive. He'll be fine. He needs to do something – he's looking much too morose. He won't be long."

"Are you sure about that?"

Connie waved off her wry comment and set a bowl of cut vegetables and a glass of water on the counter in front of Liv as she sat.

"I need to start thinking about going back to Calgary soon. I can't stay around here forever."

"So who's going to keep him out of trouble?" The corner of Liv's mouth drifted up, but she wasn't joking, not exactly.

"He's old enough to do that himself. Wouldn't get him anywhere to push things, would it?"

If Nate's mother felt she could count on him to behave, Liv

probably should too. There was nothing she could do to stop him anyway.

"It's been good to spend some time with you, even if things haven't been ideal," Connie said. "Maybe the two of you can come out to Calgary at Christmas."

"You're making assumptions," Liv responded, not quite frowning.

"And I shouldn't?"

"It doesn't seem safe to assume anything right now. But it's my own fault."

"Oh, I wouldn't say that."

"Why?" She couldn't keep the challenge from her voice.

Connie came around the counter and sat next to Liv with her cup of tea. "He's not handling this very well. He has the tendency to go off the rails a bit when something upsets him. He's done it before, I'm sure you know." Connie paused. "You need to stop being so hard on yourself and give yourself more credit. Don't let him off so easily. He needs to deal with this head on, not run away."

Liv sighed, turning on the stool so she could see out the big picture window. Who was she to talk someone out of running away, when she'd had the same thought more than once in the last three weeks? "I admit he's thrown me for a loop. He's the solid one. I'm the flake." She caught Connie's reprimanding eye and sat up straighter. "Okay. I'm the one who doubts. The only thing I know that would make him feel better, I can't give him – I can't put him on a horse. I wish I could."

"Have you told him that?"

"No. Give him an inch, you know? He'd probably talk me into it. And if something happened and he got hurt again, I'd blame myself."

Liv turned back to rest her arms on the counter. She never

would have imagined Nate's mother being the one she opened up to. At least Nate knew how lucky he was to have her.

"Should Nate be worried about Dean Taylor?"

Liv almost laughed, because the thought seemed so absurd.

"Dean's a good friend, and I love him," she said, then shook her head gently. "But not like that. Not like Nate."

She knew what she'd said, and wouldn't look Connie in the eye. She could hear the unspoken *Have you told him* that? She could admit it, but saying it out loud, in context, to Nate...especially now, in the midst of so much uncertainty...

Connie leaned over and hugged her, Liv trying to extract all the strength and compassion she was so short of. If she were to have a mother-in-law, she could do a lot worse than Connie Miller.

The door clicked, and Nate came in, dropping car keys on a side table and kicking off running shoes.

"Hey," he said, the word casual but his posture guarded. His expression morphed into a smile for his mother before he kissed Connie lightly on the cheek.

"See, he came back in one piece," Connie said.

Nate looked sideways at Liv. "Were you worried I'd wrap the Porsche around a tree?"

"No, I think you love that car too much to risk that."

"True."

He reached past Liv and grabbed a carrot, then walked to the fridge, retrieving a bottle of beer and leaving the cap on the counter.

"I think I'll go for a walk." Connie stood abruptly, and gave Liv a motherly pat on the arm.

Both she and Nate watched her disappear out the door, the awkward silence that had become far too familiar descending. Nate took a long drink and set the bottle down on the counter. Alcohol was easy companionship when everything was disrupted. She'd been there, and, ironically, he'd been the one to tell her it never really helped.

"How's it feeling?" She inclined her head to his shoulder, grasping for conversation. As predicted, the sling was long gone.

"All right. I think collarbones and ribs ache forever, don't they? It still gives a pretty good stab if I try to move it the wrong way."

Liv couldn't help her scowl, but said nothing. She couldn't tell him what to do. He was right – she still felt an occasional twinge from the ribs she'd broken in the accident with Claire a year and a half ago.

"I'm starting PT this week," he added. "Maybe shifting gears is a good exercise."

Figuratively, as well as literally? *Don't overthink it, Liv.*

"Just take care of yourself, okay?" she said, quietly. "It would mean a lot if you were back on Chique before the end of the season."

She cursed herself for not being able to do better, say something more meaningful. He didn't comment, just looked back at the bottle – no doubt disappointed in her as well.

"I was thinking of the Canadiana for her next start." Because she was already being inadequate, she might as well settle back to default.

"Why not the Mile again? I watched the replay of the Saratoga race. First race back after such a long layoff, it's only fair she needed one."

"It's going to be tough."

"Don't duck the competition."

"If you think we're going to California if she wins, you're wrong."

His lips and eyes matched, impassive, removed, and he took

another pull on the bottle. "Whatever. Not like you need my input. I won't be back by then anyway."

She stifled a sigh, and rose. "I should go."

He whipped around the counter and caught her arm before she made it far.

"Liv."

His touch was visceral, like a bite that tore flesh. It sent the cascade of events that had obscured their connection and driven this wedge between them flashing through her mind. *What doesn't kill you makes you stronger*. And this was killing her.

"I want to fix this. But I don't know how." There was a desperation in his voice that sent a chill through her, his fingers gripping hers.

"Time, Miller. There's no magic pill. It's going to take time."

"And space." His words came out mixed with resignation, and the bite she'd felt leveled off into a whole-body ache. He continued. "I'm going to go back to Calgary with my mom. Hanging around here isn't doing my head any favours. I can do my rehab there just as easily. It's just too hard to be around here right now. But I'm not running away, I promise."

He'd always given her both time and space — but it felt like failure to be going back to that, and for him to be looking for it too. Calgary was almost as far away as California had been. But what could she say? Admitting it was excruciatingly grown-up and rational.

His hands went to her face, his lips seeking something deeper than her mouth. She closed her eyes and tried to release it, to let go of everything that had happened since that last kiss, but she'd been far too efficient at locking it all up.

It hurt to push away, but she had to leave. And the words

she needed to say, *I love you, don't leave me,* stayed stuck in her throat.

"You're going to hurt that thing if you keep pounding it like that."

Faye slipped onto the edge of the bench next to him and held out a beer.

Nate shook his head. "Got any water?"

She raised her eyebrows, then shrugged, but made no move to fulfill his request. "Have the two of you talked?"

"Not in a way that was remotely productive."

"You're such an idiot."

"Because this is completely my fault?"

"Well we know Liv is..." she paused, waving her hands around, "verbally challenged. You've got to do a bit more of the work."

"You say that like I don't know her. Like I haven't been doing that for —" He stopped himself from nailing down an exact span, because it overlapped his history with Faye.

"So no progress? At all?"

"She said she needs time. So I'm going back to Calgary with my mother tomorrow."

Will wasn't going to be happy about that, but he'd just add it to the list — it was one disaster after another right now. Will had finally booked their little band for an actual gig in a few weeks. It was just for fun, but Nate was looking forward to it. It gave him something different to focus on. The timing of his decision to leave was problematic. He'd joked about doing zoom sessions last winter, though it had never happened; maybe now was the time to test it out.

Faye was watching his hands, contrary to her earlier criticism seeming to find satisfaction in the way he was attacking the keyboard.

"Could you go do something else? I'm here to play music, not debate the sad state of my so-called relationship."

She didn't budge. "Emilie and Cory are coming tonight."

That wasn't unusual, but the comment felt like a jab, because Liv never had.

Cory was riding well at Woodbine – capitalizing on his misfortune, to be honest. The trainers loved a hot bug – at least those who weren't bothered by that hot bug being female. Roger was certainly making use of her. Dave Johnson was also all-too willing to help pick up the slack. It just got better and better. At least he could feel a little bit good about Cory, because he'd done what he could to help her out.

When they were finished, he watched Faye, Emilie, and Cory talking as the guys wrapped things up. It had been a productive session, and he'd managed to keep Liv mostly out of his mind, all the while sticking to water. Day one of pulling himself together. No more feeling sorry for himself.

"Just another two and a half weeks, and it's show time," Will said.

"I can't wait." Emilie did a little jig to imaginary music. "It's taken you guys long enough. It's going to be great."

"Not sure I can handle the pressure." Nate grinned.

"Says the guy who rides racehorses for a living," Faye scoffed lightheartedly.

Or used to.

Emilie glanced at her watch, slowing to a standstill, her face falling. "I guess we'd better go. It's getting late. Not that I have to get up early tomorrow; I have the day off."

"Why didn't you tell me, Em?" Faye said. "You should stay down here, and we'll go shopping tomorrow. Unless you've already made plans."

"Great idea, but I picked Cory up from the track."

"Nate can drive Cory back," Faye said. "Can't you Nate?"

"Sure," he said with a shrug. It wasn't as if he needed to get home in a hurry. "We'd better get going then."

Cory had gotten over her shyness around him, but she didn't say a word as they walked out to the car. He didn't question it, content to stay in his own head. He let her in the passenger side before getting behind the wheel.

"Such a nice car," she said, beaming.

He'd heard that enough times now to just smile and nod. "So how was your afternoon, anyway?"

"That two-year-old filly won for me, and I had a couple of thirds," she answered, her face lighting up all over again, then dialing back down. There was no hiding of emotions with Cory. "Ride The Wave ran huge in the Breeders'. Was that hard? I mean, you did win the Plate on him."

Her comment was innocent, but he didn't like the reminder after being happily distracted for the evening. By going to Calgary, was he opening the door for Dean? Is that what Liv needed time for? To compare and contrast horse trainer versus has-been jock?

"Sure. But I guess if there has to be someone else on him, I'd just as soon it be Liv. It's not as if she hasn't helped me through all this." Even if it wasn't on an emotional level. He glanced at the speedometer, mindful to keep the car within reasonable proximity of the limit.

All the things people had said to him about Liv came back to him. Jeanne telling him he didn't pick easy spots. Faye *saying you've got to do a bit more of the work.* Cindy's voice asking if she was worth it. He'd said she was...but he was leaving without a valid attempt to breach the void. It hurt that she'd pushed him away, but he'd deserved it, thinking a physical gesture could in any way make up for all that was wrong.

"You're so quiet," Cory said, cautiously.

"Sorry. Just tired out I guess."

"You've had such a hard year."

"It happens." He didn't want her sympathy.

"I just feel guilty, having a good year, and it's partly because of you getting hurt. After all the help you've given me. I really appreciate that."

He laughed. "Firstly, don't ever feel bad for your success. You know how it is in this business. You hang onto it while you can, because you never know when it might disappear. Case in point, right? And despite everything, it really hasn't been that terrible a year. I won the Plate – how bad can things be?"

Traffic was light this time of night, and he was glad when he reached the exit for Highway 27, downshifting as they left the 427. All her apologizing and understanding only fed his self-pity.

"You parked on the frontside?" he asked.

Cory nodded, and when he saw her little VW he pulled up beside it. There were a few cars scattered in the area – not really unusual, no matter what day of the week. People left vehicles here, came back to pick them up later, just like this – or in the morning, if they'd gone home with someone. Sometimes people were too drunk to drive and slept in their cars. You saw it all around here.

He turned off the ignition, and Cory looked surprised when he got out. He just wanted to be sure she was in her car and safely on her way before he left. Things could happen in this parking lot at night, even though it was well lit and looked deserted at the moment.

"Thanks for trying to cheer me up." He watched as she unlocked the VW's door.

"The rest of the drive is going to be a step down, though."

"At the rate you're going, you'll be able to buy your own Porsche soon enough."

"You'll be back before that happens.

"I don't know, you've worked your way up pretty good. Plus you're a lot cuter than me. I can't compete with that." He was sure she blushed, though it was hard to tell in the light.

"Thanks for the ride."

Nothing felt right about the hug she gave him, as innocent as it was. He hated the thought that crept in. *This would be a much easier spot.* He wasn't even sure Liv wanted him anymore. But the affection he felt for Cory was only like what he felt for Em: they were his adopted little sisters, nothing more.

He watched until she was in the car and had started the engine, the lights flicking on, and didn't return to the Porsche until she was driving away.

A set of headlights lit up one row over, and a dark vehicle moved slowly toward the exit. His morale went from singed to full-on charred, because he'd put money on that harmless exchange with Cory distorting into something much different by the time it hit the backstretch kitchen tomorrow morning.

CHAPTER TWENTY

HE'D FORGOTTEN how perfect the weather could be in Alberta this time of year. The heat in Calgary was dry, thanks to the altitude, a welcome change after the humidity in Toronto and Saratoga. It was the ideal climate — until something like a crazy premature snowstorm decided to arrive.

He headed for the mountains at daybreak — going further west, away from everything he'd failed to fix back east. Ironic, really, considering the drive he'd made to Ontario five years ago to escape all that had gone wrong out here. He didn't know any better now what he was going to do than he had then.

Al Wilson's farm was on the way, and when he walked from his mother's car to Al's office, he caught a speculative glance as one of the staff registered who he was. *Yeah, I don't know what I'm doing here either, buddy.*

"Look who it is." Al kicked back his chair and came around the desk to give Nate an embrace that was more fatherly than anything his real dad had ever given him. "Good to see you, kid. This is a surprise."

"Ah, well, I had some extra time on my hands."

"I heard about the spill. I'm sorry about the colt. Want a coffee?" Al stepped over to the machine on the sideboard. Nate shook his head. He remembered Al's coffee. "You look pretty good now. How's it going?"

"I feel fine. You have no idea how much I'd give to get on a horse. This being hurt...it's doing a number on me."

"You'll get it back. You're not worried about that, are you?"

"I don't know. The longer I wait it out, the more doubts I have." It didn't matter that he did his rehab exercises with obsessive dedication. There was only one thing that would make it right.

"It ain't over yet. You'll be fine."

"Letting me get on the pony or something would go a long way to helping me out." Nate tried a crooked grin, but it was rusty from disuse, like the hinges of his jaw were a little seized.

Al laughed. "And I thought you'd stopped by for a visit. Not much has changed, eh kid? Still trying to talk someone into giving you a leg up." He smirked. "You're outta luck. Not gonna happen. Your girlfriend has my phone number."

The girlfriend he hadn't communicated with since he'd left; not so much as a text from either side. He should have called her to explain about Cory, instead of letting her interpret whatever skewed version was no doubt being gleefully passed around Woodbine's backside.

Al gave him a consoling pat on the shoulder. "Don't rush it, kid. It'll just make things worse."

Advice he seemed determined not to follow. He hoped the cool, clean mountain air would clear his brain; help him backtrack and find out how things had gone so far off course. Back in May, everything had made sense up there. Not anymore.

It was dusk when he returned to the house. He punched numbers into the microwave and reheated the plate his mother had saved him from dinner, listening to the hum and watching it rotate, and wished it was that easy to reheat his relationship with Liv.

His father surfaced, opening the fridge and emerging with a bottle of beer. Reid's unchanging gaze landed on Nate.

"Want one?"

Pretty sure that was a first. "All right."

Reid uncapped both bottles and surprised Nate yet again by sitting down at the kitchen table and sliding one across.

"Thanks," he said, settling into his old chair — trying his best to look grateful rather than suspicious.

"So why the hell are you here?"

Nate nearly choked on a mouthful of casserole. "If I knew, I'm still not sure I'd tell you." He grinned, chasing the comment with a swallow of beer. "How's Tim doing, anyway? Does he have a shot?"

"Maybe not this year."

Tim had been drafted by the Calgary Flames, but that didn't guarantee he wouldn't end up relegated to the farm team in the States.

"He'll be all right," Nate said.

"I know he will." Reid leaned back, hands around his bottle. "What about you?"

This was bizarre. Had his mom put his dad up to this? Well...while he didn't want to upset his mother, he wasn't all that worried about disillusioning his father.

"Me? Naw, you were right. Ultimately, I'm just a screw-up."

"Good of you to live up to my expectations. Did you actually do something, or are you just feeling sorry for yourself?"

Nate looked at him wryly. "Well, right about now everyone back there probably thinks I indulged a nineteen-year-old's crush — and I haven't called Liv to tell her it's not true. Meanwhile, Faye's brother, and Liv's long-time friend is probably going to make a play for her, if he hasn't already, and right now he's looking a hell of a lot better on paper than me. And Will is pissed because I've bolted, and our first gig is a week away. So when I go back, I'm guessing there's going to be just a little bit of animosity to deal with."

Reid nodded and tipped his bottle. "Nicely done."

"I always knew one day I'd make you proud."

Reid laughed. "So, what are you going to do?"

Nate felt suddenly sober. "I don't know."

"If Liv loved you enough to come to Phil and Cindy's funeral, she's gonna get over a bit of gossip. But sounds like you need to get your sorry ass on a plane back to Toronto and straighten that out."

If nothing else, he could count on his father to be blunt with the truth.

Someone would recognize him, despite his attempt at disguise: sunglasses, baseball cap pulled down over his hair — which was getting kind of long — an uncharacteristic shadow on his jaw. Dressed down in faded jeans and a black jacket over his t-shirt, he fit in pretty well with the crowd, the weather cool for a September afternoon. It wasn't the Plate; few people dressed up.

Why did he care if anyone noticed him? *This was stupid.* What was stupid? Being afraid of hiding in plain sight, or being here at all?

He watched the eighth race on a monitor, then pressed his way to the already busy paddock. He didn't go right to the rail, finding a spot behind the first row of people where he could still see.

Horses began to file in, and he spotted the filly between Jo and Sue. Chique looked alert, her dark coat gleaming, pretty face set off by the bright white shadow roll. All four legs were dressed in clean white polos, and she even wore bell boots on her front feet, Liv being her overprotective self. Then the filly skirted sideways, gawking at the crowd like a green two-year-old. Better to be a little cautious than risk catching a shoe or grabbing a quarter. It was good to see Chique being her old animated self, but he felt a strong pang of longing to be on her back again.

Jo led her into the number five stall. Someone waited there — tall, dark hair, lanky frame dressed in a suit — definitely not Roger, but familiar. Where was Rog? The substitute crouched down and helped Sue remove the polos, then stood, turning to Jo, so Nate finally saw his face. Dean Taylor.

Chique had settled, her ears flickering back, then out towards the crowd again. Nate ducked as her gaze shifted in his direction — silly, really. The filly wouldn't pick him out of the crowd, but he didn't want to risk her giving him away. He wasn't sure why. Why it felt wrong to be here. Why he felt out of place.

Liv emerged from the jock's room, relaxed as she chatted amicably with Steve Gordon. The paddock judge called for outside riders, so Nate jammed his hands in his pockets and shuffled away with the flow of the crowd. He cut across the horse path and decided to skip up the steps to the balcony. This really was ridiculous. But Liv had looked so much happier than the last time he'd seen her; maybe she wouldn't be glad he'd come.

Emilie, Anne, and Claude Lachance waited in the walking ring, Liv reaching them just before Dean and Sue. Liv maneuvered next to Dean, their heads going together. They weren't talking strategy. Liv would have determined that already. A hollow opened in Nate's gut. He was an outsider when he'd once been part of that.

He waited until Dean legged her up, Liv's focus switching to gathering the lines, knotting them as she tucked her feet in the irons. She reached forward and ran a hand along Chique's sleek neck, and Nate retreated into the grandstand, taking the escalator up to the second level, keeping his head down as he weaved through the punters. He found a spot to watch away from where the owners or trainers or grooms would be.

He felt displaced, observing Chique as merely a spectator. The filly was composed beside Paz, and it hit him — it had been a year since he'd last been on her in a race. He missed her, and it scared him that it was starting to feel like he'd lost them both as Liv took Chique away from the pony to warm up.

And who was he without them? Nobody. Liv and Chique had made him who he was. He didn't belong in the one place he'd come to let define him.

He forced himself to set emotion aside and studied the filly carefully, analyzing. Each stride was fluid, confident as they galloped around the turn. Liv pulled her up and faced the infield on the backstretch, and the filly stood, statuesque, before getting the cue to head to the gap for the turf course.

He glanced at the odds board as they gathered behind the gate — she was second choice with the hometown crowd. And Liv had, ultimately, decided to go with the Mile instead of the Canadiana. He wanted to think that meant something, that his words had played a part in her decision, but he was probably kidding himself.

The field sprang out cleanly, but Chique out-broke them all, surging to the front, looking every bit the bold filly he remembered. He found he was talking to himself, carrying on the discourse he would have had on the filly's back. *Easy baby girl. There you go. We'll just sit right here.*

Maybe she'd matured, and learned to rate, but the lead was still Chique's happy place. She traveled well within herself, going easily a length up on the others. She showed the way around the big, gradual turn, the slight downhill grade carrying them all along.

They came at her in the stretch.

Chique was aware as they drew closer behind her, ears pinning, begging to be released. Mid-stretch they were fanning across the width of the turf for the final charge.

Now!

"Come on Cheeky!" he yelled, forgetting he'd been trying to be anonymous.

Chique exploded, responding fiercely to Liv's driving hands. She remained on top, hooves skimming over green, light as a deer.

"You got this, Cheeky."

He stifled a victorious whoop as Liv wrapped up on her and they coasted under the wire, triumphant. Watching them gallop out, he swelled with pride Chique had turned those horses away with determination. She was back.

That didn't change that he wasn't.

The outrider brought her to the front of the grandstand, Jo snapping the shank to the bit then reaching up to grasp Liv's hand. Victory blanket of flowers draped over Liv's knees, Jo circled them on the turf for the photographers before heading across the track to the infield winner's circle.

He watched Chique pose for the win photo — you couldn't tell him she wasn't doing exactly that — then Sue dragged off the floral blanket and handed it to Em as Liv dismounted and removed the tack. Sue threw a cooler over the filly, and she and Jo started the walk to the test barn.

He could go back, surprise Liv there. Or he could catch her after she weighed in. He started to make his way through the clamour, losing tickets littering the apron, winners still waving their slips of paper, calculating spoils in their heads.

Then he saw Dean, hovering near the gate. And when Liv crossed over the track after the presentations, there didn't seem to be any reservation as she hugged him. Dean squeezed her back. His arm remained draped over her shoulders for a few steps as they walked.

It stopped Nate, like the asphalt under his soles had reached up and made his feet part of it. Any illusion he had of talking to her and ending this mess faded away. Maybe it was true then; maybe his gut was right. Dean looked too comfortable, and Liv, the joy on her face from Chique's success – he'd always thought it was something she shared with him. But it was clear now; she didn't need him. *They* didn't need him. They were self-sufficient.

He turned away, climbing the steps to the grandstand, letting himself be swallowed and spit out on the other side. Taxis dropped off and picked up the slots addicts. He slunk into one that had just offloaded its passenger, and gave the driver the address of the farm.

Liv eased the truck and trailer to a halt outside the barn so as not to disturb her precious cargo. A glance at the camera monitor showed Chique's butt, her head up, ears swiveling. Then she let out a yell, to let everyone know she'd arrived. Claire called back.

Hopping out of the cab and jamming her phone into her back pocket, she reached for the shank behind the seat. The nice thing about the gooseneck was Chique rode in a cushy box – and Liv could unload the filly without assistance, so she hadn't needed to tell anyone on this end she was coming.

But — there was Nate. Where had he come from? He was supposed to be in Calgary.

"Is she okay?" he asked, his face showing worry but his words tinged with hostility.

Shouldn't she be the angry one? It was he who'd taken off to Calgary. Or had she chased him away? It was he who'd been caught with Cory MacDonald — even if Emilie insisted it was just another rumour spread by someone wanting to make Nate look bad. It wasn't as if he'd tried to clear it up. She didn't want to listen to Faye. *You need to*...add it to the mountain they had to talk out.

"Yes, she's fine. I just thought a few days on the farm would be good for her."

She was distracted as he helped unlatch and lower the ramp. His hair fell into his eyes, and she found she wanted to brush it back, run her hand over the unfamiliar scruff on his jaw, see if it burned her skin if she kissed him. But he stood back, hands wrapped around his elbows — a little cautious, a little defensive. She held out the length of leather and chain. An olive branch, of sorts.

He took it, silent, and walked up the ramp, removed the pins, and slipped in. Liv waited on the other side of the divider, his murmurs before the sound of chain against brass tugging at her heart.

"Okay," he called, and she opened it up.

He tied Chique in her old stall, sinking to his knees in the straw to start unwrapping the flannel from her legs. The position Liv took on the opposite side should have felt more natural than it did. She was still unsettled by this quiet, careful version of him, even if the whole rough, unkempt look that made him seem dangerous appealed to her on a primal level. It brought on thoughts of giving that whole throwing herself at him thing another go, like that's what was needed to set things right — but the memory of how he'd so effectively spurned her rushed rapidly back, drowning that fantasy.

"She ran great, eh?" he said, setting the bandage and cotton behind him and shifting to Chique's hind leg. He knotted her tail out of the way.

"She did," Liv responded softly, rising and ducking under the filly's neck. "If you can grab that last bandage, I'll get some polos and some tranq. I'm going to turn her out."

They watched the filly once she was in the small pen — Chique at first standing, surveying, sending a whinny Claire's way. Then she pawed, and collapsed in the sandy spot near the gate for a good roll. She came up exploding, like she'd just realized she was free.

"How was Calgary?" Liv asked when she was convinced Chique wasn't going to hurt herself, the filly dropping her head to nibble the sparse September grass.

He shrugged. "Quiet. My parents say hi." He propped a foot on the lower fence rail, leaning on the top one.

"I guess you had to come back to get ready for the big show next week." But not in time to come to the races yesterday.

"How long are you going to keep her here?"

"A couple of weeks maybe. She can train off the farm for a bit." It hit her that she wasn't consulting him; that she should be, that he could be back for Chique's next start. "We should —"

"Let me get on her when she's here."

Liv's mouth was still open with the words she'd hadn't got out...*talk about her next race.* She'd been on the verge of suggesting they go grab a cappuccino at Triple Shot — Faye and Will's café in town — because she had to stop putting off the long-overdue discussion, about everything. "When do you see the surgeon again?"

"A couple of weeks."

"When you get the okay from him, you can get on her."

"I'm not going to get hurt, Liv. I feel great. Please."

"It's just two more weeks, Nate. Just wait it out." She sounded more pleading than insistent.

He ran a hand over his jaw, and turned away, striding for the barn.

"Come on, Nate. You can't blame me for this. You have to think about the future. Is it really worth jeopardizing?"

He stopped abruptly, his laugh hoarse. "The future. Right."

Liv didn't recognize the reflection in the mirror, and it was more than just the short, strappy dress that skimmed her contours and matched her icy grey eyes, her long hair falling straight around her bare shoulders. It was the person wearing it, the one who found herself playing the game she'd been so sure was unnecessary with Nate. She didn't want to be that person. It disturbed her she'd sunk to that level.

"Wow." Faye strolled in and did a circle around her.

Liv crossed her arms, wrapping them around her torso. "I'm staying home."

Faye laughed. "No, you're not. Come on, we don't want to be late."

"Really, Faye. I don't think I should go."

"That's ridiculous." Faye took her hand, dragging her out of the room. "You didn't put on that dress because you want to stay home. You put on that dress because he's not going to be able to take his eyes off you."

Faye insisted on driving; it wasn't an argument Liv had any chance of winning. She probably would need alcohol to get through the evening, though Faye was an unlikely designated driver.

"As soon as it's over, we leave. Promise?"

Faye looked over at her sympathetically as she started the car. "Promise."

The club was packed by the time they got there, which didn't necessarily mean they slipped in unnoticed. Of course half the backstretch was there, watching every nuance. They'd be disappointed if they were expecting drama. She hadn't spoken with Nate since the morning she'd brought Chique to the farm, and there was no reason to do so tonight.

Faye led the way to a table — near the front but off to the side, apparently reserved for them — and, being a pro at these things, made sure the server brought them two drinks each. Faye lifted her first one towards Liv. Liv glowered in response.

They had a direct view of the stage, without having to deal with elbows and jostling up front. Of course that's exactly where Emilie and Cory were, chatting to each other excitedly. Liv felt bad for Cory, because those rumours hurt her, too.

Faye talked, and Liv tried to listen, taking a conservative swallow of the cocktail. She glanced at her watch. The sooner it started, the sooner it would be over so she could go home.

An opening act got the room warmed up with a brief set. It put Liv on edge. She wished they'd keep playing, because she'd heard Nate sing before, and it was never just a performance. There was a shuffle of equipment after the first band wrapped up; a hum running through the building that rose into whoops and whistles of anticipation. The lights fell, and the room went still.

Nate's voice came first, unaccompanied, an unfamiliar edge to it. It sent a shiver through her, and now she knew where he had put all his emotion these last weeks — all of it was channeled into that voice. It was clear and dark, the melody chilling; words that spoke a challenge, of meeting in another dimension, forgetting the world as they knew it...yet still questioning if it would ultimately make a difference. She felt Faye's eyes dart toward her. It wasn't her imagination. It was personal.

"...whatever it takes..."

That had always been Nate's stand, yet she'd accepted defeat so easily, while he'd put himself out there time and time again. No matter what Connie or Faye said, it was still her shortcoming, that she'd never been able to do that in return. It wasn't really any wonder he'd lost hope since the accident.

The music that followed was all hard edges and raw emotion; nothing like the fun of the Plate parties or the gentle coffee shop vibe of a year ago. Each note went straight to her core, leaving her ragged. If there was a game being played here tonight, she was losing badly. She would have fled, but she was supposed to behave as if she were unaffected by all this. What a joke.

It should have been a relief when the tempo slowed; kinder tunes, with Will on an acoustic guitar, Nate where he was most comfortable, at the piano. Familiar songs — ones he'd played when she was stuck on the couch in Florida after her accident. At the time she'd still been clueless that he wasn't just playing, he was playing for her.

They finished where they started, full of energy and attitude, and came back with an encore that had the whole floor bouncing, while she was drained, limp in her chair. Then finally, they were gone.

Faye sat down as the lights came back up, looking at her carefully. "I'm going to go say good-bye to Will, then we'll leave, all right? I won't be long. Wait here."

A DJ took over with recorded music, and the dancing started up — the night wasn't over. Liv needed another drink. She pushed her way to the bar, lowering her eyes in hopes no one would stop her and tell her how fabulous the show had been. Faye would find her.

"Are you okay?"

She looked up at the man who had spoken, and grimaced. "I'm fine."

He laughed. "Okay. Maybe I could buy you a drink?"

Apparently her stoniest glare wasn't enough to deter this guy. She shrugged, trusting Faye would rescue her before it became too unbearable. She ordered another cranberry and vodka and he paid before she could protest.

"I'm Kyle," he said.

He was tallish, dark hair and eyes, pleasant features, wearing a dress shirt and khakis. He probably worked in an office somewhere. Definitely not a racetracker. He might be nice enough. Too bad for him he'd decided to hit on her.

"Thank you, Kyle." She didn't offer her own name, or her hand. A drink wasn't enough to buy him that.

"All right," he said, and laughed again. "They were good, eh?"

"Yes, they were," she said, wanting to hit him for making her hear that one more time. Misdirected aggression. She didn't even know him.

"Complete fluke that I caught this. I didn't know there was anything going on, just dropped by after work to see if a buddy of mine was here. Somebody said the singer's a jockey at the track over there."

"He is. An exceptionally good one."

"You know him?"

She didn't answer right away. She had no reason to be honest with this guy, and he wouldn't know the difference. She was just some girl he was trying to pick up.

"Everyone knows him," she said.

She could tell he was sizing her up physically, though at least not in a leering sort of way. It still made her self-conscious. She knew her bare arms and shoulders were considerably more muscular than the average woman's, which threatened a lot of men for some reason, but he didn't seem put off. Or ready to give up.

"What do you do, then?"

"Back off, buddy. Can't you tell she wants to be left alone?"

She flinched. Nate. He was behind her, but she managed not to turn. She took a gulp of her drink and straightened her shoulders, trying to counter the chaos that rose inside her.

Kyle actually smiled, instead of taking offence. Is this what guys out there were like? Well, better that than a fight. Nate might very well be up for that if provoked.

She turned slowly to face him. "I'm fine, Miller. I'm just waiting for Faye, then I'm going home."

"Hey, you're the singer. You guys were awesome, man. You can play some serious piano," Kyle's voice travelled over her shoulder.

"Thanks," Nate said, flashing the guy an irritated glance. He zeroed back in on Liv. "Dance?"

"No, that's quite all right."

"Liv —"

He reached out to touch her elbow, but she twisted away.

"Hey, buddy, can't you see she wants to be left alone?" Kyle said.

No doubt he thought he was being funny, but Liv shook her head and walked into Nate, pushing him away before he did anything stupid. "Thanks again for the drink," she tossed back. *You should have just taken the hint and saved your money.*

"He bought you a drink?"

"Really, Miller?"

He didn't apologize, but dropped his shoulders and lowered his gaze. His hair was damp with sweat from the lights and the effort — mental, physical, emotional — and he still had that scruff of a beard he seemed to have mastered of late. *Rock star.*

Dressed in black, of course. And he had effectively pulled the impression off.

She fought the chemistry, annoyed enough by her interaction with the guy at the bar to easily reengage her defences. Nate's whole adrenaline-rush confidence thing was fine, but she wasn't going to let him think this would be easy, like one of his choreographed schemes.

Resisting might look like she was angry, that she cared. She let him grasp her hand and lead her to the floor, and he pulled her in amid speculative glances. Liv braced her hands against his chest, trying to retain some distance between them as both his went straight to her waist.

And what was with the song? *"Strangers in the Night?* Ironic."

"Will has a sense of humour," Nate grumbled.

She was scaldingly aware of him — of his scent and the firmness of his pectorals under her palms, the bump on his healed collarbone, his eyes as she refused to meet them. The placement of his fingers on the small of her back was deliberate, but she steeled herself against its effect on her. When he leaned in, his rough cheek brushing hers, she pushed him back.

"What do you want, Miller?"

"Funny, I thought Dean might come tonight."

"Like Dean ever comes to these things. I'm regretting coming myself."

"You two seemed pretty friendly there after the Mile."

"Well, maybe that's because we're friends. How would you know, anyway?"

"I saw, okay?"

"Saw what? What are you talking about?"

"I was there, all right? I flew back for the race, like an idiot. And when I saw the two of you, well, I figured I probably wasn't welcome."

"You were there? And you didn't let me know? What's the matter with you?"

"You never said you wanted me there."

"I didn't think you wanted to be around! You went to Calgary! What was I supposed to think? And Dean? I don't know what you think you saw, but nothing has ever happened with Dean. I talked to him about it, to make sure he knew, because I — because of you." She couldn't help the exasperation in her tone, though now she was stunned. "Is that what this is about? Because if it is, you've just lost your excuse for screwing up. And I'm not taking the abuse for being the bad guy because I won't let you get on Chique. Maybe you need to go away again and not come back this time till you've figured yourself out."

"Is that what you want?" Then his eyes changed, transitioning from anger to fear. "Tell me what to do."

The quaver in his voice weakened her, but she couldn't back down. "Whatever it takes, Miller."

She shoved him away, leaving him standing there, and pressed blindly through the lingering crowd to the door. Outside she gulped in the cool air, and searched for Faye's car. She felt an arm slip around her, and Faye's voice in her ear.

"Come on, sweetie. Let's go."

CHAPTER TWENTY-ONE

NATE STALLED OUTSIDE the Triple Stripe shed, insulated by the darkness, and breathed. His emotions were firing all over the place. He hadn't been here since that day on the way home from the hospital.

He wasn't taking anything for granted, his helmet and boots left behind in the car. Honestly, if they put him on the end of a shank and told him to turn left, he'd do it.

Because Liv might just be mad enough to keep him off Chique. If that was true, well, it probably answered the question that plagued him; the one about whether or not there was any hope for the two of them. Maybe he shouldn't even be thinking about it. Maybe he should just be alone.

Jo noticed him first, hugging him with a rare display of affection, followed by Sue. Even Michel stopped what he was doing and came over. It was all strange, and embarrassing — because he hadn't stayed away for any good reason, just his own self-pity.

"Welcome back," Roger said.

Liv hovered in the background, a quiet but undeniable presence, her face a perfect mask. When the others dispersed, she remained.

"The surgeon gave you the right answer, then?"

"He did."

"Paz is tacked up. You want to come out with me?"

He nodded, the tension around his eyes easing. He'd take it. "Absolutely."

Back at the Porsche he exchanged running shoes for his boots, and pushed on his helmet. He had to lean back on the door for a minute, trying to nail down what he was feeling. Thankfulness, maybe. Relief, definitely.

He wanted to just vault into the saddle, but he took Paz a turn and let Liv leg him up. There was something symbolic in the gesture, even if there was no sentiment in it.

"Good to have you back, Miller."

He accepted that, and didn't search for anything more. It was enough that she meant it.

Waiting outside at the end of the barn, he watched Chique approach. The filly hadn't lost that swinging, sexy, walk, her head low as Liv held her on the knot. He'd missed that little thing, feeling guilty for his absence. As Liv came up beside Paz, Nate draped his hand over Chique's neck, patting her affectionately.

"We're working seven-eighths this morning," Liv said. "Don't worry, you don't need to take me to the pole. We'll just back up to the wire, gallop once around and go. I'll let you figure out how much you want to do."

A little jog, a little gallop – that would be a good place to start. No way he wanted to rush things now that he was in the tack again, even if it was pony tack. Funny, that, when he'd been in such a hurry a couple of weeks ago. He backed up with Liv and the filly, galloped with them to the backstretch, and convinced Paz to pull up there to watch Chique breeze.

Familiar faces on horses and at the rail greeted him, were happy to see him, and he tried to acknowledge their good wishes without losing track of Chique. The filly was galloping at a good clip now along the home stretch, disappearing behind the tote board, then Nate picked her up on the clubhouse turn as Liv set her down.

Now he didn't hear anyone, absorbed as the pair swept along the rail and past him, the drum of Chique's rhythmic stride in his ears. She switched leads cleanly as she approached the turn, rounding it snugly, floating down the stretch. Flawless.

He couldn't help reaching out again when Liv turned her in next to him. Chique leaned into his touch, then tried to rub her head on Paz. "She looks great," he said quietly.

"She'll work on the turf next time. Think you'll be ready to be back on her by then?"

It choked him up, keeping him from answering right away. "It would take an awful lot to stop me."

"We're not going to California," she said.

No surprises there. The Woodbine Mile that Chique had won was still a *Win and You're In* race, and the Breeders' Cup was at Santa Anita this year.

"But she's nominated for the International," Liv continued.

A mile and a half? That's just crazy. But definitely not ducking the competition.

"I think it'll be her last race, Nate."

Their eyes met, and he wanted to ask, *what does that mean for us?* He was going to have to play that one by ear.

He insisted on walking Chique, then Rog let him go out with a few more sets on Paz. At the end of the morning he started cleaning tack. Nicole shrugged and said she'd lend the grooms a hand. Emilie sorted through the saddles, separating dirty saddle cloths and girth covers for the laundry.

"How's Cory doing?" he asked.

"She's okay. She's been around long enough now she knows people will freely spread lies." Emilie looked at him, not unkindly. "How are things with Liv?"

He frowned, and attacked a bridle. "Status quo."

The next morning Liv looked at him strangely when he said he wasn't ready to get on Chique yet. He couldn't tell her it scared him, that as soon as he was up on the filly he'd be dealing with the memory of the tragic accident in Saratoga. He needed to overcome that, and reconnect with her, not only because of the upcoming race, but as part of the grieving process; the part where the inside of him started to heal.

The days were going by too fast. Just a week, and it would be International Day, the filly's career finale. Liv didn't know whether she should cling to every moment, feel every second as it slipped through her fingers, or give in to the inevitability of it all.

Nate hadn't questioned why she'd made the decision. Maybe he didn't need to, the way this year had gone. The filly had given them so much to come back after her New Year's Eve ordeal. Just one more race, and Liv would stop asking. But the last ask, at a mile and a half, was a big one.

Liv snugged the girth one more hole as he brushed past, and she watched him put the lines over Chique's head, remove the halter, and slip on the shadow roll before offering Chique the bit. He slid the headstall gently over the filly's tiny ears, clearing her bridle path before he did up the noseband and fastened the throatlatch. Liv unsnapped the shank from the screen and handed it to him, letting him take the filly a turn.

"I'll catch up with you," she said after throwing him up, and headed to Paz's stall.

Chique stood quietly, uncharacteristically so, just outside the barn when Liv emerged on the pony. Nate hadn't breezed anyone else since his return. He said Chique had to be the first.

"You okay?" she asked.

"Yeah. Let's go."

She didn't press him further. He had every right to be quiet and moody as far as she was concerned. It was part of re-entry into this world. She couldn't do anything to make it easier.

Out on the track, there was something poignant about the scene before her, as Nate sent Chique along the turf. The melancholy bounced between them, from Nate, to Chique, and back to Liv. Feste, Nate's injury, the fracture between them, and now the approaching denouement — it was all concentrated in their midst.

Nate and Chique were symbiotic, as if they'd never been apart, sailing through the stretch and heading for the wire. It was going to be hard on both of them once the filly retired. What then? With everything that had gone on in the last two months, would there really be anything left?

He turned Chique in alongside Paz, fondly caressing the filly's crest. "She feels good, Liv," he said. "But — I don't know. There's just something...different."

Maybe it was him that was different, or maybe she had missed something. Nate knew the filly better than anyone, and his comment painted on a fresh layer of concern. "As long as she's sound," she said. "She looked happy, anyway. How about you? Everything feel okay?"

Nate nodded, but didn't offer anything more.

His five-thirty arrival on Sunday turned the grooms' heads because he was there even before Roger – though the trainer had asked Nate to work a couple that morning, He found Liv in Chique's stall, of course. It was mucked, the filly's bandages off, and Liv was running a soft brush over the dark coat, leaving it gleaming like ebony. She, on the other hand, didn't seem surprised to see him.

"Hey, Miller."

A hotwalker appeared beside Nate with a fitted cooler and shank, but Nate reached for both. "I'll walk her."

"Thanks, Nate," he said, raising an eyebrow at Liv. Liv merely smiled as she went through the filly's long tail, picking out a stray piece of straw.

"Meet me outside and I'll take that poultice off." She looked strangely amused, slipping past him as he ducked in.

It was as if they'd gone back, way back, when the thoughts running through his head relating to Liv were just unlikely romantic notions. That might not be a bad thing. Rewind to when things were simpler. Rebuild something stronger from the rubble.

Liv flaked away as much dry poultice as she could before removing the rest with warm water. Chique nibbled at Nate's jacket. He was having trouble visualizing her as a broodmare, fat and hairy. The thought of her babies romping with Claire's, though, were like little filaments of hope winding around his heart. He could convince himself he didn't care if he and Liv sorted things out, as long as they could keep working together, so he could be part of those foals' lives – and still be around Liv.

Because where would he go? If, when they finally talked, she told him to leave?

California, probably. Somewhere far enough away they wouldn't cross paths. Her pushing him to stay, after Jay's accident, had done one thing — it had ensured he'd be welcomed back if he decided to ride on the west coast again. As humbling as the whole winter had been, there were worse places to be, but it would still feel like purgatory.

She probed the left front ankle carefully, and felt both feet. She probably did it a dozen times a day. Liv stood up and reached for the towel she'd left on the railing, drying both legs meticulously before wiping her own hands.

"She okay?" he asked.

Liv nodded, looking down at the black limbs. "I've x-rayed it, but they never find anything."

"But you're worried about it."

Liv finally looked at him, with a small smile. "I worry about everything, remember Miller?"

Chique pushed into him and swung her hind end when he didn't move. "All right, all right." He placed a steadying hand on her neck, and started toward the shed.

The filly was feeling good, a bounce to her step — nothing that would suggest she was less than right — but Liv's paranoia was contagious. It was just this year, the lingering dread, unbidden voices saying *everything comes in threes.* Phil and Cindy. Feste. That was two. Chique's every move defied his fears, however. She had galloped great, worked great, and dragged him around the shed now with mocking conviction. Still, he would be more critical when he got on her the next morning.

He forced it out of his mind, and thought forward to tomorrow afternoon instead. He had a couple of mounts, his first two since getting back. Was it too soon? If Chique weren't running next weekend, would he be in such a hurry? *Right.* Now that he'd made it this far, the weeks of frustration, driving everyone around him crazy, why was he second-guessing?

The filly started to settle next to him, slowing slightly from her power walk. He needed to think about something other than racing, or Liv, or Chique, or the future, before he drove himself insane. But what else was there right now? At this rate, the next week was going to be hell.

"Hey, Nate, hang on." Roger flagged him down. "Let Marc finish her. The first set is ready to go. Get your boots on."

Roger was grinning, and it broke Nate's tension. "All right, boss."

Roger put an arm around his shoulders. "Relax. You're looking a little tight."

He sighed, and took a breath. "Sorry. What've we got going first?"

Rog filled him in on Can't Catch Me, one of three two-year-olds scheduled to breeze at six. He tugged on his boots in the tack room where he'd left them, looking up when Nicole walked in.

"'Morning, Nate." Nicole smiled. She wasn't dressed to ride. "The colt you're getting on is a half-brother to Elemental. I've been on him most mornings. You'll like him. He's almost ready to run."

"You get fired, then?" He grinned.

Nicole laughed. "Yeah, jocks only this morning I guess. I'll come out and watch."

She disappeared again. Nate put on his helmet and picked up his stick. He could guess who the other rider was. He and Liv were used to functioning with a low level of unrest, but he felt terrible Cory had inadvertently been dragged into their mess.

When he walked down to Michel's stalls, the two-year-old

he was supposed to get on was gone, so he stood in the doorway to wait.

Michel stopped the colt in front of him. "Everything seems quiet on the inner-city front."

"It's far too civilized," Nate grumbled. "I kinda wish it weren't, you know what I mean?"

"Yeah, a good fight would feel so much better, wouldn't it?"

Nate laughed as he settled into the tack and Michel led him off.

"Good luck, Miller."

Roger was coming out on Paz, and Nate carefully steered to the right of the stable pony, leaving Liv and Cory and their mounts on the other side.

"Hey Cory. How are you doing?" He wasn't about to let things be any more awkward than they already were.

Cory had a determined smile, partially obscured because Liv was between them. "Hi Nate. You must be happy to be back."

"I'm only part way back."

Liv asked Cory a question Nate didn't hear, and the two of them started talking. He tried not to think Liv was intentionally excluding him.

"All right, kids," Roger said as they went through the tunnel. "Back them up down the chute, and gallop once around. You're going five-eighths. Nate, keep your colt behind the other two; let him eat some dirt and see how he likes that. Send him at the quarter pole and see if he's going to follow in his big brother's footsteps."

Nate nodded, and followed Cory and Liv off to the left, down the chute. The colt looked nothing like Elemental – his height was comparable, but he was chestnut, and rangier than his bay brother. Nate was quiet as he held the colt, galloping, content to focus on Can't Catch Me's stride while Cory and Liv chatted sporadically to his inside.

Liv glanced at him, calling over, "He's a nice colt."

"As nice as his brother?"

"Guess we'll see."

They galloped through the stretch and around the clubhouse turn, Liv dictating the pace and letting them move a bit faster. Nate started to let her and Cory inch ahead – his colt didn't like that. As they approached the pole he dropped Can't Catch Me behind them and let them go on, keeping within a length and a half. The colt shook his head as the first clods of dirt hit him, but soon put his head down and dealt with it.

As they entered the stretch again Liv was urging her colt, inching away from Cory. Nate let his mount go after her, steering him to the outside, and in three jumps they reached her. He restrained Can't Catch Me, slightly, letting him run alongside, and felt Liv's eyes. A couple of strides and he picked his colt up again, clucked once, and did, in fact, feel like yelling out, *can't catch me!* as the chestnut went right on by and had a length on the other two at the wire.

Roger waited for them on the backstretch. "There's a race for him next weekend. You want to ride him?"

Nate smiled, stroking the colt's neck. "Yeah, sure."

He came back at the end of the morning and ducked into the office to find Roger before anyone else saw him.

"Thanks for the distraction."

"I figured you needed it. You're under a bit of pressure right now," the trainer said.

Nate shrugged. "I guess. Nice colt."

"I'm hoping he's more than nice."

It wasn't until then that it made Nate think of Feste. Promising colt, next year's Plate horse...but it wasn't the same.

"So you should have a couple of live ones this afternoon, at least." Roger brought him back to the present. "That filly I'm putting you on is as close to a sure thing as I could find for you."

"Thanks Rog." Nate perched on the couch's armrest and came back to what he hadn't been able to push out of his mind. "So what's the story? What's been going on with Chique?"

Roger leaned back in his chair, and studied him. "Nothing, Nate. Every time Jake comes and looks at her, he can't find a thing. Liv's had him do radiographs more than once. Nothing shows up. You've been on her. She looks great. And it's not like Liv's given the filly anything or done any vet work. No medication. What you see is what you get." The trainer leaned forward, his forearms resting on the desk. "I know no one wants to see Chique retired, but I've got to admit it's going to be a relief. Then the two of you can figure out what you're going to do with the rest of your lives."

Nate met the trainer's steady gaze. "Whatever that means."

All Sunday afternoon, Liv watched Nate as carefully as she was watching Chique. He didn't have a lot of mounts, easing himself into it, but started the comeback with a win on a maiden three-year-old filly from their own barn. Liv had ridden the filly to a strong second in her last start. It was probably a little obvious she'd sacrificed the mount to give him the opportunity, but if Nate was healthy — and it was apparent he was — she wanted to see him return to form as quickly as possible. She wasn't sure if it was for Chique, so that the filly would have a rider with returned confidence, or something more personal.

"You're being far too nice to Miller," Steve Gordon said to her after the race when he came back to the room — where she'd been merely an observer.

"You were gonna get beat either way, Steve, so why does it

matter who was on her? It's not like he's going to catch up with anyone in the standings at this point, is it? And I wouldn't want him to have to give up the Porsche because he can't make the payments." She smirked.

Nate endured congratulations and welcome backs before ensnaring Liv's eyes, working his way over. "You didn't have to do this, you know."

Yet she did – as if that was the only way she could communicate her feelings, by letting him ride a horse he knew full well she could have kept for herself. It wouldn't change anything, though. It wouldn't magically realign them.

Liv's quiet day-to-day demeanor was typical, merely professional – neither of them had made any attempt to initiate conversation outside of work. They would do what they always did, and wait for a more appropriate time, despite how that strategy had, in Nate's mind, proven so flawed. The letdown that was sure to follow Sunday's race was going to be difficult, so how long after that would it be before they were both ready to deal with everything they'd put off? If there was one thing he'd learned this year, it was that you had to say what you needed to say to make things right before it was too late. But he knew Liv. She didn't work that way.

As she put the tack on Chique Tuesday morning, the silence between them seemed so normal he wouldn't have thought of breaking it. He didn't leave right after the filly trained, standing to the side as Liv sloshed steaming suds over Chique from poll to tail, the sharp smell of alcohol in the rinse that followed biting his nostrils and making the filly skitter as it tingled over her sensitive skin. Liv scraped off the dripping water and ran a sponge over fine-tuned muscles and down tight legs, then dressed the filly in double coolers — one large square one, clamped high at the throatlatch; a second fitted one over top to help wick away the dampness as she dried.

"I'm having Jake do x-rays again this morning." Liv fiddled with the scraper once Marc had led Chique off.

Fanatic.

"Just a precaution," she said, like she had to justify it.

He shrugged. "I'll stick around."

When the vet came, Nate stood behind Liv and Jake as Jo jogged Chique down towards the middle of the barn, then back again. Nothing but an energetic head-shake from the filly. Chique stood patiently while the vet lifted and flexed both ankles, then radiographed the joints from multiple angles.

"Nothing," Jake said, flipping through the images. "Still clean. I don't know why you're not racing her next season. I think it's more for your health than hers."

Nate suppressed a snort.

Jake started packing up the laptop. "If something changes before entry day, let me know."

Liv gathered the filly's bandages, and Nate plucked a cotton and flannel from her arms and followed her into the stall.

"Listen, Liv, if your gut's telling you something, don't run her. It wouldn't be so bad, going out on that Mile win. So I don't get to ride her again. I'll survive."

Liv rubbed brace into Chique's leg, her face set. "You heard Jake. There's nothing wrong with her. How can I not run her? She's got a lot of fans. It's a big day. We can't let them down."

"What are you talking about? Your only responsibility is to this filly. Forget about the rest of them and do what you think is right. I never thought you'd ever let yourself be influenced by that stuff."

"I have nothing concrete to go on. I don't know if I can trust my gut right now, after everything." Her fingers wound the cotton against the leg, then fumbled with the flannel wrap. "If I don't run her, it's because deep down all I can think about is Feste, and you, and whether the universe has it out for me enough to have another go."

"So don't put me on her then, if that's what your warped superstition is telling you. You ride her, if I'm some kind of curse." He'd known it — known it all along. "If something goes wrong, that's what you'll be thinking. I'm doomed to forever be tied to losing Feste, aren't I?"

Liv looked down, her eyes riveted to the bandage as she secured it. "I don't know."

He laughed, bitterly. It wasn't the unwavering denial he'd been hoping for. "I don't want to be carrying that on my shoulders going to the gate on Saturday."

"Are you saying you don't want to ride her?"

"That's not what I said."

"That's sure what it sounded like."

"Liv —"

"Just make up your mind by tomorrow." She rose abruptly, going to the filly's head, waiting while he left the stall to slip off Chique's halter.

He told himself the stress was getting to her — to both of them. He might be back, but he'd failed to resume his role as the reassuring one.

Entry day.

Liv finished putting on the bridle and looked to the door, and Nate was there. She'd been worried he might not show up. Thankfully his loyalty to the filly was greater than the canyon between them.

He dropped the stall guard, but Liv stopped the filly in the doorway.

"If you feel anything...suspect anything...I won't enter. I want you on her. I want the two of you together again." She faltered. It wasn't the time to get into anything more.

They had a little following going out to the track, Liv escorting on Paz — Roger, Jo, Nicole, and anyone else who was free, coming to watch. Chique strode like a queen, alert but behaving, like it was only to be expected she would have an entourage.

"Let her gallop along a bit when you hit the quarter pole for about three-eighths," Liv said, staying alongside but not holding the filly as they backed up. Nate just nodded, his gaze fixed between the filly's ears.

The sadness she felt was everywhere, an atmosphere like the droplets of rain that created a mist around them. Chique rolled through the lane and around the turn and continued to gallop out strongly into the backstretch.

Liv searched Nate's face when he pulled up after a mile and a half, jogging over to Paz, turning in. How many times had they stood on this track like this?

"She still feels great, Liv. How does that ankle look?"

"Fine. Even my imagination isn't seeing anything. So...am I giving you the call?" Liv looked at him, begging him not to say no.

"Yes. Please."

Then he said what he'd said to her before, what he'd done every time he'd ridden the filly.

"I'll take care of her, Liv."

There was nothing fun about Wednesday nights. He won the featured allowance on a longshot that let him feel better about his abilities than those walks-in-the-park Roger had given him on the weekend. It lifted his spirits, at least temporarily.

"Want to pick up one in the last, Miller?"

"Sure, I guess. As long as it's not too crazy." Once upon a time, crazy had been his thing.

The four-year-old gelding in question, while not picked to win, had a decent chance. Maybe he could add another victory to the comeback.

Keep In Touch was the horse's name, and Nate assessed him as an honest sort as he put the gelding through his paces in the warm-up. Lower-level claimers weren't anything to get excited about, but the horse felt good, like it was possible he could outrun his odds.

After a clean break, the gelding rated kindly for him, Nate tucking him behind the leaders. On the turn the rail opened up, and he asked Keep In Touch to go. The gelding responded, though nothing like the horses Nate had been on of late. That moment of comparison cost him, as the horse in front of him faltered and lugged in. He checked the gelding hard, but Keep In Touch stumbled, and Nate was gone. He ducked, hitting the dirt with an *oomph*, then tried to tumble out of the way. Hooves whizzed by, and he gulped for breath, his heart pounding against his chest like the safety vest was the only thing containing it. Keep In Touch hadn't gone down, and Nate hoped he was all right.

He rolled onto his back, inhaling deeply, assessing. Everything seemed okay — toes and fingers worked, neck was sore, but moved, no sharp pains anywhere — so he sat up, slowly. The ambulance pulled up and the attendants rushed to his side, helping him off with his helmet, asking him questions. He assured them he was all right, but let them help him up, and he was far enough away, he figured he might as well get a ride back.

In the room he ignored all the questions about his own well-being until he had an answer about Keep In Touch.

"He picked himself up and galloped home ahead of the rest of us, Miller. Too bad you couldn't stay on."

Nate laughed, took the ribbing, and parked himself in front of his locker. Sure he was a little shaken — but he had walked away. Getting that behind him might be the most important step in his recovery to date.

"You're all right?"

He looked up, and Liv was standing there. Trust Liv — on the one hand so modest, but on the other, completely unself-conscious as she walked into this room of men in various stages of undress. She liked to show up when he came off horses, apparently. This time was a little less dramatic than when she'd pulled the same stunt. Keeneland, after the Bluegrass, when she'd hauled him off Ricky Acosta for the foul that had sent him and Wampum crashing to the dirt. The turn-on of it had been enough to distract him from his ire. But he liked his non-existent chances with her right now as much as he had then, and was too afraid to mess up this precarious state they were in by trying anything.

"Just ate some dirt, that's all."

"Good." Her face softened a little.

"What are you doing here?" he questioned, careful to keep his tone casual.

She wasn't riding tonight, and it was rare for her to come to the races just because. She tugged at the hem of a smart black jacket she'd layered over a white blouse, open at the neck so he could see the pendant Geai had given her. Dark blue skinny jeans hugged the hard muscles of her thighs, her sleek hair down. He wanted to run his hands through it, be done with this strangeness.

She didn't answer him. "Chique's going to walk tomorrow. I'll see you Friday at six to gallop her?"

If it hadn't been so late, he would have asked her to...have a drink with him? That was so not Liv. But the yearning was almost unbearable, to be with her. They didn't have to talk about anything, just sit there...and be.

"I'll be there," he said.

CHAPTER TWENTY-TWO

She woke drenched in sweat, sheets twisted around her legs, her pulse throbbing in her ears. Horrible, empty dreams faded with the sleep that had brought them. Forcing herself to the edge of the bed, she propped herself up. *Bad move.* A wave of nausea sent her staggering down the hallway to the bathroom, bile welling in her throat.

A cold dew coated her skin as she pushed herself back to rest against the wall. When she mustered the energy to climb to her feet, she stared at her bloodless face in the mirror. She must've eaten something funky a couple of days ago — back when she'd been able to eat anything. It couldn't be stress, *noooo.*

The fear from her nightmare crept back. It had just been a dream. But what if he did leave? What reason had she given him to stay after Chique was retired? She stripped off her nightshirt, climbing under the scorching shower stream to let it wash away the clamminess, willing the water to restore her equilibrium.

It did, a bit. It was four AM according to her phone. Close enough. She dressed and headed out.

It was like *déjà vu* walking into the office barn. Like Plate Day. She'd take that as a good omen, except the apartment overhead stayed dark. Nate didn't magically appear to appease her fears. What would Geai be saying to her now? He just regarded her silently from the painting behind the desk with that timeless smile. She fed Claire and her companions, and left a note in the feed room that it was done.

At the track, Chique stood at the front of the stall, surveying the activity on the shed, and locked in on Liv as she became part of it. The filly reached out, nose butting Liv's arm when she took down the empty haynet. Chique followed her to the corner as she unclipped the feed tub, like maybe this time Liv would give her a second breakfast. It raised a lump in Liv's throat. She unsnapped the water bucket with her other hand and slipped out, gulping it back down.

"Are you okay, Liv? You look like hell." Jo eyed her critically.

"I think I must've had a bit of food poisoning. I feel a lot better now than I did an hour ago."

Jo didn't look any more convinced than Liv had been herself. "You and Nate should just book after this, go on a vacation. God knows you both need it."

What a nice fantasy, she and Nate on a beach somewhere far away, like in his song that night. She closed her eyes for a moment, pictured a Caribbean ocean that matched his eyes, the sun warm on her face, and tried to cling to the vision.

"Liv?" Jo's voice, hesitant with worry, jarred her back to the reality of the cold October pre-dawn.

"I'm fine." She ducked the concerned stare and grabbed her straw fork, returning to the stall where she began carefully wielding it around Chique's flannel-wrapped legs.

Michel scooped up the filled muck sack before she could even protest, and Jo reappeared. "Once you're done in there, grab your helmet. I've got one that can go to the field. I'm thinking it's best not to leave you idle for too long today."

She nodded, kneeling to remove Chique's bandages. After she'd shaken them out and left them on the rail, she went back to the filly's side, and performed the daily ritual: examining every millimeter of those precious legs with hyper-sensitive fingertips, then placing a hand on each foot and blowing out a breath when all four were cool to her touch. Chique rolled an eye at her, just like everyone else had been doing each time her obsessiveness surfaced. Liv turned her loose.

It was an easy morning. Too easy. She wished she'd been run off her feet, left with no time to filter the flashes of her dreams and the intermittent pangs reminding her of the significance of this day. Emilie helped get the walkers out, then the gallopers, so they were done far too early. Chique was the only one left.

The filly displayed her usual exuberance, Liv smiling for the first time that morning. It was transient, of course, anxiety slithering back as Chique kicked out, nailing a bucket hung on the rail, the resulting splash and rattle sending her scooting forward with Liv skittering to keep control. It soon morphed back into sadness. This was the filly's last full day in the barn; the last time she'd get to try to tear it down.

She jogged Chique for the commission vet, Nate behind him when Liv turned her to jog back, appraising silently in the doorway at the end of the barn. He watched as closely as the official. Liv barely registered the vet thanking her and wishing her luck, her eyes tangling with Nate's before she walked Chique to her stall.

"All good?" he asked when she emerged. Chique pushed her head out, and he absently let her lip his hands.

Liv was close enough to see lines and hollows and shadows on his face she was certain hadn't been there before, and wanted to say *no, no it's not. Will it be?* But she answered, "Yes."

"I guess I'll see you in the paddock, then."

"Nate –"

He stopped mid-stride, uncertainty weighing down his features.

"Are we going to be all right?"

The question seemed to smudge away a few of the creases and etch in new ones, like a secret thought had tried to erase the gloom. His lips didn't quite lift, and there was a painful hesitation before he responded. "Yeah, Liv. I hope so."

It was an oat-sized promise, one she chose to curl into her palm and cradle to her chest.

Killing time in the kitchen, she abstractedly watched the undercard. Jo had chased her out of the barn because her anxiety was getting to everyone on the shed, equine and human. She felt the sideways glances, but other than acknowledging the odd *good luck today,* she ignored them, isolating herself in a corner.

A travel mug blocked her view for a moment, and she looked up as Faye set it down and nestled into the chair across from her. Faye was dressed for the races, reminding Liv she still had to somehow make herself presentable for the paddock.

"I did not slip a sedative in there. I was extremely tempted." Faye's mouth curled into a smile.

Liv eyed the mug doubtfully, but the scent of warm, frothy milk and espresso seemed worth testing her stomach's recovery. "Thank you." She sipped, and raised her eyes to Faye as the flavour of Bailey's hit the top of her mouth.

"I figured you needed something, though I decided pastry would've been wasted on you today."

"Sadly, yes."

Faye didn't try to start real conversation, instead joining Liv's silence. She let her mind drift, distracting herself by conjuring up the science behind the age-old wisdom of hot milk, embracing the anxiolytic effect of casein. Activating the analytic side of her brain seemed to settle it as much as the hot drink. It was a temporary vacation from her swirling emotions.

Outside it was drizzling now. The turf was listed as soft, but that wouldn't bother Chique. Nate won the Nearctic with Elemental — another one Liv should have been riding.

"Shouldn't you be getting ready?" Faye said. "You obviously decided against going home to shower."

Liv glanced down at her muddy jeans and smeared down vest, and ran a hand over her flat hair. "Yeah. Helmet head it is."

"Your hair is so straight, it'll be fine. Do you need help, or are you okay?"

Liv sighed, and drained the last of her cappuccino. It was a legitimate offer today. She pushed the empty mug towards Faye. "I'm okay. Thank you again for that. And for this." She met Faye's eyes with a small gesture of her hand.

"I'll see you on the front side. You're going to be all right."

Nate's words trickled into her head. *I hope so.*

She changed in the office. Faye was right — when she brushed out her hair and pulled it into a tight ponytail, it looked okay. The International didn't require the same finery as the Plate, so she'd get by with a pantsuit and her black trench coat. It was basically the same outfit she'd worn for Chique's Breeders' Stakes last year — which was fine, because this was Chique's rematch with Wampum, and today she'd have her revenge.

Jo had wisely left everything to her. Liv ritualistically set out four white Vetraps and cut four rundown patches exactly the length of the radius. Four, because she was taking every precaution today. Chique was waiting for her, standing quietly in the doorway, senses in tune to every vibe. Liv tied her where she stood, and started on the task that was second nature. The neat white polos she wrapped over them would keep the rundowns clean for the walk to the saddling enclosure.

When the call came, Liv dressed Chique in a quarter sheet and surcingle, and Jo put the bridle on. Liv watched Jo buckled the halter over it and lace the shank through its brass rings.

"You walking over with us?" Jo asked, Michel ready to escort on the off side.

Liv gave her a look. *You had to ask?* She nodded. "Let's go."

Clusters of bodies gathered under the willows, more of them crowding the rail from the outside, trying to catch glimpses of the International field circling amid the connections. Liv homed in on her family, Faye and Dean and Will on the edges of her vision. She only glanced at Wampum. It didn't matter how good he looked. Chique was the right balance of composure and fire, sliding muscles and dense bone.

"She looks great, Liv," her father said solemnly, and her mother, next to Emilie, smiled. None of it could dissipate her tension as the minutes closed in on her.

She sensed Nate at her side, not needing to look his way to know he was there. No smiles, no joking, no singing, just eyes that shared her focus and heartbeat, at least in this moment. After months of division, Chique was the one thing that could bring them together.

"Riders up!"

Each step toward the filly was measured, one closer to the end of Chique's career. Liv wrapped her hand around Nate's boot and lifted him into the tack, walking alongside for two strides before she was able to let go. Did all good things have to end? She let that thought go with him, because right now none of it was in her control.

"*Bonne chance,* Miller. Come home safe." He might not have heard it, because it seemed to get caught somewhere in her throat.

In the box, she perched on the edge of her seat, pressing her binoculars to her eyes — dissecting each step as Chique completed her last post parade and broke away from Paz to warm up, just her and Nate. The gate waited on the wide green band of the E.P. Taylor turf, directly in front of the grandstand. When the time came, Chique went in, all business. One last dance.

Chique went straight to the lead. Now that Liv had ridden the filly herself, she felt every stride as the energy coursed through those limbs, to the turf and back again. Chique settled perfectly for Nate. No one else would realize it, but Liv did, especially now. The bond between those two was unmatched. And this was the last time she would witness it.

The rest of the field bunched a length and a half behind as they negotiated the irregular clubhouse turn, then straightened into the backstretch. Nate controlled the pace expertly, Chique content as long as she was showing the way. Liv glanced at the clock — perfect, equal quarters that obviously had the trailers spellbound, because no one was challenging. She let out a breath, inhaled again, and kept the binoculars glued as Chique entered the final turn, maintaining her length and a half advantage.

Wampum was stalking as Chique led the way into the long stretch, but there were no funny games for the colt to benefit from this time. When Nate let her out a notch, Chique propelled ahead to keep her advantage. The Europeans gathered like a storm cloud, but Chique started to draw away, quickening with a certainty that left Liv filled with pride and awe that overshadowed the heartache. The sorrow would return — tomorrow, when reality resurfaced — but this was a time to honour the bravery of their gutsy little champion. The crowd surged around her, cheering the sentimental favourite home.

Five lengths, then six. Nate glanced back uncharacteristically, as if he couldn't believe no one was challenging them. He wrapped up on the filly, and Chique's ears flickered forward to the wire as she coasted through.

Did Emilie and her parents follow her as she rushed from the box, down the stairs, to the turf? She didn't know; her focus was only for Chique and Nate as they galloped out. The outrider picked them up, and Liv stood rooted as they approached, wanting to hold onto this, wishing she had one of the powerful cameras the photographers fired behind her so she could freeze time, blow it up and hang it on her wall. Jo pushed her forward.

She took cautious steps toward them, like the turf would turn to glass under her feet and shatter the moment, robbing her of this. She took the shank from the outrider, registering his words of congratulations, maybe not quite able to acknowledge them, then kissed Chique between her billowing nostrils, the heat of the filly's breath warm on her cheeks. She couldn't look at Nate. Not now. Not yet.

Woodbine had revived the Canadian flag design for the blanket of flowers being draped over Nate's knees, halfway up Chique's neck because she was so tiny. Maybe the sponsor's name still dominated, but all Liv saw was the red and white against Chique's inky coat. Their little Canadian star. The Queen, relinquishing her crown. To whom?

There was the full sister, a scruffy weanling, like Chique had been four years ago.

There was Claire's unborn foal, with three months left in utero.

Both were so very far away from filling the deficit Chique would leave. As if she felt his eyes penetrating her skull, Liv glanced over her shoulder, up at Nate. Just a quick flick of her head, but enough to exchange a question. Could a human bridge that gap? Was there something left?

Their smiles for the win photo in the infield enclosure were sombre. Chique posed, of course. She would bask whole-heartedly in the glory. It was all hers. What were they, without her?

Liv hovered when Nate dismounted and pulled off the tack. She wanted to wrap herself around both him and the filly. He was safe. Chique was safe. Another exchanged glance, but he headed for the scales, following the rules to the letter while Michel threw a cooler over the filly, then joined Jo as she led Chique away. Liv almost went too — she wanted nothing more than to bypass the formalities to follow her heart.

Or half her heart. Nate appeared at her side, and she offered him a slight smile, a brief interruption to her fixation on Chique. He slipped an arm around her shoulders, ignoring those who tried to rush them away for the presentation. Liv leaned into him, aware their heads touched as they observed Chique's departure like a ritual. She didn't let herself hope it meant anything other than the respect they shared for that filly.

The rest of it made her numb. The words, the trophies, the questions from the reporters. Nate was further away now, separated from her. *All good things must come to an end.* The phrase haunted her.

She was always better than he was at dodging the questions, checking on the filly a valid excuse to escape, but before she disappeared — remembering she'd walked over, and would be happy to walk back, have that time to herself — she captured his eyes, dragging them from the microphone stuffed in his face, and mouthed, *see you back at the barn?*

A question; a plea. Of course he'd come for Chique. Would he come for her?

He nodded, his expression giving nothing away.

The sky was grey, the wind whipping up the tumultuous clouds rather than dispersing them. Everyone wore dark clothing and spoke in hushed tones, nibbling at their food and sipping their drinks. It felt like a funeral, though this time, no one had died. Requiem for a year, maybe. It had been a year.

But this should be a celebration. Sad could wait for tomorrow. At least for the sake of Chique, if nothing else.

He'd taken his time getting back. To rush would have felt as if he was trying to hurry it away. Now he stood next to the Porsche — which suddenly seemed indulgent, somehow offensive — and surveyed the subdued gathering. Chique was back from the test barn, tearing at the sparse grass on the lawn. She, at least, was free of the weightiness that hounded the humans.

He almost climbed back into the car. But he ducked in the end of the shed, avoiding the poor excuse for a party on the lawn. There were things that needed to be said before he turned that around.

Liv sat on the foot locker in front of Chique's stall, huddled in her black coat, like she was hiding from all of it. But there was no more hiding for her, no more running for him. Time to lay it on the line, once and for all. Time for them, apart from Chique, and this life.

She lifted her head, and he wondered if he had the same look of trepidation. It needed to be banished. She slid over, and he sat next to her, hip to hip, thigh to thigh. It wasn't enough. He reached for her arm, pulled it from the depths of her pocket, and closed his hand around hers.

"So, here we are," he said. "Can we talk?"

Only her fingers moved, cold within his, clenching and releasing. She didn't speak, her chin just dipped a little lower, a faint nod.

"I'm sorry for everything. I've been an ass," he started quietly. "I can't bring back Feste. But I should have done better, helped you through that, instead of feeling sorry for myself."

She shook her head, and cut him off before he could go on. "I didn't know what to do after the accident. You were so — different — and I didn't adapt. I was convinced you didn't want me around, especially because of that night."

He blew out a breath, resting his head against the rail. "I wish we could roll everything back to that night, so I could at least fix that. I overreacted. With everything that happened, I never got to explain."

"I made a fool of myself."

"Oh, no, no way. Is that what you think? You think I wanted to stop? I've just messed up enough times now to know there's no point if it's not right."

She inhaled, her palm warm against his now, but still restless. "Either way, I came up short. I couldn't blame you if you left. I'm grateful you stayed for today, and took care of her out there. But now — I understand if that's it, if it is over. Even if I don't really know what I'm going to do, without the two of you."

"Whoa — easy there." He chuckled, because he sounded like he was settling a fractious horse. "I didn't want you to stay away. You helped the best way you knew how. My head was messed up. I kept thinking, what if I couldn't ride? Why would you want me? I didn't realize how much I'd tied my whole identity to that. It was probably stupid, keeping that to myself, when you of all people would get it."

"But me, of all people, should have got it. I should have realized you'd be struggling with that."

"We were both just coping. And you were doing a way better job of it than me."

"No," she said. "I haven't been coping at all."

"I'm not going anywhere, Liv."

"I love you."

It came out breathless and precarious, like she'd tossed her heart into a chasm, where she might never see it again. Her expression was so intense, finally finding his eyes. And he started to laugh.

"What the hell, Miller?" she said, and almost pushed him off of the seat.

He wrapped himself around her, clutching her hard, his chest still rumbling. "I didn't ever think I was going to hear those words from you. Was it that hard?"

"Yes. Feeling it and saying it are such completely different things. It was terrifying." She clung to him, her pulse coming as hard as her respiration.

"That's all right. You scare the hell out of me."

He eased her back, his hands reaching to her face, holding it steady. He had to do it, dare the grand gesture, even when it might be the wrong call, might backfire on him. "So marry me."

She stared at him. Well, he'd said it. Might as well dig the ditch deeper.

"I'm serious. I love you more than you will ever know. We are not yet the good thing we can be. I can get down on one knee. I'll go ask your dad. Whatever you want. Trade in the Porsche for a house." He was grinning now, though his eyes hadn't lost their conviction. "I promise to love, honour and obey. Till death do us part. Forever and ever. Amen."

He could feel her shaking, and almost whacked her on the back as if she'd been drowning, because he was pretty sure she hadn't taken a breath. Forever was a hard thing to sell to Liv – not to mention the rest of it. She tried to pull back, no doubt to buy time, but he wouldn't let her go.

"All you have to say is yes," he nudged.

But what if she didn't?

"You can't just not answer," he insisted. "And don't tell me you need to think about it. You had a heads up."

She'd had three months – that night in Saratoga – but since the accident, everything had been wrong.

"You're crazy," she stammered. "I'm fickle and unstable."

"We're the perfect couple," he quipped, but he sobered. "Will you? Marry me?"

"Yes, damn it." she answered quietly, and her voice didn't falter, the tiniest of smiles gracing her lips.

He kissed her. It was a kiss that dressed wounds and faded scars, regenerating damaged cells like some miracle of biology; making promises that would never be broken, rewriting a future that only moments ago had seemed impossible.

"I'm not taking the blame for this," she murmured when they came up for air.

"I'm okay with that."

"Is it all right if we keep it to ourselves for a while?"

His eyebrow popped up and he leaned away, appraising her face. "So you have time to back out?"

"No. Everything between us has always seemed so public. It would just be nice if, for a little while anyway, there was something that was just between us."

He laughed. "All right. So, Las Vegas, then?"

She smirked. "Don't joke – that would suit me just fine."

"It's tempting. I'd get you on plane tomorrow, just so you don't bolt on me."

"I'm not going to bolt."

"Promise?"

"Promise."

Nate straightened when Marc brought Chique onto the shed, but Liv didn't move from his arms, even though Marc gave a start when he caught sight of them. Because when, ever, had the two of them been that entwined in this barn? Well...not since after the Plate. Not to mention that it was no secret they'd been at odds for a while.

"Thanks Marc," Liv said with a wan smile as the hotwalker hung the haynet. Another first, one of them not jumping up to do it. "Tell Jo we'll do her up?"

In other words, leave us alone.

"Sure thing." Marc nodded, the wag of his brows accompanied by an understanding grin.

Even Chique eyeballed them as she tossed her haynet, rolling it over her head before attacking it. Okay, Chique was always eyeballing them for one reason or another. She could wait a little longer. Even though this was a stupid uncomfortable spot to be sitting, he was afraid to break the spell.

"Would you have left?" she asked.

He just laughed again. "You couldn't get rid of me that easily. It would probably take an eviction notice. Maybe a restraining order. Besides, you know Chique's babies are going to be nightmares, and I'm the only one crazy enough to want to deal with that."

"True. You'd better stay."

"You probably have a stallion picked out for her already, don't you?"

Liv's smile was smug. "Maybe."

"So is it okay if I keep the Porsche?"

"Yeah. I kind of like the Porsche."

He dislodged himself reluctantly, lifting Liv to her feet, unable to stand Chique's scrutiny any longer. "Let's get her done up so she can have her dinner. Then we break out the champagne, and light a fire outside," — figuratively, of course — "to shake up the wake on the lawn."

He paused to brush back the strands of hair that had fallen into her face, and tucked them behind her ear. "We've put ourselves through such hell, maybe the rest of our lives will be easy."

"Happily ever after?"

"Absolutely."

Her smile was everything; love, and faith, and hope. "Count me in."

THE END

COMING SOON

I hope you enjoyed *All Good Things!* Reviews on your favourite retailer and GoodReads are always appreciated. They feed authors, which lets us keep writing more books for you. It doesn't have to be long — pick some stars and write a few words. Your input matters!

If you'd like to keep in touch, sign up for my newsletter at lindashantz.com/writes for sample chapters, updates, and more. Make sure you look for your confirmation email to be added. You can also follow me on BookBub. Or email me anytime at linda@lindashantz.com I'd love to hear from you. Thank you so much for taking this ride with me!

Book Four of the ***Good Things Come*** series is in the works. Keep reading for the first chapter:

This Good Thing - Chapter One

The backstretch had a rhythm—to the days, and the seasons—but this morning it was missing a beat, the arrhythmia unsettling. The treatment was obvious, but she wasn't ready for it.

Not yet. She wanted to hold onto this feeling. Celebrate the good, weep for the bad. But there could be no resting on of laurels, no holding onto sorrow, or she'd be left behind. She'd learned that the hard way. She wouldn't let it happen again.

Eyes drifting over the four stalls, she tried to muster something resembling excitement. Before her was the future. Possibility. Fresh faces pushed over the yokes of stall screens; ears wired forward and nostrils flared, funneling information from the unfamiliar sights and smells bouncing into their orbit. *Hope springs eternal in the heart of an unraced Thoroughbred.* She would feel it again. She had to, didn't she?

"Aren't they cute? They're like newly drafted juniors at training camp, vying to make it in the big time."

"How'd that one get the scar? That's nasty."

"You're rubbing that one, Mike."

"And you're getting on him, Miller!"

Liv remained silent, a careful smile on her lips at Nate and Michel's banter.

"This is what my career has come to. A barn full of two-year-olds."

She almost laughed at Roger's jaded comment because she didn't feel much different. *Auditions open. Searching for the next big horse. We're not sure what we're looking for, other than raw talent. A brain would only be a bonus. We've proven we can deal with crazy.*

The trainer's statement wasn't exactly true. There were still some older horses, but they were all reaching crossroads in their careers—the kind where decisions had to be made because they were not as competitive as they once had been, and it might be time for them to find new jobs. None of them were going to step up to be the new star. Hopefully one of these green-as-grass two-year-olds would fill that role. Maybe not. What then?

There were no empty stalls on the shedrow, though there was still a hole where Feste should have been, even if another prospect now occupied the physical space. And that filly in the stall next to the office? The stall that had once been Claire's, and most recently, Chique's? That stall was traditionally a place of honour in the barn, those two taking turns holding court there over the past four years. The quiet chestnut meeting Liv's gaze didn't care about any of that.

The filly was as opposite to Chique as a young Thoroughbred could be. Aside from appearance—Chique's inky dark bay with merely a spray of white hairs on her forehead, compared to this bright orange chestnut with generous frosting—Chique was quirky, cheeky, with a crazy-wild forelock and rude tapping foot. Every annoying bit of her was worth it because of her precarious talent. *When she was good, she was very very good. When she was bad....*she was that girl. But Chique was retired now, as of two days ago. Liv accepted that. It had been her decision. In a few years, it would be Chique's foal in that stall.

Twenty-four hours ago, the chestnut—She Sings, officially—had still been in light training with daily turnout on the Triple Stripe farm. The filly gave off a tranquil energy and was hunter-fat. She would likely spend a few weeks here, then go back to the farm for the winter to grow up a little more, waiting to be re-assessed in the spring. There was no rush here, as much as Liv felt the simmering pressure to find something, anything, to fill the vacancy left by Chique's departure.

How long does it take to get a horse to the races? As long as it takes.

"All right, let's get some tack on these brumbies," Roger said with a subtle shake of his head. "Is Emilie coming?"

Emilie, Liv's younger sister by four years, skittered in the end of the barn, helmet dangling from her fingers. She stopped short when she realized her abrupt entrance had startled the sleepy-eyed filly. "I'm here. I'm not missing this for the world. Reba is mine."

"Reba?" Nate raised an eyebrow. "You named a horse after a country singer? More importantly, you have insider information?"

"Just enough to know who to avoid." She grinned, her eyes flitting to the colt with the scar on his face.

"That's hardly fair. If I break my neck coming off Pacino, won't you feel bad? I just got back from an injury."

It had taken Nate all of two minutes to assign the gargantuan colt with a moniker, despite *Solaire* being boldly engraved on his halter plate.

"I have less than a year left in my program." Emilie held her helmet between her knees while she slipped a kerchief over her shoulder-length, dark hair. "I need to finish. I want to offer physiotherapy, not require it. I will help you for free, however, because you're practically family. Deal?"

Nate caught Liv's eye, his grin barely suppressed. *Practically.*

He didn't have to be here. He was done for the morning, and should be on his way home like any other top jock who had spent the last three hours breezing horses for various trainers—even if being sidelined after a dangerous spill had knocked him out of his customary leading rider position at Toronto's Woodbine Racetrack. Yet he was here. With her. Because of her. Ready to help initiate the next generation of hopefuls. Ready to hop on the horse the crew had deemed "most likely to earn us a case of beer"—that being the traditional price one paid for parting company with one's mount on the backstretch.

"Do we have enough saddles for four?" Nate asked, following the assistant trainer, Jo St-Laurent. Her response was a short nod as she headed for the tack room.

"It just means you get the one with the broken tree, Miller." Michel elbowed him.

"There are no saddles with broken trees," Jo grumbled.

"You need a vacation, Jo," Nate said.

"Or a sense of humour," Michel quipped.

"A vacation would help me find it!" Jo snarled.

As Jo stacked the riders' arms with saddles and pads and girths, it felt a little like the first day of summer camp, except kids at camp usually chose their mounts by appearance. Once you'd been around the block, you learned to make your choice from body language and conformation. Especially in a barn full of prospective racehorses, because though coloured Thoroughbreds were a thing, they were not a thing in this barn. Much of what these prospects had been bred for was unseen, waiting to be developed, something much deeper than an unusual coat colour. Things were boring in that department around here. Bay, dark bay, chestnut. Not even a token grey to brighten things up.

Nate started toward the scar-faced colt. If Nate hadn't been here, Liv wouldn't have balked at getting on him. She and Cory MacDonald had started this group as yearlings a year ago, and though not as humongous back then, the colt had been an agreeable sort.

Cory MacDonald was on a trajectory right now that would see her end the race meet as the country's leading apprentice jockey. Liv had never achieved that top-bug status. Once she'd gotten over the injury and demons that had interrupted her potential, she'd quietly transitioned to journeyman—woman? She was considered a good rider. She was respected by her peers. But she was nothing more than that. Wasn't that all that she'd asked for, though?

If she based her self-worth on a compilation of all the things she'd done in her life so far, she'd feel extremely inadequate.

Three-quarters of a veterinary degree. Two-thirds of a Canadian Triple Crown. She was prouder of the latter than the former. But perhaps now was the time to recommit herself to being a rider, with no training side gig. What else was she going to do with herself?

As she prepared the compact bay gelding between Nicole's assignment, the filly Justakiss, and Nate's new friend Pacino, Liv made a mental note to send in a change for the description on the towering dark bay colt's registration papers. The laceration that had given him his distinctive identifier had occurred some time over the summer at the farm. No one actually knew how he'd cut his face that day, which was never an unusual thing. If there was trouble, horses had a way of finding it—especially young, expensive horses.

"Remember this one, Miller?" All tacked up, she stood in the doorway of the bay gelding's stall with a hand on the line, while Nate waited for Michel to take Pacino a turn—she already couldn't not call him that. "This is the little horse that dropped Cory that first day you came to see Feste last fall when we were starting this group." It still hurt to say the colt's name. It probably always would.

There was a beat before Nate answered, a reminder they shared that ache. "The kid's come a long way. I'm starting to think I should've just retired and offered to be her agent."

"You don't get to quit on me yet. We're not done here. What was it you said? *We are not yet the good thing we can be.*"

The murkiness left his features, replaced with something brighter, more genuine. "Thanks."

"For what?"

"For the pep-talk." A grin emerged, though maybe not full force. They'd just have to keep telling each other those words until they became true.

"Hey Jo?" Liv called when Michel halted Pacino in the

middle of the shed. Her eyes went up and up, taking in the skyscraper of a two-year-old. "I think maybe you should hold this one while Michel legs Nate up."

Nate didn't even joke about vaulting up on his own. He just peered at the rafters, then nodded to Michel. "With feeling Mike."

"Don't forget to duck, Miller," Liv cracked.

He still made it look effortless, though he hunched once he was on top, acutely aware of the minimal clearance. Pacino stood stock-still, and when Michel took over at his head from Jo, he had to encourage the big colt to move forward. Nate reinforced the request with legs that only reached two-thirds of the way around Pacino's generous barrel, like a little kid on a pony.

Liv and Jo exchanged a quick glance at the oversized colt's exaggerated movement before Liv led out the much smaller bay gelding. Trop was his name, one guaranteed to get butchered by the track announcer, because it was French. No need to come up with a nickname for him; they'd just have to teach the anglophones how to say it.

Roger accompanied them on Paz, the set of juveniles bumping into each other as they shied and snorted at every strange sight on the way to the training track. The cinderblock structures, the laundry on lines drawn from post to post in a barn where they had, for some insane reason, not deemed it cold enough to drop their windows yet. The vet's assistant gathering x-ray equipment out of the back of a black SUV parked at the end of one shed. The set was going out late enough that it overlapped those rounds.

Nate started singing *Opportunity*.

The Pet Shop Boys, Miller? The dialogue started in Liv's head.

Don't judge, he'd respond. His musical repertoire was bottomless, as had always been his ability to press through, move forward, though right now she felt he was struggling. This time, she was trying her best to lighten the load. He'd done that job on his own long enough.

"She's tiny." He broke from his serenade, peering down at Emilie's chestnut filly from his mountain of a colt.

"Chique was tiny," Emilie shot back.

"But she was fierce. This one's a school pony."

"So? Who cares if she can run?" Emilie leaned down, draping her arms around Reba's neck. The filly's head continued to nod, and she let out a happy snort.

"I do," Roger grumbled. "At least a couple of these horses need to be able to run, or I might be out of a job."

That was an exaggeration—the benefit of being a private trainer was he was on salary like the rest of them. But Rog was in a mood this morning. Fair enough. They were all out of sorts right now, the usual feeling of limbo in the weeks leading up to their departure for Florida amplified by the retirement of a filly whose career had been paying those salaries. It surrounded them with a certain nervousness that only the emergence of a new, clear equine leader would quell.

Nicole's filly put on the brakes when they reached the gap. When Roger tried to reach over to help Nicole, the filly ducked sideways, away from him. *Yes, Paz is scary. Really?* Reba came to the rescue, Emilie grasping Kiss's rein to provide direction and confidence. Justakiss sighed, pressing her nose into Reba's neck.

"That's okay, Kiss, you can share a piece of Reba's brain," Emilie cooed. "They were best friends on the farm."

The training track was more or less deserted—which was the idea. There were just a few others galloping over the deep sand, dried out and dusty by this time of morning. Horses for small trainers at the mercy of freelance exercise help who put such mounts at the bottom of their list of priorities. Track workers who owned a horse of their own on the side, and had to wait until the ones they got paid to care for were done up before training their own. It was the other end of the spectrum from Triple Stripe, a private stable. A dying breed somewhere in between the big public trainers and these small-time stakeholders. They were all connected, though. In the same game. Even if the playing field didn't feel particularly even much of the time.

They jogged in pairs, going the wrong way along the outside rail, backing up. Liv's gelding and Nate's colt led the way, in front of the fillies, though Pacino didn't look as if he'd figured out he should care about girls. Roger brought up the rear, assessing each stride.

Trop was a bundle of nervous energy, all flicking ears and bugged-out eyes, while Pacino lumbered along placidly beside him. The bay gelding shied at a Canada Goose on the other side of the rail, bumping against his big companion. It was like hitting a brick wall. Pacino didn't bat an eyelash, and Nate looked hilariously disappointed that he was riding the easy one while it took all Liv's skill to keep her two-year-old from jumping out of his skin.

When they reached the half-mile pole, they eased. Pacino stumbled over his oversized feet, nose diving.

"Yikes!" Nate exclaimed, scrambling to gather him and line him up next to the others.

Roger frowned. "Think you'd better stay with me, Nate. You three go ahead. Once around, if they can make it."

Nicole's filly had the biggest spark in her eye, galloping on the tips of her toes with her neck a little too close to the vertical. She was a Just Lucky, like Chique, so maybe no surprise. Trop was trying to be good on Kiss's outside, staying mostly straight thanks to the brace of Liv's legs. They all rode a longer and more defensively than they would with experienced horses. Green two-year-olds were not to be trusted.

Liv glanced over—and back—to Reba on the inside. Emilie sat every few strides to drive with her legs and seat, the filly gamely responding and snorting out a breath, then dropping back again. Emilie finally shook her head and let the chestnut filly fall into a jog. Liv and Nicole pulled their two up to stay with her. No deserting one of the set. Even if Reba would have been fine, the verdict was still out on Kiss.

"We're overdue talking about Florida," Roger said when they regathered on the backstretch.

The mutterings typically commenced as soon as Ontario's temperatures dropped to single digits, which usually happened at least once in September, but this year they'd all been distracted by Nate's injury and Chique's impending retirement. As the last big race of the season, the Canadian International, which had been Chique's final start, signaled the fast-approaching end of the meet, adding urgency to winter arrangements.

"We'll take the gelding you're on, Liv," Roger said. "And that filly, Nicole. Yours, though, Em, needs more time. We'll keep her in till we head to Florida, then she can go home for the winter."

Emilie didn't look disappointed. She'd get to spend time with the filly and could leg her up in January. Just because Reba wasn't ready to be a racehorse now didn't mean they'd give up on her.

"And this one..." Roger paused with the weight of what Liv was certain was about to come out of his mouth, "...is a wobbler." The trainer said the words like he was passing a sentence, and it added another layer of disquiet to an already unstable morning.

“I’m assuming you’re staying till the end of the meet?” Roger directed his question at Nate.

"As much as I hate the idea, yeah, I'd better."

The trainer shifted his attention to Liv. "Do you have a plan?"

She nodded. Even though they hadn't discussed it, Nate's answer made hers concrete. "I'll stay too. It's about time you got to go south early, Rog."

"At this rate, there might not be anything staying till the end of the meet for you to worry about."

Two days ago they'd won the richest race in Canada. Today, life was far more ordinary.

<<<<>>>>

ACKNOWLEDGMENTS

As always I'm indebted to my beta readers, Allison Litfin, Bev Harvey, Nathalie Drolet, and Dr. Kristen Frederick DVM. Extra thanks to Kristen for our discussions about the veterinary details.

Michelle Lopez, author and business accountability partner, for helping keeping me on task and for the support.

Thanks again to Natalie Keller Reinert who once again went above and beyond with the formatting, and continues to inspire as an author herself. Be sure to check out her novels!

And a special shout out to the horse people and horses I've worked with over the years, because you're the ones who know the highs and lows in the sport. Ours is not an easy one.

ALSO BY LINDA SHANTZ

Good Things Come (Book 1)

All The Little Things (Book 2)

All Good Things (Book 3)

ABOUT THE AUTHOR

It was an eight-year-old me, frustrated that all the horse racing novels I read were about the Derby, not the Plate, who first put pencil to three-ring paper and started what would become this story. Needless to say, we've both grown up a bit since then.

I began working at the track before I finished high school, and after graduating the following January, took a hotwalking job at Payson Park in Florida. Once back at Woodbine, I started grooming and galloping. While the backstretch is exciting, I found I was more at home on the farm — prepping and breaking yearlings, nightwatching and foaling mares. Eventually I started my own small layup/broodmare facility, and in the last few years I've transitioned into retraining and rehoming. Somewhere along the way I did go back to school and get a degree. I should probably dust it off and frame it one day.

I live on a small farm in Ontario, Canada, with my off-track Thoroughbreds and a young Border Collie, and I'm probably better known for painting horses than writing about them — if you like my covers, check out my artwork at www.lindashantz.com

Author Photo courtesy of Ellen Schoeman Photography

Printed in the USA
CPSIA information can be obtained
at www.ICGtesting.com
LVHW031521110923
757821LV00042B/193